The HOLIDAY POST

L.B. DUNBAR

Cover Design: Yummy Book Covers

Editor: Emerald Edits/Nicole McCurdy

Editor: Gemma Brocato

OTHER BOOKS BY L.B. DUNBAR

Sterling Falls

Sterling Heat

Sterling Brick

Sterling Streak

Sterling Clay

Sterling Fight

Sterling Touch

Sterling Stone

Chicago Anchors

Elevator Pitch

Catch the Kiss

Parentmoon

Holiday Hotties (Christmas novellas)

Scrooge-ish

Naughty-ish

Grouch-ish

Road Trips & Romance

Hauling Ashe

Merging Wright

Rhode Trip

Lakeside Cottage

Living at 40

Loving at 40

Learning at 40

Letting Go at 40

<u>Silver Foxes of Blue Ridge</u>

Silver Brewer

Silver Player

Silver Mayor

Silver Biker

<u>Sexy Silver Fox Collection</u>

After Care

Midlife Crisis

Restored Dreams

Second Chance

Wine&Dine

<u>Collision novellas</u>

Collide

Caught

The Sex Education of M.E.

<u>The Heart Collection</u>

Speak from the Heart

Read with your Heart

Look with your Heart

Fight from the Heart

View with your Heart

The Heart Remembers - a sequel

BOOKS IN OTHER AUTHOR WORLDS

<u>Smartypants Romance (an imprint of Penny Reid)</u>

Love in Due Time

Love in Deed

Love in a Pickle

<u>The World of True North (an imprint of Sarina Bowen)</u>

Cowboy

Studfinder

THE EARLY YEARS

<u>Legendary Rock Stars Series</u>

<u>Paradise Stories</u>

<u>The Island Duet</u>

<u>Modern Descendants – writing as elda lore</u>

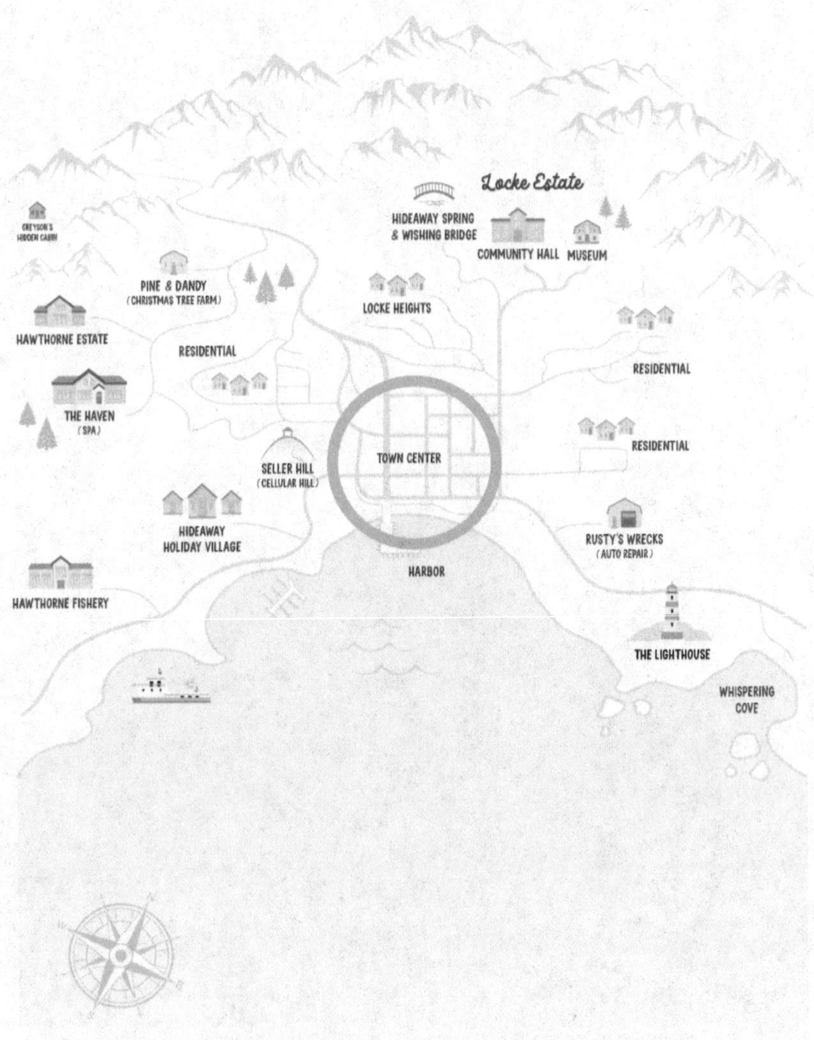

Welcome to
HIDEAWAY HARBOR
Locke Estate
GREYSON'S HIDDEN CABIN
HIDEAWAY SPRING & WISHING BRIDGE
COMMUNITY HALL
MUSEUM
PINE & DANDY (CHRISTMAS TREE FARM)
LOCKE HEIGHTS
HAWTHORNE ESTATE
RESIDENTIAL
RESIDENTIAL
THE HAVEN (SPA)
RESIDENTIAL
SELLER HILL (CELLULAR HILL)
TOWN CENTER
HIDEAWAY HOLIDAY VILLAGE
RUSTY'S WRECKS (AUTO REPAIR)
HAWTHORNE FISHERY
HARBOR
THE LIGHTHOUSE
WHISPERING COVE

HIDEAWAY HARBOR

The town center

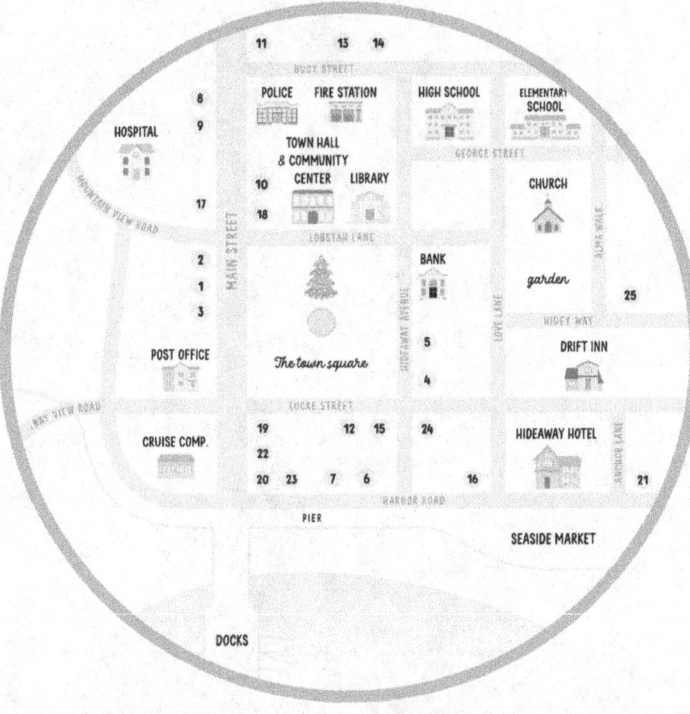

1 LOVE AT FIRST SIP (CAFE)
2 HIDDEN ITALY (RESTAURANT)
3 MAKING WHOOPIE (BAKERY)
4 HARD TO FIND (BOOKSTORE)
5 CHRISTMAS WONDERLAND (POP-UP STORE)
6 HOOK, LINE AND SINKER (RESTAURANT)
7 THE SHORE THING (BAR/RESTAURANT)
8 THE PERFECT PACKAGE (ADULT TOY STORE)
9 SCENTS AND SENSIBILITY (PERFUME SHOP)
10 THE WILDE KETTLE (TEA SHOP)
11 HIDEAWAY GROCER (GENERAL STORE)
12 PAPER MOON (OFFICE SUPPLIES)
13 LOBSTAH LIFTS (GYM)

14 HIDEAWAY CLINIC
15 HIDEAWAY TREASURES (GIFT SHOP)
16 THE CHOWDER HOUSE RULES (RESTAURANT)
17 ALMANAC (TOWN PAPER)
18 KIPPIS (SMALL BAR)
19 THE SWEETEST THING (CANDY STORE)
20 BEAUTY PARLOR
21 SALT & EMBER (RESTAURANT)
22 HOUSE OF PEARL (CLOTHING BOUTIQUE)
23 THE MASTER BAITERS (BAIT & TACKLE SHOP)
24 HAMMERTIME HARDWARE
25 OFF THE BEATEN PATH (ADVENTURE COMPANY)

CHAPTER 1

December 4
20 days until Christmas Eve

[Saint]

Fuck! I was lost. Late and lost.

"Da is going to kill me," I mutter to no one as I continue my death grip on the leather-wrapped steering wheel of my forest-green Aston Martin DBX707. The car is a total luxury.

And one not built for snow.

About an hour ago, the wind picked up and the snow swirled, and I'd hiked my baby girl into high gear, like I could outrun the weather.

I have, on occasion, but that's a different story for a different time.

My GPS went out around the time the weather kicked in, the snow changing from pretty, dancing flakes, like the inside of a snow globe, to vengeful crystals of ice, angrily pelting my car.

My subscription radio service went out at roughly the same time, and I switched to a regular FM station, hoping for a local weather update.

No such luck.

Certain I'd made a wrong turn because the road grew narrower and curvier, I could hardly make out the blacktop that should have been in front of me. Instead, it was snow, snow, and more snow, obscuring my windshield, blanketing the road, and weighing heavily on the thick trees surrounding my highway path.

Yep, definitely lost.

Eventually, I break through the trees, and a vague emptiness appears on my right, as if nothing exists over there.

"Am I on a cliff?" Squinting to better see through the barrage of flakes and the dark night reflected back at me by the sports car's headlights, my breath catches.

"Is that the fucking ocean?"

I'd been crossing through Maine on my way to Bangor, the final destination of a three-month cross-country road trip. I could have ended the trip in Chicago, where I'd been visiting my brother Nick, or grabbed a flight from New York, but I'd wanted to continue the journey in my beautiful green machine until the last possible minute, and the last minute meant from Bangor to a private plane in Nova Scotia to take me home.

North. The place was waiting for me.

Only, I don't appear to be anywhere near Bangor, possibly not headed north, nor south, as I'd hit the edge of the Atlantic Ocean. Trees tower to my left, water is somewhere to my right, and I pray I don't end up in it. Neither myself nor my car desire a winter dip in that certain-to-be freezing water.

With brief thoughts of icebergs and polar bears and the state of the polar cap, I mutter aloud another thought. "Do not let me die in snow."

My entire life I've battled frozen temperatures and frigid

nights, and I've survived fifty years of the wintery mix Jack Frost tosses into the air.

"Snow will not be the end of me," I vow, again to no one as I am alone in my green machine.

Always without a partner at my side in this adventure called life. Been that way for fifty years as well. There'd been plenty of women in my life, but not *the* woman. The right woman. The one who would understand what I do. Believe in me. Accept me.

With my chest pressed to the steering wheel, my hands are covered in leather driving gloves and perfectly placed at midnight. Narrowing my eyes, I'm certain I've seen something dash into the road.

Blinking rapidly, I pray out loud again, "Don't be a deer." Or worse, a reindeer. Those beasts can cause some serious damage to a vehicle. I don't want to think about what they'd do to a human inside a low-to-the-ground sports car. Then again, caribou are not common in Maine.

With my thoughts scrambling once again, two bright eyes flicker to life in my headlights, blinding me like an old-fashioned camera bulb. The level of the pair is too low for a deer. Plus, the dark, furry patches around each eye, outlined by white fur on a large, round head suggest that this four-legged creature is a Saint Bernard.

In the middle of the road.

Instinctively, I swerve left, hopeful the big dog goes right, but as my car starts to tailspin, I'm worried it isn't going to matter which way the dog runs, if he even ran.

Why the fuck was he sitting in the middle of the road during a godawful snowstorm?

All these thoughts continue to whirl in my head in the blink of an eye as my car spins in a circle at high speed, while feeling like slow motion, until I come to an abrupt stop, jolting me side to side inside the Martin. The thud on the right side of the car means impact with something solid and sturdy.

Closing my eyes as the air bag deploys, punching me in the face, I hold my breath, wincing at the sting in my nose and the burn in my eyes at the swift release of protection. Taking a moment to catch my breath, I keep my eyes closed.

Please let the dog be safe.

As the airbag deflates, I slowly crane my neck to the right. The front side of my car is pressed up against something circular and firm. A tree, perhaps.

Oh fuck, not my car. Not my sweet baby girl green machine.

Reaching for my phone, I notice there is no reception. Probably due to the storm. And now I have no way to call for roadside assistance, not that anyone would find me in this blizzardy mess right now anyway.

Squinting into the darkness, my headlights are the only illumination.

Tilting my head forward, I correct my assessment about a tree, deciding instead that I might have hit a utility pole.

Great, just great . . .

Only as I narrow my gaze, resting my forearms on the steering wheel, over the burst airbag, I see that I've hit a pole of some sort. A mile marker, maybe.

Either way, I'm off the road a bit, and now, I'm not only late and lost, I'm stuck.

And the dog.

Quickly, I glance out the front windshield, slanting my eyes.

"You have got to be kidding me," I glower.

With a heavy press against the driver's side door, I force the opening into the fierce wind. Bracing myself for the cold, I slowly stand, using my gloved hand as eye protection and the door as a shield as I holler over the top of the window.

"What the hell are you thinking?" I shout at the giant Saint Bernard, who looks at me with a puppy dog gaze despite his grown size. The expression suggests I'm the stupid one.

Not to mention, he appears to be in the exact same spot he

was sitting only moments ago, having shifted his body to face my new direction. Not a scrape or scratch on him, thankfully. Also, apparently, not a single care that a blizzard rages around us.

"Come here," I call out to him, stepping to the side of the open door and waving toward the warmth of the car, which will quickly be lost the longer it takes this beast to hop inside.

He's lucky I didn't hit him. He might not be so lucky a second round, especially as he continues to stare back at me with those large, melancholy eyes like I'm the one he feels sorry for.

With a quick, sharp whistle, one that demands he follow my command and works on other animals in my care when I want their attention, I motion toward the car again.

This gentle giant, however, does not move.

He turns his large head slowly, like he's heard someone call him. He pauses a second as if listening, then lazily lugs the lower half of his large body upward and sluggishly runs off, back toward the trees.

Having no idea where I am, I lean into the wicked wind, stepping forward as best I can to both assess the damage to my car and hope the post my baby girl is now wrapped around will give a hint to my location.

First, I glance at the way my front right tire bends in the wrong direction and the front fender panel kisses the post, offering it a hug I'd prefer it not give. Next, I glance up at a sign attached to the post and narrow my eyes once again against the blinding wind and bitter cold to read it.

Welcome to Hideaway Harbor.

"Well, this certainly has been quite the greeting."

CHAPTER 2

[Saint]

$\mathcal{T}$his isn't the first time I've had to hunker down for a winter nap in a vehicle. Hopefully, it won't be a long one.

With no cell service, my phone is of no use to call for help. I'll need to tough it out until daylight and hope for a snowplow or another lost traveler on this vacant road. A quick glance at my watch shows it's after two a.m. Definitely late. I think of Da again. December is our most hectic month. The last-minute purchases. The backorders rushing in. Christmas sales project our business needs for the upcoming year.

But for now, all I can concentrate on is the cold creeping into the car, as I've let a great deal of heat out by having the door open, intending to offer shelter to a stray dog.

"So much for trying to be on the nice list."

I'd chuckle at the idea if I weren't so grumpy. And growing colder by the minute.

With my arms tucked into my pits and the travel blanket I keep in the backseat over my legs, I huddle against the steering wheel, laying my forehead against the spent airbag. With my eyes closed, I dream of warm things.

Sunshine on the beach. Hot chocolate in a festive mug. Crackling logs in a blazing fireplace.

Imagining heated items isn't helping, so my thoughts shift instead to thinking about a warm body beside me. The gentle curve of hips. The strength of feminine thighs. The softness of a pair of—

A sharp rapping from my left, like knuckles against glass, jolts me and I jerk my head upright. My eyes rapidly blink due to the brightness of daylight and the glare of freshly fallen snow. My shoulders ache from the initial reaction of gripping the steering wheel so tightly last night. Twisting my neck, I wince at the pain from sleeping with my head against the leather-wrapped steering wheel. I cup my nose, finding it tender as well. Then I turn my head and glance out the driver's side window, blinking once again to clear the fog in my brain.

Because a pair of the brightest blue feminine eyes I've ever seen stare back at me. The woman's cheeks are rosy. Her lips lush and pink. Her nose wrinkles as her gaze scans my face.

"You okay?" she says, or at least I think that's what she says as it's difficult to hear her through the window. "Are you hurt?"

She motions with her mitten-covered hand for me to roll down my window, but I pop open the door instead.

With a giant step backward and both hands in the air, she watches me warily as I exit the low riding Martin. My legs are cramped and cold, and my knees crack after hours in the hunched position. Something snaps along my lower lumbar region. And even lower, I'm sporting morning wood that rivals the post against my car because of the dream I'd been having.

One in which the beautiful woman in front of me could have been a star.

Then I glance down her body, clad in a long, puffy, dull-green coat that falls below her knees. Thick fur-trimmed boots are laced tight around her mid-calves. A thick scarf circles her throat. Her hair is covered by a cream-colored knit cap.

Fuck, she looks warm and toasty and—

"You can't park your car here, mister," she says, her voice soft with an East Coast accent, rolling *park* and *car* over her tongue as if the words don't contain the letter *R*.

"I'm not—"

"I'm teasing," she quickly interrupts, lowering her eyes from my face and glancing toward the post the Aston Martin embraces.

She steps around me and the hood of the car to assess the damage. Her lips twist side to side, like she's calculating the cost of repairs. Dollars signs fill those bright eyes.

"Must have made Santa's nice list to get a car like this."

"Santa's—" I choke. *Does she know?* I scrape away the thought as quickly as it comes.

"Yeah," I mock. "I've been *really* good this year."

Production is up. Damages down. Returns are at an all-time low. I'd say it's been an excellent year, and I deserve to treat myself once in a while.

Call it a mid-life crisis car, if you wish.

Da would say I'm spoiling myself. Ma would say I've earned it. Nick would just be thankful he isn't in the family business. My younger sister Kaye would simply roll her eyes and suggest I'm overcompensating for something.

"Alright, let's get you hooked up." She nods over the roof of the car, and I spin to see a tow truck I hadn't noticed parked behind me.

She bends, looking at something beneath the front bumper of my green baby.

"Dammit, these fancy cars are so complicated," she grunts, lowering even further, lifting her backside in the air.

I don't have the slightest hint how she's shaped beneath the bulk of her coat, and her figure should be the last thing on my mind, especially when she straightens, catching me squinting like I can see through the layers of her outerwear.

She gives me a stern smirk, mumbling under her breath. "I do not have time for this today."

"Towing my *cah*?" I counter, poorly mimicking her accent, before instantly regretting it. My intention is not to offend her. The accent is actually cute coming from her.

Her face is stoic, not giving away anything other than irritation. I've heard that before.

Without another comment directed at me, she continues muttering to herself.

"This is what happens when you offer to give Neve a day off. A snowstorm hits. And suddenly I have twenty extra things to do today other than what I'm supposed to be doing."

My shoulders sag as she grumbles to herself, hating that I'm suddenly one of the inconveniences derailing her day.

I watch as she easily climbs into the tow truck and pulls the larger vehicle around to the front of my car. The alarming beep of the truck reversing has me scrambling toward the hood of my baby girl, watching with bated breath as the tow hook swings over the precious emblem signifying the prestige of this vehicle.

With a hardy shove of the driver's door, she hops out of the truck, still muttering to herself as she walks toward the rear and assesses her position. Pulling at a lever, the hook lowers with a sudden rush before she yanks the lever forward again, bringing the heavy curved metal to an abrupt halt.

I watch in horror, certain the giant tow hook will crash onto the smooth hood, adding more damage to my green girl.

"Easy," I snap, glaring at this woman with my hands jammed into my jacket pockets. I try not to wear red but 'tis the season and as I was headed home, well . . .

Her gaze roams my stature from top to boot tip before she disregards me and returns to the lever, reaching for the tow hook with her other hand, which is just beyond her grasp.

"Here," I scramble forward, catching the hook and angling the curved metal piece away from the hood as she returns to lowering it.

"Thanks," she mumbles. "I'm out of practice."

Out of practice at what? Towing cars? This does not make me feel better. I'm all for equity and equality, but if this woman doesn't know how to tow a vehicle, maybe . . .

"Is there another tow service in town?"

The descending hook comes to another abrupt stop as she slams the lever forward once more. She straightens her body, shoulders tight, head held high.

"Rusty's is the only place around here."

"Rusty's," I repeat, instantly anxious because of the name.

"Yes. Rusty's Wrecks, proudly serving Hideaway Harbor for sixty years." Her tone turns tight as those blue eyes blaze like large outdoor bulbs decorating homes this time of year. She speaks like a canned voiceover in a commercial.

Rusty's Wrecks. The name does not ease my concerns.

"You want me to tow your car or what?" she challenges, hip possibly jutted to the side. Hard to tell beneath the thick layer of her coat, but her mitten-covered hand fists near her waist.

"Yeah. Okay." I swipe off my own knit cap and scratch at the back of my neck as I spare a glance at the damage to the Martin.

Her breath hitches, drawing my gaze back to her.

"What?" I snap, worried she sees something else wrong with the car, or worse, she's done additional damage.

Instead, her eyes fix on my face. Or maybe it's my hair. The silvery-white combination. I can't exactly say, and I don't bother to ask as she drops her eyes and grabs the tow hook from my hand.

She squats, removes a mitten from one hand with her teeth, then uses the free hand to tug off the other one, shoving both into her pockets before she struggles and fumbles with the giant hook, muttering once again to herself.

"I can't find . . . Oh wait . . . got it . . ." She exhales heavily as her face scrunches, causing her nose to wrinkle and freckles to pop despite her rosy cheeks. "Nope . . . Okay . . . maybe to the left . . ." She sighs. "That's it."

"That's what *she* said," I mutter, unable to stop myself.

With the hook attached, she slowly stands, swiping her hands together. For the first time, I notice how delicate her fingers are. The digits are long and thin but marred by black grease and pale from the cold.

"Actually, unfortunately, most of the time that is what *he'd* say." With her hands on her hips, she takes a second glance at my now-hooked car, and it takes me a second to realize what she's just implied.

Does she mean some knob has had trouble finding the right spot on her?

I choke at the boldness, and she spins toward the tow truck. "I can give you a ride but keep your hands and your dirty thoughts to yourself."

"I don't have dirty thoughts." I chuckle. Following her, my booted feet crunch over the thick snow. My toes are cold; my fingertips too, but I've experienced frostbite before, and this isn't anything like the prickling sensation. It takes a lot to stiffen my body parts.

Like a smart mouth and blue eyes.

Good thing she can't read minds, because mine keeps me indefinitely on the naughty list.

CHAPTER 3

December 5

{Lumi}

An overnight snowstorm was the last thing I needed. Mondays are always the worst.

In an effort to help my younger sister Neve, I'd told her she could take today off. The shop is always closed on Mondays anyway, but Neve is typically on call or tinkering. She needed time out of the office, though, and I'd told her I'd *woman* the phones. What could possibly go wrong?

As I'd mentioned to the stranger now seated beside me in Dad's old truck, Rusty's Wrecks has proudly served this area for sixty years. The locals use us for their day-to-day vehicle needs, but our busiest season is typically summertime, when tourists arrive for the beach and the harbor. Oil changes. Flat tires. Dead batteries. Car wrecks are mostly fender benders since the speed limit through town is snail-paced. Crowds only accumulate during the summer season.

Well, and fall, for the leaf peepers. And winter has its charm as well.

Hell, all year through, the charm of Hideaway Harbor packs in the extra visitors.

Our little corner of Maine is an alcove of sorts with lush mountains in a horseshoe shape facing the giant bay, which is a slice of the Atlantic Ocean. Our town features a typical East Coast flair with a quaint downtown area, residential niches up the hills, and the harbor, which is a focal point. We have a rich Nordic history, but we're an eclectic mix of locals now. And we attract a plethora of visitors, anywhere from families to party groups to celebrities. Or singles, like this guy.

Clearing my throat, I state, "If you're here for the Bachelor Auction, you're a few days late."

Hidden Italy, an Italian deli and delicacy shop owned by the Cafiero family, kicked off the month of December with the brainstorm to auction off the single brothers who share responsibility for the place. If you ask me, it was a ploy for one particular brother to get a girl he had his sights on.

"The bachelor what?" Mister Tall, Silver, and Handsome chokes in the passenger seat. Oh, yeah, I didn't miss how good looking he is, with that silver hair slicked back from his knit cap and the right mix of snow and tinsel on his jawline. He looks like a solid man, but it's hard to tell with the waist-length puffer jacket he's wearing. But his legs are thick in a pair of khaki-colored jeans.

"You know . . . an auction. For the single women in town." Personally, I had not attended the shindig as most of the men were younger than me. "Unless you aren't a bachelor."

Way to sound like you're probing for answers, Lumi.

However, I'm not interested in what out-of-towners do in this town. Been there, done that long ago, and learned my lesson. I also have no time in my life for short-term dalliances.

We have a name for people not from here. Flatlanders,

pronounced flatland*ahs*, are typically not from Maine. We espe-cially toss the title on people from Massachusetts. This guy doesn't look like he's from anywhere near the East Coast.

Anyway.

Between Rusty's Wrecks and my job with the postal service, plus being a single mom, I hardly have a spare minute, which is why a snowstorm, resulting in a car towing, has set off my day.

My passenger doesn't answer about his relationship status, and it's better that I don't know. I don't want to know. I'm not interested in some guy who looks like that Santa-actor from the 2024 holiday campaign for Target. I'd never admit how hot I found the man in those commercials.

My sisters would never let me hear the end of it if I owned that fact out loud.

"Sounds . . . interesting," he finally states.

I hum, side-eyeing him as he stares out the window at the harbor on our right. The mountain to our left is how our town of Hideaway Harbor got its name. Your typical young and in love runaway couple, fleeing families that were enemies, and who disapproved of their union, thus hiding away here.

"Maybe Santa's Speed Dating Event?" I chime next, still unreasonably curious about what brings him to our small town.

Love at First Sip, my personal favorite coffee shop in town, hosted the speed dating event the other night as well. As another love-matching event, I graciously skipped. Eileen Burrows, owner of the coffee shop, and the unofficial and self-appointed town matchmaker, designed the night.

"Santa's what?" The stranger barks, startling me with the strength of his voice.

"Speed dating," I clarify, sparing him another glance. "You know, like a round robin of dates, each only so long, to get to know someone." With my right hand on the large steering wheel, I curl my forefinger and middle one to make air quotes. As if you can know someone in minutes.

Then again, I side-eye my passenger, taking in his leather boots, the fancy driving gloves laying on his lap, and his winter jacket which costs more than my monthly utility bill. He drove a car that could have covered Danny's college tuition, for heaven's sake. All four years of it.

This guy not only screams out-of-towner, he shouts pompous and rich and out of my league.

No matter. I don't want a league.

"Eileen suggested that Santa found his match that way." I smile.

"He most certainly did not," the man scoffs, turning his head and scowling with a glare that attempts anger but there's something too cute about the expression on his face.

I'd be frightened if he didn't appear soft in some manner. Not *soft*-soft, just kind perhaps. Friendly, maybe. Oh, what did I know? I'd misjudged a flatlander once before and look where it landed me.

Permanently grounded in this town.

Then again, I couldn't fully fault *that guy*. I'd been the other half of the situation, and the result was Danny. My son.

"You haven't heard the great Christmas fairy tale. How Santa found his wife in thirty seconds or less." The corner of my lips slowly curl, and the man beside me chuffs.

"You're pulling my leg," he snorts.

"Better than pulling other parts," I quip.

"That's *not* what he says," he mutters.

I bark out a laugh before catching him watching me. Without much sleep last night, I'm a bit delirious this morning. The wind howling and the house rattling always keep me up, especially now that I'm all alone in that creaking old house.

"Guess you must have been here hoping to catch the Viking queen's fundraiser." Our resident Viking romance novelist, Jocelyn Collins, hosted the fundraiser for the local library.

A second bachelor auction happened, and I couldn't have

afforded to bid on a single guy, let alone want one of the men offering himself up for who knows what. I'm certain it wasn't about sex, just a charity event for the local library, but still . . . I didn't want to *pay* for a pity date.

To an outsider, two bachelor auctions and a speed dating event might make Hideaway Harbor sound like matchmaking is our number one attraction outside of the harbor. The area *is* steeped in romantic history, but I've never been lucky at love. It isn't for a lack of trying so much as from a major failed attempt. Then life got in the way.

My passenger is already shaking his head in response to the second auction. His mouth lifts in a lazy curve, surrounded by that delicious silvery mix along his jaw and cheeks, dismissing my ridiculousness. His eyes are dark as coal with a hint of innocent mischief in them. At the corners of his eyes are laugh lines, or maybe smile stitches, like he's often practiced the facial motion. He looks a little bit like a Viking, albeit one with a trim beard and shorter hair than the unruly characters. Still, there is something Nordic about him, like a sexy version of Santa Claus.

And now I've really lost my mind.

"Anyway," I groan, placing both my hands at the top of the steering wheel as we slowly roll through Hideaway Harbor, along the actual harbor, and head toward the lighthouse on the other side of town. Rusty's Wrecks is located just outside of town proper near the old beacon. I typically walk to work because you can get anywhere important in Hideaway Harbor within thirty minutes max on foot. Even in the cold, I enjoy the crisp, fresh air to wake me up in the morning or clear my head in the evening, but today I drove to the garage to pick up the tow truck. I'd gotten the call from Neve after she got a Good Samaritan call from a passerby about the accident.

"How *did* your accident happen?" Perhaps other than the obvious snowstorm.

"Fucking Saint Bernard in the road."

"Skippy?" I shriek, turning my attention to the near-Viking.

The truck swerves as well, and he reaches for the dashboard, crying out, "Eyes on the road."

Sharply straightening the tow and giving a quick glance through the rearview mirror at his fancy car hitched to the hook, I then spare him another anxious peek.

"Who is Skippy?" he asks.

"The Saint Bernard." The town dog is claimed by many but owned by none. He once belonged to the lighthouse keeper but when the old guy fell ill and passed away, Skippy was adopted by all. His home is anywhere he wants it to be, but mainly he roams the business district of Hideaway Harbor.

"What kind of name is Skippy?" the silver Viking asks.

"*His* name. He plops down wherever he wants to, and people just skip over him. Skippy," I repeat the beloved dog's name.

"Well, Skippy decided the middle of the highway right outside your town's entrance was a good place to squat a bit last night."

My brows crease. That doesn't sound like something Skippy would do.

"Are you sure it wasn't a moose in the road? Maybe Santa's reindeer?" I lower my voice while mentioning the mythical creatures. Although caribou do exist, they do not live in Maine. However, when Danny was young, we called the first sighting of an antlered buck a reindeer spotting, which meant Santa was busy working toward Christmas.

The thought of my now-adult son gives me pause until Mister Sportscar speaks.

"It was most definitely not a reindeer. Nor a moose. It was a dog." He motions with his hands. "Yay big. This wide." He spreads his arms to emphasize Skippy's size. "Sad eyes."

"Skippy isn't sad," I defend the sweet mutt's disposition. However, I'd be sad if my owner died, and I was left to the town.

Then again, in many ways that's exactly what happened to me. Not that my dad was my person, but he did own Rusty's Wrecks, and I'd inherited the place, along with my sisters, keeping me doubly grounded to this town.

With a heavy sigh, I snap on my blinker and nod. "Here we are."

Home not-so-sweet home.

Pulling into the lot, I take in the three garage-bay doors, along with the saltwater-weathered sign and ocean-air-stained windows. My grandfather took pride in this place. Dad, too, for a while. But as the name implies, the auto repair shop is a bit of a wreck itself, thanks to previous poor management and lack of business. Most days, I don't know how we'll keep the place running for another year, let alone another month.

I don't have to hear Mr. Fancy Car, Viking imitator, Santa wannabe, to know he's internally groaning at the sight of the shop. My only hope is that Neve can fix his car quickly and send him on his way.

"So, tomorrow my sister will be in, and she can have a look at—"

"Tomorrow?" he interjects before I've punctuated my sentence.

"Tomorrow," I repeat, setting the tow in Park in front of one closed garage door.

"What about you?" He sniffs, shifting his body to face mine.

"What about me?" I turn my head toward him, tilting it in question.

"Can't you fix it?"

"Do I look like a mechanic?" The question is unfair. I did drive the tow truck to pick him up, and it isn't really his fault I'm in a piss-poor mood. I'm late for work, and while every other business is understanding about the weather and able to slow down to accommodate, the post office is still open.

Wind, rain, sleet . . . *or snow.*

"My sister Neve is the mechanical one, and she's off today."

My responsibility toward Rusty's is to check the books once a week and, occasionally, drive a tow truck.

His forehead furrows, and he glances toward the closed garage doors plus the front door with a CLOSED sign hanging against the glass.

Neve put potted Christmas tree toppers on either side of the door to give the place a festive appearance, but Rusty's Wrecks still looks sad.

Like a Saint Bernard without a home.

And the four daughters who inherited this garage.

"Do you need me to drop you somewhere?" I ask, despite being disgruntled that I'm already late for work. A small pinch of concern for the guy settles in my chest along with a weak attempt at displaying Hideaway Harbor hospitality. He looks tired and he is starting to show evidence of the airbag bursting in his face. Purple crescents mar the underside of his eyes.

"I'm not certain anywhere has vacancies, but The Drift Inn is down the street, or The Haven is up the hill a bit."

He looks a little lost for a moment, staring through the windshield at the repair shop for another second before saying, "Yeah. The Drift Inn is fine. I just need to grab my bag from my trunk."

However, he doesn't immediately move other than pulling his phone from his coat pocket and jabbing at the screen.

"We get spotty reception here on a good day," I tell him. "Probably worse today because of the storm last night."

He tips back his head and exhales toward the ceiling. Frustration expels in the heavy breath and misty cold puff of air coming from his mouth.

I get it, sexy stranger.

I'm not thrilled I still live here either.

CHAPTER 4

[Lumi]

*A*fter the day I've had I need a drink.

Hideaway Harbor's post office is located downtown across from the town square at the corner of Main Street and Locke Street. Because of the small size of our town, most businesses and residents pick up their mail from the office, thus giving me a daily stream of town gossip. The latest information is about our newest celebrity arrival, Amanda Willis, a rom-com queen, doing research on small-town life for a future holiday movie she wants to produce.

I have a sliver view of the harbor from the front door but face the town square. Some days, I consider how ships once came into the bay, depositing letters from family and lovers across the seas to this very location, although the building is much improved from our 1620 origins. The brick structure had a good pressure wash and internal polish a few years ago.

The town square, across Main Street, is another highlight of the area. Once night creeps in, the town's Christmas tree lights up. The annual tree lighting ceremony took place roughly a week ago, and the brightly lit evergreen has a magical glow about it. The town square tree is different from the harbor one, which will be lit in a few days.

With the holiday season in full bloom, excitement swirls in the air along with the scent of tourists, and I cannot seem to rid my nose of the fragrance that tickled it earlier. Peppermint and chocolate. What an odd combination on a man. Even more surprising was that I'd gotten close enough to smell him.

He needed to sign some paperwork, granting permission for Rusty's to inspect the damage to his car. He'll also need to call his insurance agent and confirm his deductible, etc. Then again, he is not my problem.

The post office was hectic today. As the sole counter worker, I take in the outbound mail from locals and visitors, and help Judy, our part-time staff member, sort the incoming mail and packages. Judy and I have worked side-by-side for decades.

She looks the other way when I read postcards coming in or going out, dreaming of the great travels and diverse locations I've never visited.

And I occasionally overlook her little flask and the drops she pours into her midday coffee.

Martin is our mail carrier, who covers the residential areas. He's a friendly enough, thirty-something aged guy, but quiet, preferring his headphones to human conversation. Music isn't the only thing he listens to. I've heard the distinct sounds of an audiobook or two coming through his earpiece, especially the grunts and groans from some Viking romance.

Because of the chaos of the day, and the ease of eating quickly at The Chowder House Rules, I step into the restaurant for a bowl of soup, before heading to The Shore Thing.

The bar is a bit dark and moody, and covered in kitschy nautical décor, complete with a giant, wooden sailboat steering wheel on the wall, now decorated with tinsel and lights for the holiday. The only anomaly in the place is a large cactus by the front window. The bar typically hosts a younger crowd, looking for exactly what the name implies: a sure thing. However, I'm not on the prowl, and in the mood for one of their holiday specialty drinks. I'm grateful Summer is the bartender tonight.

"What will you have tonight, Lumi?" The pretty blonde offers a friendly smile. She's young and studying psychology, hoping to be a counselor one day. Being a bartender, she's getting lots of unsolicited practice.

"I'll have a candy cane martini. It's been a Monday, and martinis go with Mondays, right?"

"Martinis go with any day ending in a y." She winks, gives a little laugh, and steps away to mix my drink.

With a slow turn of my head, the first cause for my rough Monday is seated three stools down from mine. Without his puffy jacket on, I have confirmation that his shoulders are broad while I already know he's taller than me. He's still wearing the Carhartt brown pants from earlier with a dark green sweater. The bruising underneath his eyes from the airbag is becoming more prominent. Still, there's something vaguely familiar about him which makes absolutely no sense. Even stranger, he gives off an aura that he could bring comfort and joy which is just plain weird and a sign I need a stiff drink.

I smirk at Mister Tall, Silver, and Handsome, and he lifts what looks like a whiskey on the rocks.

"Here's to Mondays," he offers, saluting me with his short glass and taking a sip of the amber liquid.

"Here you go, Lumi," Summer says, bringing my attention to her as she slides me a pretty pink drink in a Y-shaped glass, complete with a candy cane hooked over the rim.

I lift my glass toward my earlier passenger and salute him. "To Mondays." Then I sip the super sweet, extra minty, liquid treat. With pressure on my lips, I pop them apart and sigh. "Ah."

"Lumi? That's an interesting name."

"Lou-me," I correct of his pronunciation. "It's Finnish for

snow. Ironic considering my last name is Snowe. Snow with an e." There is no earthly reason to explain the spelling of my name or the pronunciation but I'm feeling generous after the first sip of candy cane dreaminess.

My unwanted stool-mate slides one stool closer to me. "I have a double name as well. I'm Astan, pronounced As-tan." He quirks a silvery brow, mimicking my instructions. "Santos." He holds out his hand to shake mine.

"But people call me Saint." Clarifying what his last name means.

"Astan? Like your car." How pretentious that he owns a car that sounds like his name. I do not reach for his hand.

"That car is an Aston Martin." He draws out the *aw* like he's almost from Maine. But everything about him says the East Coast is not his home.

"So where are you from, Ass-tan?"

"Saint," he corrects, his dark eyes darkening, and warning me that his real name is not to be trifled with. It makes me want to *trifle*.

"I live . . . north."

"North?" I question, taking another sip of my delicious martini while eyeing him over the rim. "That's vague."

"No, the town's name is North."

"North?" I repeat, finding we are both full of doubles. Whether that is a negative or not is yet to be determined, but as he's clearly from out-of-town, it shouldn't matter to me where he's from. He isn't from here and that's all I need to know.

"What's its zip code?" I ask.

"Just . . . North."

"Huh." I nod, dismissing this vague conversation. Instead, I turn toward the bar as Summer approaches again.

"Wicked cold out there today," she says, tipping her head toward the door.

"Wicked," I repeat, emphasizing the chill, but it isn't as cold as it can get around here. Considering it snowed last night, the temperature is a bit mild for winter. We still have January and February to contend with, and I shiver at the thought.

"How's Danny doing?" Summer's cheeks turn a sweet shade of pink, nearly matching my drink as she asks about my son.

"He's busy." I try to infuse enthusiasm into the statement. My boy graduated in the top five of his university class and got a job right out of college with a firm in New York. Business analytics. I didn't even know what that meant, but some days I think Rusty's Wrecks could use some analyzing. Then again, I never wanted Danny to work at the shop. He was destined to get out of this town, even if I've never been able to escape.

"Comin' home for the holiday?" Summer asks, wiping at the bar top like she's simply making conversation when it sounds a little like she's probing for answers.

"He's . . . busy." I sigh, pinching my forefinger and thumb around the thin stem of my glass and slowly spinning it side to side.

"Yeah," Summer exhales, understanding my answer.

Danny isn't coming home for the holidays. A first.

Having kids, you experience all their firsts. First step, first tooth, first word . . . and the first time they miss a holiday.

Lifting my glass, I take another sip of my martini, the sweet taste slightly bitter with the harsh reality.

While two of my three sisters are in town, and we'll get together like we always do, Christmas morning isn't going to be the same without Danny. His stocking will hang empty next to mine.

A throat clears beside me, and I notice Saint has moved next to me. His knees spread, one knocking mine beneath the counter, and I shift my leg, assuming we've accidentally touched. Leaning forward, I straighten my back and fold my forearms on the bar top.

"Who's Danny?" he asks softly.

I shrug. "My son." Fully looking at him, I meet his dark eyes. Ones that were black as coal when I teased him about his name are now more like freshly poured coffee, softer, smoother. "He's twenty-three and this will be his first Christmas away from home."

Danny called me minutes before I left the post office this evening to share the news. Like a lump of coal in my stocking, the announcement topped off my shitty Monday.

The melancholy in my voice sounds like I'm the one who will be absent from this place, when all I've ever wanted was to leave Hideaway Harbor and travel the world. I didn't understand homesickness because I've never suffered from it. I've never been anywhere but Maine.

"I'm sorry. For you and your husband."

I glance down at my naked fingers where my nail polish is chipped. "It's only Danny and me."

This stranger doesn't need to know all the particulars, even if his eyes are suddenly kind and compassion is wafting off him.

He sighs and turns for his drink, which has made the move closer to me as well. "I'm never home on Christmas. It's my busiest day of the year."

I snort. "The only reason Christmas would be busy for you is if you were Santa Claus." I chuckle at my own joke and take a drink of my martini, feeling Saint's gaze press at the side of my head.

"Yeah, Santa Claus." His voice lowers. "Ridiculous." With that, he lifts his drink and takes a healthy slug. My eyes follow the way his lips wrap around the rim of the glass and how his throat moves as he swallows. As much as I'm trying to ignore him, I seem to be cataloguing every move he makes, causing my own mouth to go dry.

After setting down his glass, he turns only his head. "So, know anywhere with vacancies around here? Looks like I'm staying a while."

I arch a brow. "Really?"

"My car needs parts that might take weeks to get here. And there doesn't appear to be anywhere in town with openings for a last-minute traveler who needs longer than a few days' stay."

My sister hasn't assessed his fancy sports car yet, so his explanation suggests he's familiar with the needs of his damaged car.

"No room at the inn," I tease.

"No room at the inn. The Hideaway Hotel. Or The Haven."

"I'd suggest sleeping in your car, but you did that last night." I'd seen the leather interior and extra-thick traveling blanket. Despite the mean exterior, that car looked cozy inside.

Saint shivers, exaggerating the experience of sleeping in a freezing, dark car. "That's harsh."

His words suggest my tone was harder than it needed to be, cold even. I'm not always known for my tact or grace, and I'm embarrassed that he has misunderstood my quip.

"Too soon?" I grimace.

"Definitely too soon." He slowly smiles, like his lips have all day to form a grin, and he lifts his glass for another sip of his whiskey. "But seriously, there isn't a place to stay in this town."

"Lumi has a room."

The statement comes like a flash of light streaking behind us, and I lean back to see who made the comment.

Eileen Burrows. The mid-sixties former beauty queen who still looks every bit the part, is mad at me for skipping her Santa Speed Dating experience, after I've told her, repeatedly, I'm not interested in speed-anything, dating or otherwise, with a man. The last time I rushed a relationship, I ended up pregnant, and at forty-three, that lane is closed.

With annoyance, I frown at Eileen's retreating back. She's always trying to interfere in love lives, or those lacking one.

Dismissing her suggestion, I sit forward and lift my martini for a sip.

"*Do* you have a room?" Saint asks, his tone hopeful.

"Only Danny's room," I state. The discussion is closed as that space is my son's.

Besides, why would I let a strange man into my home? A strange, hot, man who looks a little like Santa but a whole lot hotter than the official man in red.

Darn it, Eileen, I groan, taking another drink of my martini, the peppermint flavor going down a little too easily and reminding me of the man sitting a little too close to me.

It strikes me that Saint wore red earlier. His puffer coat is the authentic color of the holiday season, which causes a tickle in my throat that leads to a coughing kind of chuckle.

Maybe he is Santa Claus.

The laugh turns into a giggle until Saint reaches over and snags the candy cane inside the edge of my glass. I watch as he boldly sticks it in his mouth, sucking on it, and giving me a wink before biting off the end.

Summer comes to check on the progress of my drink, which is nearly empty, but I'm flabbergasted by the audacity of Saint and his cheeky wink, so it takes me a minute to finally say, "I'll have another. And so will Santa Baby here."

Saint pulls the candy cane from his lips, and I watch like he's performing candy cane porn. He points at the bartender with the now-sharp end of the sugary stick. "Put them on my tab."

Well, how very holly, jolly of him.

Then he returns the red and white striped candy to his mouth and gives me another pointed glance. I swear a fleck of light gleams in each of his dark eyes. Like a mischievous twinkle.

Strangely reminding me once more of Santa Claus.

Only this one is quite a bit sexier.

CHAPTER 5

[Lumi]

When I wake in the morning, I'm reminded why my forty-three-year-old body can no longer handle martinis like it did when I was twenty-one. My head is throbbing. My stomach sloshing. And my limbs are sluggish.

I need coffee. Stat.

Dressed in a loosely tied flannel robe over a T-shirt with a giant lobster on it, and long underwear leggings, I amble down the stairs from my second-floor bedroom, and stumble past the living room on a mission to the kitchen where I find the coffeemaker on.

"Huh." I don't recall turning it on. For that matter, I hardly remember getting home. As I live close to town in a section of older homes, the walk isn't long, although with the storm two nights ago, it wasn't my best move. Hideaway Harbor is safe enough. The snow is what can be dangerous.

Taking a mug from an upper cabinet, I pour myself a cup of fresh brew and inhale the steamy contents. While it doesn't smell particularly appetizing this morning, the mysteries of coffee need to work their magic because I need to check in with Neve about her newest service project and then get to work.

Closing my eyes, I inhale again as I turn, placing my backside against the countertop.

When I open my eyes, I scream, nearly dropping my full mug of hot coffee. "What the Christmas?"

"Hi."

On the opposite side of the small butcher block table I use as an island stands Saint, dressed in a white, long-sleeved Henley and gray joggers, sporting delicious silver bedhead and . . . *holy peppermint sticks.*

I quickly glance away from the bulge in his sweats and slam my coffee mug on the counter beside me.

"What are you doing here?" I shriek, turning back toward him, and noticing he has slipped his hands into the pockets of his joggers, which does nothing to make the evidence of his morning wood disappear.

He slips a hand free and scratches at the back of his neck, sheepishly glancing at me. "You invited me to stay?"

"Did I?" Because the way he's worded it, it doesn't sound like I actually invited him.

He straightens, slipping his hand back into his pants, *and baby Jesus in a manger,* why am I noticing him adjust himself? Gripping the countertop harder for support, I glance to the side again.

Then another thought leaps into my head, and I swivel mine back in his direction so quickly my stomach pitches. "Did you and I—"

"What do you think?" He arches a brow, taunting me.

It would certainly explain the stiffness in my body, but surely, I'd feel something more, as it's been so long.

He removes his hand from his pocket and rubs up his belly, dragging his shirt upward just the slightest bit to reveal a hint of dark hair leading below his waistband.

"We couldn't," I whisper as my stomach drops sickeningly at the thought I might have had sex and don't remember it.

"We didn't." His eyes intently focus on mine, playful one minute, serious the next, as he rounds the island, lessening the distance between us. "I would never ever take advantage of someone like that." He pauses a beat, letting the earnestness of his tone sink in. "I want my partner to be coherent and consensual, involved and invested."

He takes another cautious step closer to me, but somehow not close enough.

"Because I want her to experience every lingering touch, every breathy sigh, every pleasurable moan I've extracted from her."

Holy hotcakes. Is it suddenly hot in here? Did someone light the fireplace?

"And . . ." He arches a thick brow. "I'd want her to get my name correct."

"Saint?" I question.

"Astan. You started calling me Ass-tan, though."

Shit. I swipe a hand down my face, catching a whiff of my morning breath, and then wondering what my hair must look like. I swipe around one ear, brushing back the long loose locks before repeating the motion on the other side.

"I'm sorry," I mutter. "But it still doesn't explain what you're doing here." I tip forward as if I'll find evidence of breaking and entering or something.

"You had a lot to drink."

My head swings back in his direction as he scratches at the back of his neck again. His face pinches for a second.

"And I walked you home." He glances up at me. "You really don't remember that?"

"So, you let yourself in?" I snap, desperately trying to remember how many martinis I actually drank.

"You invited me in." His hand falls from his neck, his expression a mix of crestfallen and concern, like he's truly upset that I don't remember inviting him into my home. Which was a damn risky thing to do as a single woman in a small town.

His brows crease, the severity of his concern deepening. "You offered me the couch." He nods toward the well-worn couch that faces the opposite direction which explains why I didn't see him when I walked past it this morning. Then again, I shouldn't have missed the large, leather duffle bag in the corner of the living room, or the neat pile of clothes folded on top of it.

"You can't stay here," I say next, like he's made himself comfortable when he hasn't. *I* made him comfortable by inviting him in. I might need to rethink candy cane martinis on Mondays.

A thunderous knock comes to my front door, causing me to flinch, before the lock clicks, opening the door with the key I've provided only to my sisters and Danny. Within seconds, Neve is standing in my kitchen dressed in a short-waisted puffer jacket and wide-legged jeans.

And I'm standing in front of Saint as if I can hide the larger man behind my smaller stature.

"Well, hello." She gives Saint an appraising glance that sends a quick streak of envy through me. Neve has raven-colored hair, like me, but I dye my waves to match red wine. Her hair is chopped into a cute bob and often held back with bobby pins to keep the weight out of her face, giving her the appearance of a 1930s beauty. Men are quickly attracted to her wit and sarcasm. I'm not really jealous of Neve as much as I'm skeptical of her interest in Saint.

Saint acknowledges her with a quiet, "Good morning."

Neve glances at me, arching a brow. "Who have we here?"

"This is Saint," I shift only slightly as I present him, then turn back to shield him once more. "And he was just leaving."

Neve pouts, shifting her gaze from me to him and back. Her brows arch even higher on her second glance at me, demanding immediate details about him despite him standing only a foot behind me.

"He's the Aston Martin."

Neve's eyes widen, and she whistles long and low, glancing back at Saint. Neve loves cars, hence her serving as the shop mechanic.

"He didn't have a place to stay, so he crashed here last night." The explanation sounds innocent enough until you consider that I don't invite anyone to my place. *Ever.*

Learned my lesson once. Won't fool me twice.

"How . . . convenient," my sister drags out the comment, glancing between Saint and me once more before narrowing her gaze on me and my haggard appearance. I look more like I've crawled out of the attic than spent a night rolling around in bed with a hot Santa wannabe.

"But he's not staying another night," I clarify.

"Why not?" Neve and Saint say in unison before sharing a glance with each other.

I lower my voice, directed at my sister. "Because I'm not a fucking inn." I'm a single woman, living alone, who likes her space, even if she has room for a guest.

"Everywhere else is booked," Neve says, as if she's part of the hospitality industry in this little village, and not the town mechanic. She casts another side-eye toward Saint, assessing him another second before muttering rather loudly toward me, "And you have room."

"Neve," I cry, quickly turning to look at Saint and then away because his mouth does that lazy curl, like he has all year for those lips to form a smile. He also looks like a little kid who has gotten a coveted gift on Christmas morning.

"What?" Neve lifts her hands, shrugging at the same time. "It's Christmas. Hideaway is packed. And his car is going to take weeks to repair."

"Really?" Saint and I say at the same time, then I scowl at him.

"I haven't had a chance to look at your vehicle, but knowing the make and model, the parts will take a while to get shipped to our little corner of Maine."

Based on my experience at the post office, I understand shipping demands and delays.

Saint hangs his head a second, and my shoulders fall, mouth twisting as I fight a twinge of guilt. It would suck to be stranded here. Then I remind myself it isn't my fault he crashed his car. Or that it happened in Maine. Or he's too damn good looking.

The last one throws me off, and I briefly close my eyes.

Once upon a time, I invited a man into my space, and he broke my heart. I can't go through that again. Then again, we aren't discussing love here. We're talking about letting a stranger stay in my house.

Saint exhales before glancing up at me. "I know this is awkward, but I could pay you."

"I don't want your money," I gripe, but I could use the money. *Rusty's* could use the money.

"A hundred dollars a day," he counters, and my brows lift. Quickly, I do the math. For seven days, that would equate to seven hundred bucks a week and a good chunk of what's owed for Rusty's mortgage. The re-mortgage Dad took out and didn't tell anyone about, before he passed away.

But I'm already shaking my head, declining his offer.

"Two hundred," he bargains like we're in an open-air street market instead of in my small kitchen where his presence seems to be taking up too much space. Why does he have to look so good tumbling out of bed? *Er*, rather, off a couch.

I glance at Neve, who watches the exchange between Saint and me with curious interest. A soft smile forms on her face.

"What?" I snap at her.

Her head whips in my direction. "I didn't say anything."

"But you have a look on your face."

"What look?"

"I don't know," I huff, flailing out my arm. "Just a look."

Neve shakes her head, like I'm a chestnut roasting on an open fire. Cracking under the pressure.

"I stopped by for the spare keys for the tow. I can't find the original set." She glances at Saint. "And I have an Aston Martin to inspect."

Then she looks back at me, shifting her shorter body so Saint can't see her face. "Take the money," she mouths.

"What?" I glance up at Saint and back at Neve. "No."

Because the man cannot sleep on my couch for a week, even if my calculator brain doubles the fee and realizes the amount he's offering would make nearly one month's mortgage payment. A thirty-day financial reprieve for Rusty's.

However, money is not the point and—

Neve steps closer to me. "Let him stay," she whispers. "It might be fun." She twitches her nose before glancing over my shoulder at Saint and wiggling her fingers in a wave.

"See you soon," she says to him, swiping the spare keys from a hook near the fridge and stepping out of my kitchen, leaving me in a standoff with my wannabe housemate.

"I don't *know* you," I whisper, slumping against the counter again.

"You could get to know me." His typically rugged voice is softer somehow, causing our eyes to meet and hold. The depths of his dark eyes has that spark again. Just a single gleam and then it's gone. "Think of it like speed-dating."

"What?" I shriek.

"Get to know your new roommate in thirty seconds or less."

"Absolutely not," I argue, although I chuckle.

"I'm Saint Santos." He flattens his hand on his chest. "Local car accident victim. Fifty years old. Gainfully employed."

"What do you do?" I ask like this *is* a speed dating moment. Then I think better of myself. "Never mind. Don't answer that."

I don't care that he's employed or fifty or a victim. He's

standing in my kitchen looking healthy as a caribou and too sexy for *my* own good.

"Last night, you told me you're super busy, so you'll hardly be bothered by me. And at night, I can . . . I don't know . . . go somewhere for a while."

"You'd still be sleeping in my home," I remind him. Or is he implying he'd sleep with someone else and then come to my place to actually sleep . . . and what the heck do I care? Let him have a sleepover at the imaginary sleepover's house.

"It didn't matter to you last night." His rough voice remains soft. Not threatening. Not teasing. Just stating a fact.

True. Maybe. I don't know.

"On that note, I don't like that you don't remember inviting me in." He tilts his head, his initial concern returning. "You need to look out for yourself. But as long as I'm here, I could look out for you, too."

I'm stunned by the offer. I don't have any idea what that would feel like. Someone looking out for me. And the suggestion certainly shouldn't be coming from a stranger, but the vague sense of familiarity I experienced last night returns.

Would it really be so bad to have him around?

I glance at Saint one more time, taking in his broad shoulders, the strength in his arms, those grey sweatpants. Plus, the softness of his smile and hesitation in his eyes.

"I—" I rub at my throbbing temples, pressing my skull with my forefinger and thumb as if I can erase the lingering headache. My brain isn't in a condition to process. It hurts to think.

Rusty's mortgage. Danny's absence. Stranger on my couch. The offenses hammer through my head.

"Here." His voice comes closer to me, returning to our earlier position when he approached me and told me all the things he'd want a lover to experience with him.

"May I?" Holding up his hands, he pauses them near my face.

His dark eyes are swirls of chocolate, teasing me, taunting me to give in. And for some unexplainable reason, I nod.

The second his thumbs come to either side of my temple, massaging in slow circles, I start to melt, needing my grasp on the countertop to support me before I puddle at his feet.

"Holy Rudolph and his fellow reindeer, that feels amazing," I groan, with my eyes closed and his peppermint and chocolate scent filling my nose. The fragrance should be a reminder that I drank too much last night but with his thumbs working their magic, I can't think. I simply relax until he removes his fingers.

"I don't think reindeer can give massages." His voice is light, teasing, and my eyes slowly open.

"Better?" he whispers. Even his voice is soothing, deep and rumbly.

With my eyes open, I'm met again with those black orbs, dark as coal this time, yet sparkling with something I don't recognize.

I swallow thickly as he steps back. "You should probably get ready for work, right? I don't want to get you in trouble and place you on the naughty list."

However, another gleam in his eye says he's all sorts of trouble and doesn't mind being on the naughty list.

I can think of a few other things I'd like to do to put me on that list as well. However, being late for work would not be in my best interest, nor would remaining here, staring at him, like he's who I'd like to cause all kinds of trouble with.

CHAPTER 6

December 6

[Lumi]

$\mathcal{D}$espite the busyness of the post office, at the end of the day a walk is in order to clear my mind. From the post office, I live near the opposite end of Locke Street in an older section of houses east of town proper. The location is close enough to Rusty's I can walk there. Anywhere in Hideaway Harbor is walkable, within thirty minutes, even the old Locke Reserve.

Striding north on Main Street, the garland-wrapped lamp posts and lights strung above the street from business roof to business roof create a festive air. The buzz of the upcoming holiday hums along the street between window shoppers dallying and after-work locals rushing by. I wave at Noelle Clarke on the opposite side of the street, who runs Christmas Wonderland, a pop-up shop over on Hideaway Lane, and then turn back to thinking about my day.

Inside the post office, we have a red, imitation postal box for children to mail letters to Santa. Each year, we collect a handful of notes, and I pass them out to local businesses in hopes of support in helping a little one's dream come true for the holidays.

When I was a little girl, I loved to visit the local library and look through books about foreign places. The colorful maps. The vivid cultural photographs. The lists of sites to see. One year, I asked for a Barbie airplane so I could pretend my doll traveled to wherever my imagination took me. Unfortunately, I never got the plane or the sleek-looking Barbie flight attendant who whisked away on grand adventures.

With that thought, I recall the strangest thing that happened today. While children rarely enter the post office, as typically picking up mail is an errand done by adults, today we had three separate little kids enter, walk directly to the Santa-approved red box, and slip their request through the slim slot.

One young mother explained, "He couldn't wait to get here today."

I offered her a compassionate smile. Christmas is a magical time for children and a frazzling one for mothers.

Still, I couldn't get the excitement on that little boy's face out of my mind, and memories of my own son at that age flipped forward.

Danny loved the idea that Christmas was Christ's birthday, and he demanded that I purchase a present for the newborn babe. We settled on a teddy bear, as a little baby needed something soft to cuddle. With his three-year-old hand in mine, he led me to the manger scene inside the church on Christmas Eve and placed his gift bag right on top of the plastic baby Jesus in the manger. After the service, I mentioned to the minister what Danny had done, a little embarrassed that the red and green gift bag sat on top of baby Jesus during the service.

"Happens all the time," he assured me, although I'd never noticed gifts on the swaddled infant before that year or after.

Smiling at the memory, something up ahead catches my

attention. A distinct red, puffy jacket and matching red cap on a solid male frame. For some reason, I suddenly walk faster, especially as he disappears into a shop near Buoy Street. Rushing faster than I intended, as if suddenly on a mission. I crane my neck to peer into businesses as I near the corner of Main and Buoy, until I pause before one particular shop.

With a black curtain behind the large window, the gold embossed lettering is highlighted: The Perfect Package. An Intimacy Shop.

I glance at the hot pink door marking the store's entrance.

He couldn't have, could he?

Taking the final steps to the entrance, I tug open the door and enter the warm shop.

Lola Monroe owns the place. To complement her name, Lola is in her early thirties and a bombshell. Voluptuous with powder blue hair that reaches her waist, she is a cross between a mermaid and a 1950s sex siren. She's gorgeous, and we get our hair done at the same place, although mine is a deep, red wine color.

The store has a luxurious aura about it, like stepping back in time yet with a modern flair. Alcoves and deep wooden cabinets line the walls around an open center area that provides intimate seating arrangements with velvet settees and classic loungers. With the blackout curtain on the front window and low interior lighting, the space feels like a cross between a boudoir and a high-end jewelry store, complete with glass display cases for some items.

One wall features portraits of female icons, boasting feminine trailblazers and pleasure revolutionaries, because, as the name suggests, this place is all about adult sensual satisfaction.

Which is probably why I shouldn't be standing in here, breathing heavily like I raced a mile, chasing after someone I shouldn't care about who entered Lola's store.

But my eyes catch on the gold-scripted sayings painted on the wall, empowering sexual awareness.

Own Your Yes. Touch Yourself With Kindness. Pleasure is Power.

These are among my favorites and a reminder that I've been the sole instrument of my personal pleasure for years.

On that note, I catch sight of the only other person in The Perfect Package at the moment. With his shoulders hunched, head hung in deep concentration, Saint stands with a dark box in his hands. My face flames just thinking about him and what he might purchase. What he might use it for, and with whom, how, and when.

As my entire body warms, I summons courage and slowly step closer to him.

"Looking for a gift for that special woman in your life?" I tease, slipping my hands into the pockets of my long, green puffer jacket.

Not flustered in the slightest, Saint looks up from the package in his hand and scowls at me. His thick, gray brows squeeze together.

"Actually, I'm looking at the packaging of this product." He holds up the black box with gold script.

"What is it?" I chuckle, realizing too late what I am asking in relation to *where* I'm asking it. I'm also noticing that no man should look so confident in a sex store.

"It's a sensory box." He flips the package to read the back. "Contains products for taste, touch, and smell, plus a toy as a tool."

"Sounds . . . nice?" I hesitate, uncertain what any of that could mean.

"Would you buy this for the special man in your life?" He positions the box so I can see it better. With its dark color, the packaging is rather dull and not overly appealing, not that I'm an expert on sex toy products or their marketing. However, I'd probably pass it up for something a little more . . . enticing.

There is also the obvious, and I scoff before stating it, "I don't have a man in my life."

Saint arches a brow. "Would you buy it for yourself?"

As my face heats fifty shades of red, I avoid eye contact a second before admitting what I shouldn't admit. "I don't think I understand the product."

"How to use it?" The corner of his mouth hooks.

Bolstering confidence I don't actually feel, I nod toward the box. "That description is a little vague." I mean, what am I tasting, touching, and smelling? Also, I want to know the specifics about the toy inside. I'm not a prude, but it's been a while, and while I'm open to experimentation, I'm still cautious enough that I want to know what I'm getting myself into. Plus, how would I use any of that on myself? And suddenly, I realize I'm in over my head, standing a little too close to sexy Santa, looking at sex products.

"Exactly," he states a little too loudly for the intimate atmosphere, before slamming the box back on the wooden shelf inside a large wardrobe. "I'll need to talk to Kaye."

"Who's Kaye? The special woman in your life?" I playfully prod, circling back to my initial question, when I really don't need to know, or care, if he has a special woman in his life. I definitely do not want to picture him tasting, touching, or smelling whomever Kaye is.

"No." He chokes, almost like he's gagging at the thought. "She's my sister."

His sister? Why the hell would he need to talk to his sister about a sex toy?

He picks the box off the shelf again and points to the logo in the lower corner while he reads the name.

"Kringle Toys. This is her company."

Oh. "Sounds holiday-ish." I chuckle.

"It should. And this is supposed to be a holiday product." Then he runs his finger along the item's name. "Wonderlust. An experiment in wonder and lust." He scoffs, like he doesn't approve of the name or the tagline.

"I'm only familiar with *wanderlust*," I comment. "But it sounds like you know a lot about this product." Has he used it? Tested it? With whom? And why am I asking . . . at least in my head?

"I should. I sit on the board of her company." He sighs heavily, sets the box back on the shelf much gentler this time.

So, he's a board member for a sex toy company. What exactly does that mean? Unlimited access to pleasure items? Free range of samples? What other perks might there be? And why does my mind race to wonder if he'd share all those advantages with me?

When he turns his entire body toward mine, he slips his hands into his jacket pockets, mirroring my stance.

"Do you have any siblings other than Neve?"

The question feels like it fell out of the sky. "Three sisters. I'm the oldest."

He chuckles, jolly and light, before glancing back at the package he'd replaced on the shelf. "Yeah. I'm the oldest as well. I have a younger brother, Nick. Kaye is the youngest." He shakes his head, pursing his lush lips, before glancing up at me.

Our eyes lock for a second, like he wants to tell me something. The space around us seems to hum. With the dim lighting and the velvet lounger in my periphery, my imagination races.

Would he lay me out and use that sensory kit on me?

Suddenly, he blinks, like he read my thoughts, and he shifts his body, letting the potential for him to speak, and my dirty thoughts, to pass.

From behind him, Lola approaches us. I hadn't heard her because of the carpeted floor, but the way Saint's body twists suggested he sensed her approach.

"Hey, Lumi," she addresses me.

Saint offers Lola a soft smile as a greeting, and she takes him in for a second. When her eyes leap to mine, they widen the slightest bit. Yeah, she sees it. *Sexy Santa.*

"Anything I can help you and . . . your man . . . with today?" She quirks a brow, insinuating something that does not need to be insinuated.

"Oh, he's not my—"

"I'm her roommate." He looks over at me and winks.

"He's not—"

"Saint." He holds out his hand for Lola, and if she expects more of a name from him, he doesn't offer it.

While they shake hands, I turn back to the package on the shelf. "Saint has questions about this—"

"No, I don't," he interjects, low and warning, as I pull the box off the shelf and hold it toward Lola.

Was my voice too loud? I feel like I've been shouting. Suddenly, I'm too warm and flustered, but I battle on.

Lola glances between Saint and me, giving us both a curious look. She is all about sexual freedom and expressing sexuality with confidence, so our bumbling act is certain to be confusing.

"He wants to try this with the special woman in his life." I power on, leaning in like I'm whispering a secret to her, sharing what he'll be purchasing for that certain someone for Christmas.

"I—" When I glance up at him, he clamps his mouth shut. His expression shifts from objection to mischief.

"Actually, Lola." He pauses after addressing her. "I'd like to gift Lumi something." He leans toward Lola like he has a secret for her, as well. "To take the edge off. She's a bit tense this holiday. I'd also like to gift her something, as a thank you, for hosting me at her house for a few weeks."

"A few *weeks*," I screech, because I thought he was continuing to look for other options. He can't stay at my house for a few weeks, let alone another night. He's already stayed one too many.

Lola looks at me, puzzled for a second, almost uncertain how to navigate this shitshow in front of her.

"What do you recommend? Maybe something holiday-themed?" Saint continues, like he has the attention of a personal shopper. "It's going to be a *long*, hard couple of weeks."

CHAPTER 7

[Saint]

*P*urchasing an emerald-green dildo that looked more like a giant pickle than a penis was worth the crimson shade of Lumi's face.

After we exit The Perfect Package, I hand her the distinct bag.

"For that special someone in my life," I jest, my sarcasm playful. "My roommate."

However, while I'd intended the purchase as a joke, now I'm plagued with thoughts of Lumi using it. Would she moan softly or cry out loud? Would her head fall back, her mouth open, her body beg for more? Something real and long and—

"Well played." Lumi snags the pretty bag from my hand, tucking it unceremoniously beneath her arm and sticking her hands back into her pockets. "Now the whole town will be talking about us."

Securing my place as her houseguest, insinuating she's sexually frustrated, and purchasing a pleasure toy for her, certainly will give the town something to talk about. I'm not evil by nature, but *that* sure was fun, and I haven't had enough of these moments in my life. I'm surrounded by jolly folks and well-wishers, but outright silliness that's just for me is rare.

"Dinner?" I ask, in an effort to make up for my bad behavior.

Lumi ducks her head. With her hat on, I can't see all that lush red-wine-colored hair that hangs long and loose, at least first thing in the morning. When we met, it was tucked into her knit hat. When she left for work, it was pulled back into a tight knot at the base of her neck, which I suspect is the current style beneath another knit cap.

I'd like to see all that hair, dark and richly red, spread out on a bed pillow.

"Oh." She hesitates. "I was just going to stop by The Chowder House Rules and take something home." She glances upward but away from me, possibly still embarrassed by how things turned out in The Perfect Package.

"Didn't you eat there last night?"

She shrugs. "Yeah, well, it's tough to cook for one." Her eyes meet mine only briefly before she glances away again, and I see what I saw last night. She misses her son.

His absence brings guilt because I shouldn't be in this town. *I'm* a son who has a huge responsibility this time of year. I need to be in North. I promised I'd be there by December first, and I've missed the date. I could blame the snowstorm and the accident, but I'd already been running behind.

As I've quickly learned, cell service is spotty around here. I haven't had the chance to connect with home, other than a hasty message about the accident and my unexpected delay. Since sending the initial message off, I've been avoiding any responses.

And what better way to continue to ignore my family than to take this single mom to dinner.

"Chowder House Rules," I state. "My treat. A thank you for letting me stay at your place last night." I'd love to reach out and wrap my arm around her. Pull her into my side, like it's a date, but Lumi has this air about her. A wall thicker than a snow barricade.

Is it because she's the oldest? Because she's a single mom? Because she's alone?

I know all about loneliness and the burden of bearing it. The sense that you must continue to do everything on your own, in silence. It's a strenuous, heavy sensation, and just for the night, I'd like to remove the pressure from her shoulders.

I knock my elbow into hers, forcing her to turn around as I'd noticed the chowder place on Harbor Road, appropriately located near the local harbor, which is at the opposite end of Main Street.

"The Chowder House Rules," she agrees, her blue eyes still sad and her smile weak. But I intend to change both those things.

As we walk along Main Street heading in the direction of the restaurant, I admire the devotion this town has to Christmas. Garland-wrapped lamp posts and holiday lights highlight almost every store window. One thing I noticed earlier on my stroll was an easel in front of a local business with a giant calendar number on it.

"Explain the calendar to me," I nod in the direction of the wooden easel still outside a boutique.

"Each day, a business can request or volunteer to host the traveling calendar for the day. A business owner or someone of their choosing rips off the large calendar date." Lumi waves her arm in the air, dramatically imitating the removal of a date. "It's a photo opportunity. Helps advertise the businesses and counts down until Christmas."

Lumi smiles at the town tradition.

"Creative," I state, noting once again how much this town loves the holiday season as we continue our stroll to the famous chowder spot.

Once seated in the cozy restaurant, with blue paneling that resembles waves above darker wood, like the bottom of a ship, we each order a cup of their famous corn chowder, plus a meal. After last night's drink-a-thon, Lumi declines an alcoholic beverage, but I opt for a beer.

"So, tell me more about these three sisters," I ask, making them sound mysterious.

Lumi laughs, the sound lighter than soft Christmas bells tinkling. Her smile is more genuine than it had been outside The Perfect Package.

"As I told you, I'm the oldest."

I don't dare ask her how old she is, although I'd guess around forty, give or take a few years.

"Which means I've inherited responsibility for Rusty's Wrecks."

"I totally understand." She has no idea how much responsibility I shoulder as the oldest son as well.

"Then comes Neve, two years younger than me. She's the mechanic in the family and runs Rusty's. I don't know anything about cars."

I nod. I checked in on mine earlier today, informing said sister about the parts I'm certain I will be needing for my damaged green baby.

"Then we have twin sisters, who are three years younger than Neve. Isolde and Icelyn."

"More snow references." I arch a brow.

"Yes." Her face brightens, like she can't believe I recognize the names, but I'm familiar with tons of names. It's why hearing her name yesterday evening struck me. Lumi is rather unusual in the States, not to mention, I haven't ever heard it used on someone her age. The name seems like a modern identity. Still, it's lovely and fits her, although I can't put my finger on why I think that.

Lumi Snowe. I run the name silently over my tongue while she explains what her twin sisters do.

"Isolde is a local teacher. Icelyn doesn't live around here." She glances out at the cold harbor view through the window at her side, like the second twin is a difficult topic.

"Any *special someone* for each of them?" I tease, not missing how often Lumi asked me the same question while in the adult shop.

She shakes her head, smiling down at the table. "Haven't we all had that certain someone at least once in our lives?"

No. But I don't answer her. Instead, I offer a warm smile like I understand when I don't. I haven't been able to have someone exclusive because of my position. My experience is unusual to say the least, and it's a large commitment, one I've never asked someone to share with me.

"Sounds like a story," I admit, leaning forward like she's about to reveal all her secrets to me, which would be a preposterous assumption. I only met her two nights ago.

"No story." Lumi sighs and stretches back in her seat. "It's your typical girl comes home for a funeral and sleeps with the wrong guy. A flatland*ah*."

"What?" I sit up straighter, staring at her as she lowers her lids, embarrassed either by her explanation or my outburst. I have so many questions.

"I was in college when my mother died." She leans forward, slipping her hands beneath her thighs, and glances toward the wintery harbor again. Her expression is melancholy, like a deep well of emptiness still lingers after all these years.

Swallowing thickly, I don't want to imagine the day I'll lose my parents.

"I'm so sorry," I offer while my fingers itch to touch her somehow, comfort her some way.

When she turns back toward me, her eyes are a little darker than normal. "I let someone who wasn't intending to stay in this town into my heart." She shrugs again and lowers her gaze to the table. "It happens."

Does it? Is it that easy? And then, that easy to dismiss? I don't like that someone hurt her, took advantage of her, and the desire to wrap her up in comfort strikes again.

After a silent minute, in which I sense she doesn't want to further discuss the passing away of her mother or the wrong guy she slept with, I ask, "What's a flatland*ah*?" I repeat the word how she said it.

"Someone who doesn't live in Maine." She gives me a look because I'm a flatlander.

My beer is delivered to the table along with our cups of chowder before I can ask for more details about this flatlander and what happened with him. What he did to her.

"So, tell me about your siblings?" She points her spoon at me before digging into the piping hot, thick soup and swirling it around as if the motion will settle the steam rising above the cup.

"One brother. Nick is a few years younger than me. He didn't want any part of the family business, so he's a firefighter in Chicago."

Lumi stares at me across the table, brows pinching like she understands. Again, that responsibility thing.

"And Kaye . . . she wanted to take on a different division of the company."

"Adult toys," Lumi clarifies. She blows on the steamy mug in front of her. There is no reason that move should look sexual, and yet it does. The perfect, tight O of her lips. The rosy color of that delicate skin. Her soft exhale.

Jack Frost, I need to get it together around this woman. I'd nearly busted my personal pipe this morning in her kitchen, watching her suffer through a hangover in that loosely-closed robe and cute lobster shirt. Not to mention, being near enough to rub her temples.

Temples, Saint? Honestly? Like I've seen her ancient petticoat when I'd give anything to know if she wears a thong or boy briefs or nothing at all.

Nope. Bad Saint. Very bad.

"You seem to know a bit about the packaging," she adds.

I'd become acquainted with *my* package, especially after she left for work and I helped myself to her shower, luxuriating in body wash that smelled like green apples and her. Taking a little too much luxury, I allowed her to play out in my fantasy, which would be highly inappropriate to admit.

"Yes." I clear my throat. "I happen to know a thing or two about packaging and marketing. I'm in the toy industry. *Children's* toys." Although I also dabble in electronics and accessories for older kids.

"Gainfully employed." One side of her lip tips upward as she sits up taller. "That's so interesting because earlier I was thinking about a toy I never got for Christmas."

"What did you ask for?" I clear my throat again, noting how easily it clicked into a familiar tone.

And what did you ask Santa for this year, insert any name you'd like.

I take a sip of the hot chowder to distract myself while I listen.

"A Barbie airplane." She giggles afterward like she's still a child and not a forty-something woman.

"Why?" I ask, offering a smile.

"I always wanted to see the world," she says a bit wistfully, then sighs to further emphasize her desire.

"And did you?"

Her gaze snaps back to me, like she was far off for a moment. "I've never been anywhere other than Bangor."

"Bangor, Maine?" I clarify.

"Is there another Bangor?"

"There are at least ten cities named Bangor in the U.S. alone."

"Really?" She laughs again, deeper, throatier. "How do you know that?"

"I've visited all of them."

She stares at me a moment, blue eyes bright and deep like I

imagine the ocean outside the harbor might be in the summer months. Her lips tip up on one corner again.

"Really?" Skepticism fills her voice.

I've set a trap for myself. *Why would I be in all ten Bangors?* Turning the situation around, I ask, "Where would you go if you could go anywhere?"

"Everywhere." She blows out a breath again, her shoulders lowering as she twirls her spoon around her chowder mug, staring into the cup once more. "Africa. England. Cabo. Antarctica."

"Antarctica?" I chuckle.

With her eyes still lowered, head bowed, she continues to spin her spoon round and round, like she's circling the globe in her head.

"Why haven't you ever been anywhere?" I ask gently, hoping to encourage her to keep talking. I like talking to her.

"Another classic tale. First, I was a single mom in a small town who gave up her education."

I'm not liking that excuse.

"And then, when I had more time and a little bit of means, my dad died four years ago, leaving me in charge, with a four-way split of Rusty's Wrecks."

As she's clearly unhappy about this inheritance, I'm curious .. . "Why didn't you sell?" Take the money. Go on her trips. See the world.

Lumi gazes back out the restaurant window, focusing on something out there, before bringing her attention back to me. She shrugs again, and I'm beginning to dislike the motion.

"Neve was the closest to our dad, and she didn't want to give it up. Not without a fight." Lumi fists her hand around her spoon, holding it upright over her chowder mug like a weapon. "I told her I'd give her five years max."

"Five years for what?"

Lumi lowers her gaze again. "Turn the business around. Or buy us out. Or sell."

"And what year are you on?" I know the answer before she says it.

"Four."

"One more year," I offer, like it's an easy solution when I know that when it comes to family and business, it's never that easy, especially when the business *is* your family.

"Yeah." I hear the disagreement and disappointment in her soft voice.

Our food is delivered although we haven't finished our chowder, and we move to easier topics while we eat.

I wanted to know where she went to college before she left school. She asks me where I went, and I admit I've never been to college. I learned on the job. A lifelong education of predicting the toy market and monitoring societal change. Purchasing. Production. Marketing. Gains and losses. Worker equity. Every single facet of the business I've worked, from the ground up and literally since I was a toddler until present day.

"And you were headed back to the business? North." She holds up a French fry, pointing at me, displeasure in her tone at the vagueness of the location. "Before Skippy got in your way."

"Couldn't skip over him," I counter, feeling the pull of my lips into a smile.

Lumi chuckles before biting her fry.

As we near the end of our meal, the waitress returns. "Can I interest either of you in dessert?" She holds out a special dessert menu, and Lumi reads the top, then gasps.

"Is today December sixth?"

"All day," the snarky waitress states with a friendly grin.

"What's December six?" I question, curious why the date would be important to her.

"It's the Feast of St. Nicholas. I forgot—" She abruptly stops herself.

"What?" Curiosity has me by a throat hold.

She waves me off and then shakes her head, declining dessert.

"I'll take a coffee, please." The caffeine will keep me up for hours, but I could use the hot drink to clear my head. No more sexy shower thoughts about my housemate.

As the waitress walks away, I point at Lumi. "Explain yourself."

"I just . . . for half a second, I realized I hadn't set out shoes for St. Nicholas Day, and then realized I had no one to set them out for." She laughs at herself. "Which is silly because I haven't set shoes out for years."

Setting out shoes for the feast of St. Nicholas isn't widely practiced, but here and there in the States, the patron saint known as the original Santa Claus is celebrated. People honor the day by encouraging their kids to set a pair of shoes by the front door or in a front hallway. The activity is similar to hanging stockings by a fireplace, which is how Santa delivered the first toys. The premise of St. Nicholas' Day is that if a child has been bad, he'll receive coal in his shoes. St. Nick is displeased with his behavior, but the child still has a few weeks to right his wrongs. If a child has been good, he might receive candy or a small treat. Some even receive something holiday-themed in their shoes, like a Christmas Lego set or a snowman book, adding to the excitement of the season.

I've never been involved in the tradition, although I've grown up hearing about it. We leave St. Nicholas Day up to parents to handle.

"Aren't shoes set out the night *before* St. Nicholas Day?" I nearly laugh every time I say Nicholas, as it reminds me of my younger brother, who always wants to claim this day as his day when it's really mine.

"Yes." She smiles softly to herself. "I don't even know why I thought about it just now."

Danny. Her son won't be home for Christmas, and the memories of past holidays are dancing in her head like sugarplums.

I don't mention my thoughts. Instead, I say, "Well, we can still celebrate, because today is my birthday."

I don't typically make a big deal out of the day. December birthdays tend to get lost because of the holiday. Still, I want to distract her from her sad thoughts about her son and his absence. I'm here. Not that *that* is any consolation, but I'd still like to give her another reason to honor the day. Celebrate it in a new way. Sharing my birthday with someone special would be a first for me.

Her head pops up, and those blue eyes are saucer-sized again. "You're pulling my leg?"

After our banter yesterday about pulling body parts, I roll my lips before I blurt out what other parts of her I'd like to pull. Like sucking at that pouting lip. Or tugging at her nipples to see how peaked they get.

Dammit, Saint. There you go again.

I can't take out my driver's license to prove my birthdate, so I smile as convincingly as I can. "Elf's honor. I'm not pulling your leg."

She watches me for a minute, taking a drive around my face. My eyes. My cheeks. My chin covered with a heavy growth after a few days without trimming.

"If it's your birthday, then we *should* celebrate."

"That's what *he* said," I jab a finger into my sternum, because I did say that. Plus, I'd like to distract her from her sadness about Danny's absence. Her responding smile is worth the joke.

Lumi turns in her seat and waves for the waitress, who quickly returns.

"We need two whoopie pies, please," she orders, before pointing at me. "It's his birthday."

"Happy birthday," the young woman says before clapping her hands once and stepping away to retrieve the famous Maine treat of vanilla cream fluff slathered between two soft, cake-like chocolate cookies.

When the waitress returns with our dessert, Lumi hands one to me and picks up the other one. Holding hers up, she nods for me to follow her lead.

"As we don't have a candle, we'll toast to your birthday, and you should make a wish before you take the first bite."

"Is that a Maine-ism? Like when you see the new moon, wish before you speak, and you'll receive your wish before the end of the week."

Lumi laughs, sharp and loud. "I don't know, but we can add it to the list."

The naughty or the nice one? Because being around Lumi is nice, which makes my thoughts all the naughtier. Birthday spankings? For me or her.

But seriously, spending time with her has been refreshing, and I'm grateful she's giving me her time. I've asked a lot in suggesting that I stay in her home. I understand her hesitancy, it's just . . . I like her, and she's safe with me. I don't like to think about what could have happened to her, walking home in the cold and dark, a little too tipsy to remember inviting a stranger inside her house. The thought of anything happening to her, especially on my watch, sends an uncomfortable shiver down my spine.

Shaking the thought, I hold up my pie and tap it against hers, making a wish before I take a bite.

I wish for more time with her, but know immediately it's only a wish.

"Okay, you can stay," she says before biting into her pie.

"What?" I ask, a little confused by the suddenness of her comment.

"At my house." Her brows lift. "Unless you found somewhere else?" I watch as those pretty brows of hers lower and pinch, like she doesn't like the idea of me finding another place. Maybe even questions why it bothers her.

"Actually." I clear my throat. "I haven't found anywhere to stay." In the back of my mind, I'd been hopeful she'd change her mind, but my backup plan was to sneak into Rusty's Wreck and spend the night there.

"Well, as long as you've already started the rumor that you'll be my housemate for a few weeks . . . I have a spare room."

Her shoulders fall like she's given in on a hardship, but she also softly smiles at me before taking another bite of her whoopie pie. I counter that smile before taking a bite of my own, deciding this might have been the best birthday I've ever had.

And when we get back to her place, I set a pair of her shoes at the base of her staircase in the front hall and unpack the poorly packaged Wonderlust items, filling her footwear with holiday-print, textured fabric, winter-scented oils, and chocolates in hopes her holidays are a little brighter, even if she will be alone.

St. Nick already knows she's been a good girl all year.

CHAPTER 8

December 7

[Lumi]

$\mathcal{I}$ don't get to Rusty's Wrecks until my lunch break on the next day, although Neve and I have discussed the tragedy of the Aston Martin over the phone.

"Do you have any idea how much that car is worth? How much *he* must be worth?" My younger sister asked, but I didn't respond. I don't want to know the answers, and I'd be worried about my sister and materialism if I didn't know her better.

When I step into Rusty's waiting area, I'm gobsmacked by what I see.

Next to the forest green sports car is Saint, dressed in a white Henley with mechanic bibs rolled down to his waist and wearing a baseball cap. He's gone from Santa heartthrob to auto shop bad boy, and parts on my body start to pulse in ways they haven't in a long time. For lack of a better comparison, my engine is suddenly revving when the battery has been dead for a while.

57

Saint is bent beside his car, removing the side panel over the right wheel well.

"What is he doing?" I whisper to my sister, like Saint can hear me from our position inside the waiting area, which has a window that provides a clear view of Mr. Bent-over with his firm backside in the air. The small lobby has a few stackable chairs, which look dingy no matter how often we've cleaned them. Neve stands behind the front counter.

"He said he couldn't sit still, so he decided to start taking damaged pieces off the vehicle."

"Is it really going to be weeks before it's fixed?" I ask. The timing cuts awfully close to Christmas.

Neve stares through the cloudy window. "Yep. Fancy car. Fancy delays on parts, especially up here. The axle is bent. The front wheel alignment screwed, and he needs a new tire, which happens to be a specialty one."

Any more details, and Neve is going to lose me. The bare basics about automobiles are the extent of my wheelhouse. Neve was the one who followed our father around after our mother passed away. She had always been close to him. The female counterpart to the male child he never had. Dad loved his girls, but he still wanted a token son, and Neve tried desperately to fill the role.

"Interesting what a change of clothes can do for a man," she blurts, pulling my attention from ogling Saint's ass in those mechanic's bibs.

"What do you mean?"

"He walked in here wearing khaki pants." Neve dramatically shivers before pausing a second. "Negative ten."

I laugh, loud but light, recalling the game Neve and I used to play, rating guys. For her, khaki pants have always been a negative number. She wants a man who is rugged and rough, not smooth and silky.

"Was he wearing that three-quarter zip sweater?" He'd had

one on the morning I picked him up, which reminds me his pants were not classic chinos, but Carhartt jeans. My sister is so silly.

"Yep." She pops the word, slipping her hands into her own bibs, which are fastened over her breasts.

"You know what that means?" I pause for effect. "Health insurance."

Neve barks a laugh so loud, Saint stands and narrows his eyes in our direction, catching us watching him through the window. We both turn our heads, leaning over the front counter as if something fascinates us about the chipped countertop.

Only within seconds, Neve lifts her head, side-eyeing the bays. "He kind of looks like a hot Santa."

I whisper, "I know, right?" I peek over my shoulder, hoping to catch another glimpse of Saint without getting caught. My thoughts flip back to this morning when my shoes were stuffed to the brim with sex-enhancing sensory products. Whether a joke or not, he'd gone out of his way to make me feel better about Danny's absence and my absentmindedness, momentarily thinking I'd forgotten the special day.

He gave me a new reason to celebrate. His birthday. While he'd tried to play it off as no big deal, he still shared the evening with me, momentarily distracting me from sad thoughts about Danny's absence. The gesture was rather sweet, if not a bit enticing.

Whatever shall I do with all those pleasure items? Use them alone or with that someone special in my life?

I pull my gaze from Saint and look at Neve. "He looks like that Target one."

"What? No." Neve grimaces, but her gaze drifts toward the bays again. "More like that book with the naughty next-door Santa-like character."

I chuckle as my sister is terrible at remembering titles and author names.

When she gasps, I glance at her startled face, then follow her gaze aimed at the garage.

I turn my head in time to watch as Saint finishes twisting the baseball cap on his head from bill forward to flipped backward.

Neve slams her hand on the countertop, causing me to jump, and I let out a squeak as I turn back toward her.

"Sweet Christmas." She whistles low. "Plus fifteen for the backward baseball cap."

We collapse over the counter in a fit of giggles, like when we were teens checking out the various mechanics our dad hired.

I'd worry about Neve's attention on Saint, but I know she's only ever had eyes for one man. One who eventually broke her heart.

With a hesitant glance, I gaze back toward the bays, watching Saint squat in intense concentration while working on something near the wheel well.

"I see that look," Neve says, drawing my attention again.

I meet eyes that match mine. The Nordic blue coloring is something we inherited from our mother. "What look?" The question is innocent enough, but I'm worried that Neve can read my thoughts. The naughty ones I've been having since discovering a shoe full of sensory items and chocolate this morning. And then imagining how I might use those items with my temporary housemate.

"Like you want to take a bite of him."

"He does smell like peppermint and chocolate," I tease, pressing my forearms on the counter and leaning toward my sister on the other side. Despite the quip, my face heats, like she's caught me stealing said chocolate out of a holiday gift box of them.

"And we know this how?" She arches a brow.

I smile at the collective *we* and ignore her question.

"So, you decided to let him stay at your house." Neve lets the comment hang a minute, like mistletoe in a doorway.

"You told me to," I remind her. "Remember . . . it's Christmas. And Hideaway is packed. There's no room at any inn." I spin my finger like it will jog her memory. "You said it might be fun."

She hadn't been wrong. So far, I have had fun hanging out with Saint. It'd been nice to have dinner with someone new. We walked back to my place mostly in silence, but it wasn't awkward. Just Saint taking a moment to point out the stars and I took a second to appreciate the magic of them. Twinkling so bright, yet pinpricks on a dark canvas, light-years away from Hideaway Harbor.

"Lumi." Her tone is a warning. And a reminder. This is how I got myself in trouble the first time. The only time. When trouble knocked and I let him in.

"He had nowhere to go," I defend, like I take in strays on the regular when the decision had been a total whim. It also was the fault of candy cane martinis. Plus, that something so familiar sensation about him. The beard. The hair. The color red on him. I cannot place it.

"Just be careful," she warns, like she's the older sister.

I round the counter and bring her into me for a hug. "I always am."

She knows I am. I've never been anything but careful, except that one time.

When I release my younger sister, I take a final glance toward the garage, catching Saint watching us.

He looks concerned until I wave, and the tension on his face eases. His smile is lazy, looping up on one side like the hook that holds up my Christmas stocking.

I'm in so much trouble. Again.

CHAPTER 9

[Lumi]

$\mathcal{A}$fter work, the house is empty, and I assume Saint is still at the shop with Neve. Despite the early evening, the sky is pitch black, and the house is quiet. Almost too quiet. No Danny rushing up and down the staircase. No race for dinner before a sports practice, or an actual game, or a holiday play. No extra hustle and bustle as I'm the only one present.

It was silly to think about that long ago past as Danny has been away for years. Off to college. Living a dream. As he should.

So, I decide to make Christmas cookies. The kids who come into the post office might enjoy them. Lord knows if I keep them all to myself, I will eat them all by myself as well.

I'm in the midst of pulling out ingredients when a short rap comes to the front door. When I open it, Saint sheepishly stands on the front porch.

"I don't have a key."

And I'd locked the door as I do when I'm home alone, even if Hideaway Harbor's crime rate is extremely low.

"I'll . . . I'll give you the spare." I hold the door as Saint enters. A whiff of peppermint and chocolate follows him, lingering with the crisp cold coming off his coat. He hangs that red coat on a hook in the entryway directly next to my long jacket, and I'm caught for a moment, staring at the bright red puffer coat beside my olive green one, looking a little too right hanging there together.

"Lumi?"

"Yeah?" I swallow and glance at Saint, realizing I'd been staring a little too long at those two jackets hanging together.

"I'm going to shower quick. Then maybe we could share dinner again." He scratches at the back of his neck like he's nervous to ask.

"Dinner?" I pause. "Oh gosh. I hadn't thought about dinner. I was about to make Christmas cookies."

"Cookies for dinner?" He arches one thick brow.

"My Nana would approve." Although my grandparents are long gone, Nana loved any excuse to eat cookies, often having them for breakfast with her coffee.

"Well, you should probably eat something a little heartier. Pizza?" His expression looks sheepish once again.

"Would *you* like pizza?" I ask, brows pinching at the strange expression on his face.

"We don't exactly have delivery where I live, so the concept of ordering a pizza to be delivered is kind of a novelty."

My forehead furrows, eyes wide. What kind of remote place doesn't deliver a pizza? But then I think of hundreds of places I'd like to visit, and none of them would involve a pizza delivery service nearby.

"Pizza it is then." I step toward the kitchen while Saint heads for the stairway. The soft thud of his feet reminds me of my earlier thoughts about the house being too quiet. The clang of water pipes rustling and the knowledge Saint's using the shower brings strange comfort that I don't have time to consider. I have a pizza to order.

When Saint enters the kitchen, his hair is still damp, and the peppermint scent overpowers the chocolate one. To prevent myself from fully sniffing him, I focus on the sugar cookie dough clumping together in a bowl beneath the mixer.

"Whatcha making?" Saint asks, sliding up beside me. My kitchen isn't large, and just like the other morning, his presence seems to make the space even smaller.

"Sugar cookies. Half the batch I'll frost and the other half I'll add crushed peppermint and extra peppermint extract to make them peppermint starbursts."

Saint leans toward the mixing dough and inhales. "Already smells amazing."

"It's just dough." I laugh, no extra ingredients added yet.

Saint stands to his full height. His chest almost presses against my arm as I face the counter. He rests his hip against the edge, standing close, almost too close.

"I still can't wait to taste it."

My gaze leaps to his eyes, noticing them trained on my lips for a second. My mouth suddenly goes dry, and I swallow thickly, glancing back at the whirling dough. Staring at the twirling clump like I'd almost forgotten what I'm doing. *What's my name again?*

"Lumi."

"Yeah," I exhale, making the word breathless as I turn my head, catching on his lips this time. Watching as they slowly curl. Taking their time. One side hooking a little higher than the other.

"Would you like a glass of wine?"

I don't think I can be trusted with alcohol around him. Candy cane martinis and men who look like Santa are clearly a danger for me. Then again, I didn't drink last night, and he still came home with me. I'd invited him in.

"A small glass would be nice." I'm about to explain where the glasses are kept and the wine opener, but Saint easily helps himself, popping open a bottle of red in the corner of the counter space near my fridge. He pours each of us a small amount in a stemless glass.

Offering me one glass, I shut off the kitchen mixer as Saint holds up his glass. "To holiday housemates."

I chuckle. "Housemates." I clink my glass against his, then stare at him as I bring the delicate container to my lips. Watching him over the rim, I see him watching me back, and I almost choke on the first sip. His eyes are intense; the bruising beneath them has faded. That pinprick gleam sparking once like the stars we witnessed as we walked home last night.

As I slowly lower my glass, still holding my gaze on his, he lifts his glass, keeping his eyes on me. He takes a sip, and I watch his throat slowly roll. Mine follows as if the motion is contagious. My mouth is suddenly dry again despite the burst of peppery wine on my tongue.

A sharp buzz causes me to flinch, then giggle, and Saint turns his head toward the front hallway.

"Pizza?" He turns back toward me, excitement filling those dark eyes and turning his cheeks a light rosy pink.

I don't think I've ever seen anyone so excited for a delivered pizza.

Before I can respond, he's turning for the hall and I down the remainder of my wine. The racing of my heart. The pulsing in other places. If him only looking at me has me this turned on, I can only imagine what his touch might do. Or his kiss.

Then again, I shouldn't imagine either scenario. I might implode if I do because I'm already so worked up. Thankfully, my imagination is brushed aside as Saint enters the kitchen with a piping hot box and sets it on the table-island.

"Pizza. Cookies. And a beautiful housemate." Saint pauses, looking up at me. "Sounds like a perfect Tuesday."

At this point, I might not make it to Wednesday. Between

compliments and that mischievous gleam in his eyes, I change my mind about him. He isn't Santa, but the devil. A really attractive one.

Because I've already started the dough-making process, we eat standing around the island before I start another batch because the dough needs time to chill in the fridge. The next set of cookies will be for me.

"Russian Tea Cakes?" Saint gives me a hopeful glance after pointing at a bag of walnuts and one of powdered sugar.

"Good guess," I admit, impressed. "And my favorite."

Saint slowly smiles. "I consider myself a Christmas cookie aficionado." His expression turns thoughtful.

"I used to help my mom make them as a kid." The hard edges of his face soften. "I'm better at sampling than baking, though." He pats his belly, which responds with a sharp clap because those abs are tight as I witnessed the other morning when his shirt rose up, exposing a trail of hair leading downward and—

"Well, I'm happy to let you sample my cookies."

Our eyes lock at the invitation, innuendo not intended but interpreted underneath. Am I willing to let him have a bite of me? I can't even remember the last time someone had a taste of me, down there, where I'm hot and damp and desperate for a little attention.

That bright green *toy* he gave me might get used after all.

On that note, I look away from him and assign him the job of chopping walnuts.

"Have you ever wanted to go to Russia?" he asks me, remembering I told him I wanted to go everywhere.

"Yes. Because I've heard it's a beautiful country. But Europe is the first location on my list. London. Paris. Rothenburg ob der Tauber." The last one I infuse with the worst imitation of a German accent, but I still smile around the name.

"That's rather specific." Saint smiles.

"I've read it's the ultimate Christmas town."

"I don't know. From what I've seen of Hideaway Harbor so far, this looks like the ultimate Christmas town."

I laugh. "Well, you haven't seen anything until you've seen the harbor tree."

"The harbor tree?" Saint questions. "You mean the big one in your town square?"

"Oh no, we have another one. We take our Christmas trees very seriously around here."

Saint glances over his shoulder while still holding the chopping knife. "I don't see a tree in here."

I shrug. "Well, I don't know if I'm going to bother getting one. With Danny not coming home and all . . ."

Saint gives me a questioning look. Then it passes into compassion. And I don't want to turn our pleasant evening into another pity party centered around me.

"So, what about you? Tell me where you've been. Some place really special or magical."

The next few minutes pass with Saint explaining incredible locations from all over the world that he's visited. And all the while, we work in tandem, like a team, circling one another like we're well-practiced at sharing the small space of my kitchen.

He chops walnuts. I mix wet ingredients.

He adds the walnuts. I stir in the dry mixture.

Then we each take turns forming the dough into small balls and placing them on the baking sheets.

With the timer set, I turn toward Saint, prepared to ask him if he'd like a little more wine. But as I face him, he reaches for my forehead, near my hairline.

"You've got a little . . ." He traces his finger along the border of skin and hair and then continues along the side of my cheek. "Powdered sugar in your hair."

I could question how that happened, but I swiped at my loose hair a time or two with the back of my hand while my palms were doughy and fingers covered in powdered sugar.

"Messy baker," I whisper, still trying to catch my breath as the stroke of his finger lingers along the lines of my face.

He smiles, then assumes the role of refreshing our wine glasses. Only a few short minutes pass before we remove the first set of pans, and the warm cookies need to be rolled in confectioners' sugar.

We work quickly, whimpering and hissing at the heat coming off the hot treat, while we attempt to cool it with a dusting of powdery sugar. Once finally clear of the pan, Saint grabs my hand and brings it to his mouth.

"Here," he says, keeping his eyes on me as he sucks at the tip of my finger, cooling the sizzle of heat lingering, while at the same time starting a new crackle and spark. The kindling already buzzing all evening as we worked around one another. A flame shoots through me like a flare gun shot into the night. An SOS cry for help. Or in my case, a whimper of need. Deep-rooted desire to be taken to the kitchen floor and experience this man.

This should not be happening. I should not be reacting to him so fiercely, so fast. I've known him less than three days. My attraction to him doesn't make sense.

The Santa vibe should be a distraction. But everything in my body says put me on your lap and add me to the naughty list.

"Thank you," I whisper as he pulls my finger from his mouth and takes my thumb next, concentrating on the two fingers we used most to roll cookies.

He only holds the tip between his lips, but the salacious swirl of his tongue against the end of my finger has me wondering about other *lengths* on him and how they'd fit inside me.

This is so messed up, and yet my body refuses to pull away from him. If anything, I want to be closer. Press up against him and wrap around him and—

"Better?" he asks, keeping his eyes on mine as he removes my thumb and blows on the moistened tip.

"Yeah." The word is a breathless exhale, and the opposite of how I feel.

My insides are a churning volcano, ripe for eruption, from the single act of him sucking on my finger.

CHAPTER 10

December 8

[Saint]

Baking cookies newly tops my list of foreplay after last night.

Saved by the oven's buzzer once more, Lumi and I broke apart and finished covering our next batch of cookies in silence.

No second round of finger sucking in sight.

We ended the evening by cleaning up Lumi's kitchen, while stealing glances at one another. I held firm every time she caught me. She ducked her head each time I caught her.

First, I was worked up over massaging her temples.

Now, I'm a mess over sucking her fingers.

I wanted to shovel away whatever snowy line is between us and take Lumi down to her kitchen floor to explore all the sugary sweet places on her, as well as the crunchy bits that needed softening.

Instead, we worked quietly, washing bowls and utensils, like a couple who'd made cookies together for forty Christmases instead of their first.

Sugar cookies were put off for another day and my body buzzed at the thought of another night spent in Lumi's kitchen. The small space kept us in close proximity to one another. Allowing me to experience the intoxicating mix of fresh-baked cookies and Lumi's green apple scent.

The anticipation of a second night together only stoked the heat swirling inside me. A sudden, visceral need to unwrap Lumi Snowe. Read the instructions. Assemble the parts. And see how she works.

As she'd made the sugar cookie dough last evening, and it needed time to chill, she left it in her fridge overnight. The evening starts out innocently enough by rolling out dough and cutting out shapes. Christmas trees. Five-point stars. Santa heads.

Lumi also has sprinkles and cinnamon candies for additional decoration on the food-colored frosting.

We each fill another sheet with cookie dough shapes and wait as they bake, eating leftover pizza between baking times.

Our conversation from last night continues as well, me asking her about more places she wants to visit, making a mental list of all the places I wish I could take her one day.

If only . . .

"There are plenty of places on this side of the planet I'd love to visit. Maybe even the mysterious North," she teases, like it's a place easily found on a map.

"I'd like that," I admit, finding the response truthful. I'd love to show her new-to-her places and bring her home, but it's not possible.

Bringing home a woman has never happened.

There isn't a rule against it so much as a hesitation on my end. I'd have to trust someone with family secrets that I'm not willing to share with just anyone. Again, the right woman will get all the keys to the mystery.

The thought has me glancing at the spare key Lumi left on the counter for me earlier. The newly made gold key had a little red ribbon slipped through the end like a key chain. I didn't want to appear overly eager and swipe it off the counter, shoving it into my pocket like a greedy man, but something about that key made my chest ache. Almost like I longed for a place to turn that key, unlock the door, and call home.

With a glance at Lumi, I realize she's given that to me in a small way. She's opened her home to me, provided a key for the door, and she's slowly letting me in to know more about her.

In no time, the sugar cookies are cool enough to decorate. We laugh at our lack of skill. Some cookies end up with lumps of frosting instead of a smooth surface. I overshot with the sprinkles container, and a pile of multi-colored candy lands heavily on one end of a Christmas tree, making the cookie look lopsided. Lumi puts cinnamon drops on her trees like ornaments.

"Here." She holds an extra one out, pinched between her fingers. "I overcalculated how many my tree could hold."

Taking her wrist in my hand, I hold her hand steady as I suck the spicy candy from her fingertips, reminding us both of how I took her fingers in my mouth last night.

While I'm still holding her wrist, Lumi swipes at my nose with her other hand. "You have a little something . . . right there."

I release her hand and brush at my nose, coming away with a glob of frosting on my fingers.

"And, you just happened to have a little something . . . here." I swipe at her nose in retaliation, passing frosting from me to her. As the glob was heavy, some drips down to her lips, and Lumi swipes at it with her tongue.

She's quick to stick two fingers into the frosting container and stretch toward me, only I'm faster and capture her wrist again, bringing her fingers to my mouth where I suck at the sugary goodness. Only this time, I show no mercy.

I slide my tongue around her fingers, spreading them apart

and forcing one from my mouth to savor cleaning the length of it from webbing to tip. I don't let it escape but draw it back into my mouth, swirling my tongue around the digit one more time before I brush it aside and treat her other finger in the same manner.

While I close my eyes to enjoy the experience, I sense Lumi watching me. When my lids flip open, she flinches like I've startled her. Catching her eyes on mine. But she doesn't pull away. She actually is leaning toward me. The neutral space over the table-island has become the peak of a mountain. Our eyes hold a moment like we stand on a literal precipice. Which way will the wind blow? Which direction will it take us?

Suddenly, Lumi's hand caresses the side of my face, but I feel the stickiness the second she makes contact. The mixture of frosting in the coarse hair along my jaw.

"You have more . . ."

"You'll pay for that." With no mercy, I stick my finger into the frosting container again while still holding Lumi's wrist. She struggles, but I'm stronger.

"You wouldn't," she choke-giggles.

"Wouldn't I?" I round the table, still clutching at her wrist as I near her, and at the same time I pull her closer. Then I swipe at her neck, coating a swath of her flesh in green frosting. My favorite color mixing with my new favorite scent, green apple. But I'm only concerned with a possible new favorite flavor.

Lumi.

I lick up her neck, cleaning off the mess I made, forcing her head to tilt back, and a deep moan to escape her.

Fuck!

Her reaction wasn't something I'd considered, and yet everything I'd hoped it would be. I cup the back of her neck and bring our foreheads together.

"Lumi," I groan as my heart races. My chest heaves with the effort to hold myself back. I want to kiss her when I shouldn't. I don't want to take advantage of her hospitality or this friendship slowly brewing between us. I'm not staying long in this town, and I don't want to complicate us.

Oven timer buzzers make it to the top of my sounds-I-hate list, as the interruption instantly separates us, like a cookie cracked in half. Lumi slowly pulls back, her eyes avoiding mine.

"Lumi, if I crossed—"

"You didn't." She smooths down her shirt and wraps her hand around the front of her neck like she can still feel my tongue rushing up the column. Then she clears her throat and steps toward the oven, which continues to beep its warning blare.

She removes the trays from the oven, setting them on top of the stove.

"I don't want to take advantage here, Lumi," I start again, wanting to explain myself. It's not that I'm not attracted to her. I'm overly attracted to her, but that isn't good for her. She told me how she let someone not intending to stay in town into her heart. I cannot be that guy again.

Although no one is taking hearts here, something tells me that deep beneath the sarcasm and wit is a sensitive woman. A survivor of broken bits. Her mother's death. Her father's too. Some man who casually came and easily left from her life.

I don't want to do that to her because I will go. I have to leave.

"I know," she whispers, eyes still on the cookies. But then she looks up at me. The clear understanding in the blue sea of her eyes is overwhelming. She knows I don't want to hurt her. She knows she's done me a favor by letting me stay here. A mere stranger.

I glance toward the key on the counter. The one which opens her home to me.

Lumi Snowe is a good woman.

Any man would be a fool to leave her.

CHAPTER 11

December 10

[Lumi]

"What the tinsel town is this?" Saint laughs as he stands on a dock in the harbor, and I savor the chuckling sound that's thick like falling timber.

It's been two nights since our playful frosting fight. We haven't mentioned it again, letting the strain of a failed moment linger between us. I understand his hesitation. He's going to leave town as soon as he can. He's actually doing me a favor. Protecting me. Still, my heart aches at the loss from both a missed kiss and the day he'll eventually leave.

"It's the lighting of the harbor Christmas tree."

Although there isn't an actual tree in sight. Instead, a pile of lobster traps is stacked to imitate the conical shape of a pine tree with a miniature cutout of Larry the Lobstah, the town mascot of sorts, on top.

Saint stands beside me on a dock as we watch the approach of the town's mayor, Mr. Locke. He's dressed like Santa and waves at the crowd from the front of a lobster boat donated by Hawthorne Fisheries. John Locke loves Christmas. At fifty-seven, he's still a good-looking man with salt and pepper in his hair. He grows a beard each holiday season for the chance to play Santa when any opportunity arises. He'll be the person to officially light the harbor tree, turning the pile of weathered crates into a multi-colored light display, complete with small buoys and giant plastic candy canes.

This year, the donated boat is being driven by Greyson Hawthorne with Wren Wilde by his side. The two look very cozy, but my attention is more focused on the man beside me, caught between humor and offense at this production.

In addition to the town Santa, Larry the Lobstah is present and represented this year by Ralph, a man in his mid-thirties who still lives with his mom. As he's fumbling with the costume, trying to keep the claws up on his hands and the head-piece righted on his head, Saint lets out a hearty chuckle beside me.

"What is that?"

"Larry the Lobst*ah*," I exaggerate my accent on the town's mascot, and Saint laughs even harder. His shoulders shake while his arms are crossed, one hand lifted and fisted by his mouth, like he's trying to contain his mirth at this community event.

"It's okay to laugh." While we take our traditions seriously in this town, we also appreciate the good nature of them.

Ralph looks ridiculous in a costume too large for his non-athletic build. Mayor Locke is waving like he's the king of England, and Greyson is so distracted by Wren at his side, the boat keeps swerving like a drunken sailor is steering its course.

"It's fun." He smiles wide, as he continues to watch the approach of the lobster boat.

For all the years I've stood out here, freezing my backside off, listening to Danny whine about the cold and begging for hot chocolate from a nearby vendor, I'm having fun as well. A different sort of fun from being a mom worrying about her kid to a woman standing next to a hot man.

One who I'd like to wrap my arm around the crook of his and press against.

Instead, I continue watching the lobster boat dock, then Mayor Locke light the tree that almost looks like a tree once the lights come on, disguising the crates a bit. However, that bright orange cut-out of Larry the Lobstah reminds me that the crate stack is indeed *not* an evergreen.

The festivities will continue as tonight is a big drinking night for the adults in town. Most will gather at The Shore Thing. In the past, I've met up with my sisters, and I plan to do the same thing tonight, with a plus-one.

"Thanks for helping Neve at Rusty's this week," I state once the official lighting is over, and the crowd becomes restless to move on.

Saint has been at the shop since Wednesday, working on his own car, having told me earlier in the week that he likes to tinker.

"I can't sit around and watch Christmas movies all day."

I'd beg to differ, but don't argue with him.

"Hot buttered rum?" Saint arches a brow as we make our way in the direction of The Shore Thing, like many others, after the official lighting ceremony.

For the night, the town council approved a local vendor to sponsor a booth selling hot buttered rum, another tradition of the season, near the harbor. While every bar in town is certain to have the drink as a specialty item tonight, instant gratification suggests having one here and now.

Without waiting for my answer, Saint takes my mitten-covered hand in his leather-gloved one and guides me through the crowd to the vendor. My preference is to include cider instead of water in the drink, which adds to the sweetness of the beverage, and once Saint and I each have a disposable cup with the steaming treat, it does not disappoint. After a savoring sip of the hot liquid, I lick my lips and catch Saint watching the motion. With his eyes on me, he lifts his own cup for a drink.

The moment feels charged, crackling with heat despite the cold temperature around us. My insides light like the harbor tree as we stare at one another for a long beat.

Saint opens his mouth like he wants to tell me something. Only, he's jostled to the side, jerking his gaze from me.

"Sorry, bub," a man says to Saint after he bumps into him.

"Ayuh," Saint answers, like he's from the area, instantly forgiving the disruption to our staring contest when I am suddenly desperate to know what he was about to say to me.

Before turning back in my direction, Saint does a double-take as a little girl stands rather close to his side.

He smiles warmly as she waves for him to bend down. As he does, locking his gaze on me, she cups her hand around her mouth and whispers something into his ear. His brows hitch, the expression both full of surprise and glee. Like he's humoring the young girl.

"Really?" He turns his head toward her as he slowly stands to his full height.

She nods, eyes wide and expectant.

"Well, I suppose if you've been very good this year, I don't see why not." He winks at her and her grin is so wide her entire face illuminates as bright as Larry highlighted on top of the harbor tree.

Saint looks over her head, glancing around for a parent, and within seconds, a woman presses through the adults nearby.

"Samantha." The mother breathes in relief. "You can't walk away from me like that."

I recognize the panic and fear in her voice. While the crowd is safe, the collection of people is tight and daunting.

Taking the little girl's mittened hand, the mother apologizes to Saint before giving me a nod. I recognize the local schoolteacher and offer a sympathetic smile. Every mother has been here.

As the two make their way through the crowd, Samantha turns back and gives Saint another wave. He responds by wiggling his fingers toward her.

"What was that all about?" I chuckle once they are out of hearing range.

Saint turns back toward me. "She told me what she wanted for Christmas."

"She what?" I choke on a laugh before realizing what that little girl must have thought. *He's Santa Claus. The* Santa Claus. The idea makes me laugh harder.

With his brow arched, suggesting I've answered my own question, he takes another sip of his hot buttered rum.

"That was sweet of you." He clearly played along with Samantha's thought process.

He smiles.

"What did she tell you she wanted?"

His mouth pops open. A stream of warm heat escaping. "I cannot tell you that. It's the Santa code of confidence."

"The what?" My smile is nearly as wide as the child's.

"The unbreakable code that I cannot divulge what a child requests directly from Santa." He moves his finger in the air in a complicated motion of up, down, back and forth, and zigzag. Then he clumps his fingers together and presses them apart as if dispelling something into the air.

"What the heck was that?" I chuff, glancing at his fingertips as he wraps them around his to-go cup again.

"I made the international symbol for Santa-direct requests and then shot it off for the big man in red."

I chuckle, throaty and deep. "Now you're really pulling my leg."

"I would never joke about something so serious as a Christmas wish." His smile is pure Grinch, delicious and lush, as he watches me once again over the rim of his cup and takes a drink of the warm rum.

My insides are heated from the drink, but that smile just turned up the temperature.

Saint steps closer to me, brushing back a wisp of hair hanging out of my knit cap. His eyes twinkle as he leans toward me.

"What's your Christmas wish this year, Lumi?" The crook of his smile is pure seduction, which causes my cheeks to warm.

I scoff, laughing off the blatant flirt because I have an inkling he knows what I want. At least from him.

I shake my head at him, like he's a naughty boy. "Thought I wasn't supposed to share, or the wish doesn't happen."

Saint laughs.

"Should we head to The Shore Thing?" I suggest, which almost sounds like I've announced I'm a sure thing, willing to let him pull body parts, like my legs apart and my hair in his fist.

With a final sip of my hot buttered rum, scorching the back of my throat, I try to drown out the naughty thoughts.

Then I make my own complicated symbol in my head and toss my wish into the universe, mentally watching it burst at the impossibility of Saint and me ever being together.

CHAPTER 12

[Saint]

I shouldn't have done it.

Not listen to the girl's request. Not make the symbol in front of Lumi. Not even make a joke about it, like I have the power to make wishes come true.

But I want to. Whatever Lumi is thinking, whatever she's wishing for this holiday season, *I* wish I could make it happen.

I'd garnered that having her son come home is her greatest desire, and if I could make that happen, I would.

Instead, we walk to The Shore Thing and press through the mass of bodies to make our way to the bar for another drink.

While I enjoyed the hot buttered rum, I'm going to need something stronger to prevent me from making more mistakes near this woman, like almost telling her who I am and what *I* wish could happen between us.

Thankfully, someone knocked into me, knocking sense into my thoughts.

With the bar as crowded as it is, I tug Lumi in front of me, positioning her back to my front, and using myself as a shield against the press of eager residents and holiday visitors wanting a drink after that interesting tree lighting ceremony.

I chuckle to myself. People love Christmas. And they love to decorate anything and everything to show their pleasure for this time of year.

A time for hope. A need for brightness. A desire for peace. Because that's what light in the dark represents.

Let there be peace on earth.

With that heavy thought, I sigh and place a hand on Lumi's hip to keep her steady in front of me.

"What do you want?" she shouts over her shoulder as we inch closer to the bar.

You.

The answer comes swiftly, and nearly knocks me backward, but shouldn't surprise me. Lumi and I have been circling one another for almost a week, coming together to share dinner or a drink, plus our cookie-baking escapades.

Between her shift from eight-thirty to four-thirty at the post office, plus one night a week at Rusty's when it stays open late, and another night to do their books, she stays very busy.

I wonder if the busyness helps with the loneliness.

Most times, it works for me. But other times, I want to slow down and I want to do it with someone by my side.

As an opening arises for us to move forward, I step in that direction, but Lumi steps back to allow the person in front of her to slip past us. The movement brings her even closer to me. Her body lines up with mine. Her back to my chest. Her ass to the zipper region of my pants. My hands grip her hips tightly, holding her in place.

"You okay?" she says, glancing over her shoulder again. Her hair is brushed to the side now that she's removed her knit cap. The second we walked into the overheated bar, we tore off hats and gloves and unzipped our jackets, but the space is still too warm. I'm even hotter with Lumi so close to me.

"Ayuh," I say, having picked up on how the locals respond in the affirmative. Yes.

But really, the answer is no, because I want to clear this bar, press Lumi up against the counter, and nip at the section of skin exposed on her neck. Her green apple scent fills my nose. Her hips fill my hands.

I want—

"Saint?"

"Yeah." My voice cracks.

"We need to move forward."

I hadn't realized I was holding her so tightly that we weren't even moving. Loosening my hands, Lumi steps up to the bar counter and leans over it to speak to the blonde bartender from the other night. The noise level is loud, like every resident of Hideaway Harbor decided to hang out for the night in this exact spot.

Lumi places our drink order and then leans back from the bar, but the bartender points upward. Lumi and I both look at the same time.

Mistletoe. *Fuck.*

"Come on," the blonde bartender encourages. "It's a Shore Thing." Her play on the bar's name would be funny if my throat weren't suddenly so dry.

Space has opened up for me to slip next to Lumi as she shifted to lean her side against the bar.

"It's not a sure thing," she says, as her gaze flicks over our heads a second.

Only, I hear *she's not a sure thing.* Or maybe it's that suddenly I'm not certain of anything, other than I want to kiss Lumi. Despite the crowded bar. Despite the mistletoe. Despite needing to leave this town sooner rather than later.

Quickly, our drinks are plopped in front of us, and I hand over my credit card, finding my chance to act passing.

Lumi's brows hitch. "American Express Black. Impressive."

Only she doesn't seem impressed. The Aston Martin. An elite black credit card. This woman, running a rundown auto repair shop and working at the post office, couldn't care less about my wealth, which is a little refreshing, but also disconcerting.

Why not?

I'm not a material man, even though my business is based on *children* wanting material items. Yet, it has not escaped my attention that some women are typically turned on by a fancy car or a sky-high credit limit.

Not this woman. She's been an anomaly from the start.

That Christmas gift you didn't know you wanted until you unwrapped it.

However, I haven't fully unwrapped Lumi Snowe.

When my card is returned, the bartender asks if I want to keep the tab open. I glance at Lumi, who shakes her head.

"I don't like to say I'm old, but I'm feeling my age tonight." She glances around us where a large percentage of the patronage is under forty.

Stepping to the side so the next person in line can order drinks, Lumi huddles close to me once more with the press of people around us. She greets a few who easily recognize her.

"Hazard of living in a small town all your life. And never leaving." She smiles weakly as she sips her drink. Another hot buttered rum for consistency.

However, when someone pushes her from behind, she pitches forward and her drink lands on me.

"Oh shit. I'm so sorry." She's twisting side to side with no hope of getting closer to the bar for napkins, while the front of my green flannel is soaked through to my skin.

"No worries." I wince while I brush at the warm liquid seeping through the cloth. Thankfully, my shirt is absorbing the heat, but I'm done here.

"Let's just get out of here," Lumi says, her voice almost relieved over the idea of leaving the crowded bar.

I down my whiskey in one smooth gulp before handing my empty glass to Lumi, and she passes it to the person behind her to set on the bar.

Zipping up my jacket, I grimace as the sopping wet flannel clings to me. When Lumi and I step outside, I shiver against the rush of cold after being overheated in the bar.

The main area of Hideaway Harbor is within walking distance of Lumi's home, and Lumi walks everywhere, especially tonight when she thought she'd be drinking. Without a car, I'm at her mercy, so we walk in silence the few blocks to her house.

As we walk, I note the canopy of stars like I did the other night. There is something magical about them, twinkling from light years away, and yet almost so close I can reach up and touch one. What I'd really like to touch is Lumi's hand, holding the warmth of it in mine. Instead, I admire the garland on lampposts and wreaths on front doors. The quiet of a winter's night, where people are cozy in their warm homes, or in the case of tonight, filling up the downtown district of Hideaway Harbor to celebrate their pride and love for this place.

The one thing I ignore as we walk is that traveling countdown calendar, not wanting to be reminded that time is ticking on my stay here.

A layer of white snow blankets the lawns, but as we walk, a fresh dusting falls from the sky, adding to the magical aura and holiday atmosphere.

"It's like being in a snow globe," Lumi whispers, and I glance at her. She tips her face upward despite our slow walk. Her long lashes blink as snow tickles her face. She smiles toward the heavens. She looks . . . peaceful, and I gaze upward as well, as if I can capture that peace.

Quickly, I look back at her, realizing she's the tranquility of this night.

Lumi eventually lowers her head and peers at me, offering me the same warm smile she gave the stars. My chest fills, my heart skips a beat. I've never wanted to kiss someone so badly in my life.

Once we reach her front landing, I'm suddenly nervous. Lumi's place is narrow and upright, and clad in the classic cedar shingles of a New England home. Her yard is tiny with thick bushes on either side of the wooden steps leading to her front door. A string of white lights drapes over the lower-level windows, outlined with white trim.

Our walk to her place shouldn't have felt any different than the other nights I've walked her home, and yet tonight feels special. Like I've been on a date, which I haven't done in decades. Panic seizes me about her opening her front door, like a spell will be broken once the key hits the lock.

"Wait." I catch her forearm as she inserts the key into the lock. Releasing the key, she turns to face me. Her rosy cheeks illuminate from the simple light over our heads in the small triangular canopy.

"I just wanted to say that I appreciate you letting me stay at your place. And I've had a good time hanging out with you this week."

Slowly, her lips curl. "I've had fun with you as well. You aren't half bad as a houseguest."

I've graduated from the couch to her son's room. *As he isn't coming home*, she'd said, allowing me to take over the vacant space that's still decorated like a teenage boy lives here.

She turns back for the key in the lock.

"But, I—" I catch her arm again, and Lumi turns back toward me, her eyes questioning mine.

I lick my lips, and Lumi's gaze follows the stroke of my tongue.

Dammit, this shouldn't be so difficult. I'm out of practice, I tell myself. Only the truth is, this woman makes me nervous in a good way.

Reaching for her jaw, I cup the soft edge of her face.

"I want to kiss you," I admit, giving her a chance to reject the idea.

"There's no mistletoe in sight," she teases.

"I don't need mistletoe to want to kiss you, Lumi."

"Okay," she whispers, giving me that shy smile she'd share with the stars. She looks hopeful, shyly eager, but reality slams into me, like a blizzard throwing me off course.

"But I can't make any promises to you." And a woman like Lumi deserves promises. She deserves oaths and vows and everything she desires. She's already been hurt by one man who didn't stick around.

"I'm not looking for promises." Her voice is still quiet, like we'll disturb her neighbors.

My thumb strokes her cheekbone while my gaze falls to her mouth.

"Just a kiss," I whisper, leaning closer to her. That's all I can give. It's what I want to take.

"Is that *your* Christmas wish?" she teases, while her voice is so low, it's raspy, nearly breathless. Her throat rolls.

"Yes." Slipping my other hand against her cheek, I pull her closer to me.

As our lips meet, my body heats, like the sudden flash of a tree being lit or the star on the top bursting into color. I step even closer to her, despite layers of winter outerwear and my wet flannel shirt that doesn't even register while her lips connect with mine.

Promising that this moment will live in my memory forever.

Lumi kisses me back with the same strained patience I'm offering her. Taking my time to sip at her lips and outline her mouth before breaking the seam for a slight swipe of her tongue which tastes like hot buttered rum and more.

The more is what I want to savor, and I tighten my grip on her cheeks, holding her closer to me, as our mouths move, continuing the stroll over each other.

Lumi is all the warm things I imagine when I'm cold.

Sunshine on a beach. Hot chocolate in a mug. Crackling logs in a fireplace.

More.

I want to get closer and yet I know it'd be selfish to take advantage of her kindness.

Pulling back sooner than I'd like, I rest my forehead against hers, breathing her in. Green apple and warm rum and everything I wish *I* could ask Santa to deliver on Christmas.

But cannot.

CHAPTER 13

[Lumi]

We stumble into my house. Unfortunately, not because we are ripping our clothes off, which I'd really like to be doing, but as an aftereffect of that kiss.

Forget the hot buttered rum or a candy cane martini. I'm drunk off this man's kiss.

I've never had a front porch kiss and then had my date follow me inside.

Not that this evening was a date.

But that was still some kiss.

In the tight entryway, Saint reaches for my hat, tugging it off my head, allowing my hair to go wild with static. He swipes off his own cap next and tosses both in the basket I keep below the coat hooks.

When I reach for my scarf, his hands pause mine.

"Allow me."

My heart races, lungs expanding, as he slowly peels the wrapping from around my neck free. Then he pops the snaps on my jacket, spins me around, and removes the outerwear. For some reason, I remain frozen in place as he hangs up the long coat, watching it dangle from its typical hook.

The strangely loud ripple of Saint tugging open his own coat, sluffing it off, and hanging it beside mine, keeps me pinned to the wood floor beneath my feet another second. When Saint takes a seat on the low landing of the staircase to remove his boots, I bend at the waist to unlace and remove mine, but when I stand back up, Saint is watching me. His gaze rises to my face as I stand upright.

He stands as well, although it seems like he moves in slow motion. Taking his time to unfold from the low seat and rise to his full height. His peppermint and chocolate scent becomes more pronounced when exposed to the cold, like we were when we walked home. He also smells a little like hot buttered rum, and my mouth opens, prepared to suggest I'll wash his soiled shirt for him.

When his hand touches my cheek again, his thumb stroking over the cool flesh, crackling beneath his warm touch, words elude me.

"Fuck it," he whispers, before his mouth crashes with mine, both startling me and striking a flame, like a match newly lit. Instantly, I'm pressed against him, clutching at that still-damp flannel, while he spins me until I'm falling against our hanging coats. And yet, none of this matters other than the weight of him against me. His mouth, warm and eager. The kiss more intense than the tender exploration on my front porch.

I make quick work of unbuttoning his flannel and shoving it over his shoulders, keeping our mouths connected but with more hunger, more passion. Quickly, Saint pulls back and takes a deep breath before tugging off the shirt he wore beneath the flannel and tossing it to the floor. I want to explore every ripple and ridge of his firm chest, but he cups my face and brings my mouth back to his.

Wrapping my arms around his neck, the warmth of his skin

struggles to breach my sweater, and I pull at the neck, removing the thicker covering to expose a fitted base layer. Saint glances down, runs his hands from my waist to the sides of my breasts, teasing me with the nearness but not getting near enough.

"You're perfection," he whispers to my chest, taking in the outline of my shape in the form-fitting shirt. Then, he cups my jaw again and kisses me, long and deep, with tongue seeking tongue.

My arms are back around his neck and within seconds, Saint cups the underside of my ass and lifts me up. He doesn't press me into the wall, covered by the coats dangling from the hooks, but spins us instead, blindly walking into my living room, circling the couch, and then dropping me on it.

I giggle as I bounce once before Saint lowers over me. The move resembles a dropping push-up, in which he never gets back up but covers me. Our legs entwine. His hand cups the back of my neck. His mouth returns to mine, and we kiss, and kiss, and kiss.

I can't remember the last time I simply made out with a man. In no time, things heat more as Saint drags his hand down my chest and over my breast, pausing only momentarily to give it a firm squeeze. Then he travels to my hip and bends his leg, forcing his thigh higher, spreading my legs wider.

"Lumi," he hums against my mouth as my hips move to the rhythm of our hearts. My fingers comb through his hair and around his neck. Down his firm back to the base of his spine. I feel the heavy length of his stiffness just off center, against my hip bone as he uses his thigh at my core to bring me higher and higher.

"Saint," I whimper, startled once more at how quickly he's wound me up. Then again, I've been spiraling for days, working to deny my budding attraction to him. I'm twisted tighter than the red and white on a peppermint.

With little warning, other than the sharp cry of his name

again, I unravel, coming undone like stripping the red from the white candy stick. I clutch Saint's fine ass, holding him against me as my body releases a week of building frustration. From not wanting him to stay to not wanting him to ever leave.

The instant thought is dangerous, and Saint must sense the shift. He slows his kisses as my body flows back to the couch, settling into the cushion beneath me. After he kisses my nose, he slowly presses up and off me, then stands beside the couch. Staring down at me, he offers me a soft smile. Not the lazy one, but one I cannot properly read.

"I'm going to shower," he says softly.

"Wait. What?" I rush to sit upright. "What about you?" I wave toward the bulge in his pants which is eye-level in my seated position.

"This." He strokes his finger around my face. "I just want to memorize *this* for tonight." His smile warms and he inhales, like drawing in my scent and taking in my post-release face are enough for him.

I can't find words to argue, before he leans down, kisses the top of my head, and rounds the couch, heading for the staircase.

As soon as he clears the staircase, I toss myself against the cushions on the couch and cover my face with both hands.

What the holly and ivy am I doing? Why did I kiss him? How did he make me orgasm so fast?

Flinging my head back to rest on the sofa, I blink as I stare up at the ceiling, giving myself a list of reasons why I shouldn't be upset.

He isn't staying. He isn't meant to be here. He has somewhere to go, and he's been counting down the days until he can return home.

North.

Whatever the hell that means?

"It means none of your business, Lumi," I say to the room, realizing I've never confirmed if he has a wife. Kids. He doesn't mention family other than his siblings, although I've caught him looking at his phone a time or two, scowling at it.

When I'd asked him if everything was okay, he'd simply respond, "Work."

I don't really know exactly what he does or where he lives. I only know he has a time limit on him, like a giant stamp that reads priority mail.

He has somewhere to be, and it isn't in this small town.

On that note, I press myself off the couch and slink to the kitchen, turning off the over-the-stove light I left on for us. A Saturday night and I'm turning in early, which isn't anything new, yet tonight, it weighs heavily on me.

As I reach the top of the staircase, the bathroom door flings open and a rush of steam releases into the hallway.

Saint steps forward with his clothing clutched in one hand and his other hand holding the towel wrapped around his waist.

A waist that's rippled by washboard abs and highlighted by a trail of dark hair leading below the loose wrap around his hips. Slowly, my gaze travels up that trail and along the firmness of his pecs, dusted with another patch of silvery hair. My fingers twitch, eager to comb through the curly, coarse mix.

The roll of his Adam's apple brings my eyes to his throat. He trimmed his beard the other day, and the clean line distinguishing growth from shaven skin makes my mouth water.

Finally, my gaze crosses to his jaw where the hair is thicker. A mixture of white and chrome, like snowflakes and tinsel.

He licks his lips, and I swear if I don't move, I'm going to melt right in front of him.

While water drops sprinkle his flesh, I'm soaking wet down below.

"Want to—"

"I'm going to read," I rush to say, hardly recognizing my own voice. The hush. The groan. The breathlessness.

The sound alone suggests I'm turned on and want him, but I won't act on my desire.

He isn't staying, I remind myself.

Once upon a time, I was attracted to a man who didn't plan to linger. I'd wanted to escape with him. Instead, I rooted deeper into this town after his exit. I can't do that to myself again.

With a stunned face and a blankness in his eyes, I excuse myself for my room, rush to shut the door and lock it, then fall against the closed barrier.

Despite our little make out session and the startling orgasm, I feel a little rejected by his sudden desire to shower. I'm also still on edge.

After a deep inhale, I dive for my bed, lunging over it for that damn holiday-green pickle pleaser Saint bought me from The Perfect Package.

He has no idea how suddenly handy this gift is or what I will do with it with my own hands.

My clothing feels like wet wool, scratchy and irritating, and I can't get undressed fast enough. Naked, I slide between flannel sheets, imagining the fabric is the shirt Saint wore earlier, minus the buttered rum fiasco.

The first hum of the vibrator sounds too loud, and I quickly shut it off, sliding it down my sternum and between my thighs. Hoping the thick layer of duvet, blanket, and flannel sheet will mute the noise, I flick it on again.

With my eyes closed, Saint is all I see. His taste lingers on my lips. Whiskey kisses. His scent fills my nose. Peppermint and chocolate. And his touch. Imagined.

His fingers between my thighs, easily finding where I ache to be worshipped.

His mouth, blowing heat against the sensitive nub.

His licks, warm and wet and eager to taste me.

Within seconds, I explode like holiday fireworks and crackling logs and the first flick of Christmas tree lights turning on.

I tug the flannel sheet to my mouth to muffle a moan, fighting the urge to cry out his name.

Saint. Astan Santos. Santa Claus.

The last thought flicks my eyes open, and I stare up at the ceiling a second before I turn the vibrator off and roll my head on the pillow, giggling into the stuffing.

Why the heck would I imagine praising Santa?

But in my heart, I know the answer.

From here on out, in my imagination, Santa will always look exactly like Saint.

CHAPTER 14

December 11

[Lumi]

On Sunday, I'm a coward and slink off to breakfast with my sisters. Isolde will be working the gingerbread competition later in the afternoon at the community center, and Neve and I promised to attend, but I need an emergency meeting of the Snowe sisters.

"What happened?" Neve asks without greeting as she takes a chair opposite me in the hole-in-the-wall diner near the docks.

The bright red door with a porthole is the only hint this place exists. The inside contains mirrored portholes with drawn curtains as fake windows. A long bench lines one wall with several rectangular wood tables and chairs opposite the bench. The bench and chairs are red to match the front door. The locals like to keep this spot a hidden treasure. I especially love this place for its quick and greasy breakfast. This diner was our father's favorite.

"We should wait for Isolde," I state from my seat on the bench. I don't want to have to repeat myself.

"Wait for me for what?" Isolde asks, sliding in next to me on the wooden seat.

Being five years younger than me and one half of a set of twins, Isolde has the classic Snowe features. Bright blue eyes and dark hair, only she keeps hers in an elaborate braid that dangles over one shoulder while long bangs frame her face. Today, she's wearing a pink knit cap on her head.

As soon as Isolde sits, the waitress, Gladys, approaches. She's almost an institution as much as this diner. She brings over two cups of coffee without needing to ask if Neve or Isolde want a mug. Gladys dumps the sugars and creamers clumped in her hand on the table and announces, "Be back in a second, girls."

"I kissed Saint," I announce without preamble once Gladys walks off.

"Who's Saint?" Isolde asks.

"What?" Neve drags out the word like a teenager, her eyes wide, her face bright. Then she glances at Isolde. "Saint is Lumi's sexy Santa roommate."

"You have a roommate?" my younger sister turns toward me.

"Not a roommate. An extended-stay houseguest."

She still gives me an expression like *what's that* while Neve interjects, "How was it?"

"Why am I always the last to know things?" Isolde mutters, clearly not caring about my kiss.

"You haven't heard the rumors?" Neve continues.

"Rumors?" Isolde glances back at Neve. "I work in a middle school. The only rumors I hear is who likes whom, and who is dating whom, and who broke up with whom. Who was mean to whom, and who had the latest non-important drama. It's enough to make my head spin. I don't have time for town gossip."

I chuckle. My head would spin as well, and I remember when Danny was in middle school. He wasn't exactly into girls at that point, and I was grateful. Then he hit high school, and his hormones hit the accelerator.

"We all know town gossip is only gossip," I remind my sisters.

"Still, Lady Lovewatch would enjoy this morsel of romance." Neve leans closer so the table next to us won't hear her next words. She rolls her wrist, twirling her finger. "Now, tell us about this kiss."

I sigh, falling back against the hard bench seat. "It was just a kiss."

"Just a kiss." Neve is loud enough the customers at the table next to ours *can* hear her.

"If it was just a kiss, I don't think you'd be asking us to meet like this," Isolde adds, as the voice of reason.

"Okay. You're right. It was more than a kiss." My cheeks instantly heat, and I lean forward, glancing down at my steaming cup of coffee.

"Holy cinnamon. Your cheeks are bright red," Neve points out as if I don't already feel the warmth.

"You like him," Isolde states the obvious a little more gently.

Peering at her, I smile, shy and timid. "Yeah. I do."

"Then what's the problem?" she asks, grinning, pleased with this new development in my life.

On that question, Neve and I meet eyes before I say, "He isn't staying in town."

"Ah," Isolde says. "Houseguest." Like the information has finally clicked into place. "How did that happen?"

I give a short rundown of Saint's accident, Eileen's suggestion, and my invitation for Saint to stay at my home. I toss in how Neve convinced me to let him stay long-term until his car is repaired.

"Once his car is fixed, he's out of here." With my hand over my coffee cup, fingers on the rim, I slowly twirl the cup side to side.

My sisters remain quiet a second, certain to be sharing a look with one another, before Isolde places her thin hand on my arm.

"Lumi. They aren't all him."

Him. The reduction of Danny's father. We never speak his name. It doesn't matter who he was anymore.

"I know." I blow out a heavy breath. *I know.* "It's just . . . I haven't really felt this way since then and I'm scared."

"Aren't we all a little afraid of love?" Isolde continues, like I'm a hormonal teenager and she's a sympathetic teacher. "But fear only keeps us from what might be life-changing experiences."

"Tell that to your students about sex, do yah?" Neve interjects with a laugh.

"We aren't talking about sex. Or students," Isolde defends. "We're talking about matters of the heart. Being open with your emotions."

Neve rolls her eyes, which pretty much sums up her opinion on emotions. "I say bang him. Make it your Christmas wish."

"Bang him?" I snort. "Who even says that anymore?"

"Have sexual intercourse with him." Neve uses sarcasm to season her comment. "Does that sound better?"

I glance over my shoulder at the table next to us which is close enough to be getting an earful. The couple are staring at their plates proving they *are* listening to our conversation.

"Girls," I lean over the table, lowering my voice in hopes that at least Neve will lower hers. "I'm not talking about having sex with him."

But aren't I? I mean, that is what I want. I want to bang him. Rail him. Take the Polar Express straight into Saint's pants so both of us can let off some steam.

"Then it's only a kiss?" Isolde questions, her eyes wide as she focuses on my face, as if trying to read me.

My shoulders slump. "Okay. No, it was more than a kiss." It was an unpredicted, unprecedented, unbelievable orgasm that came on a rush. *Pun intended.* Then it led to two more self-induced ones. I was like a runaway sleigh last night, and I wanted to hand over the reins to Saint.

Only, he walked away. His shower excuse was a gentle rejection.

"He's leaving," I remind my sisters one more time.

"At least you know he's going," Neve adds.

"Neve!" Isolde scolds at the insensitive quip.

I'd always known Danny's father would leave as well, I just thought I'd go with him. But when he left without me and never turned back when I told him I was pregnant, everything crumbled inside me. At least Saint has been upfront. He isn't staying.

"I'm just saying you don't need him to stay," Neve defends. "Have some fun with him, then let him go."

What if I want to go with him? The question halts on the tip of my tongue, knowing I have my own setbacks. I can't just leave with him. Mainly because he hasn't asked me to go anywhere with him.

North. The elusively vague location not found on a map. There are only two cities in the entire world named North, and neither of them is truly north of the East Coast. I know; I looked it up.

Neve softens her tone. "You deserve to let loose. It's okay to have fun with him."

Her comment isn't an insult, like I'm too uptight, but a gentle reminder I'm more than a mom and a postmistress.

"Have a one-night stand." Neve waves toward me. "Or a holiday fling. Summer ones are overrated." She chuckles.

"Not all of us are like you," Isolde argues a bit too defensively about our sister's proclivity to like flatlanders because they come and go. She doesn't want them to stick around.

"And not all of us pine for someone instead of telling him how we feel. Speaking of feelings." Neve arches a brow, and I gaze at Isolde.

"What is she talking about? Do you have a crush on someone?"

"It's nothing." She brushes at a loose strand of hair. "It's not like that."

Neve snorts.

"Sounds like I'm missing additional town gossip," I tease, but gentle my tone, hoping Isolde will talk to me. She used to come to me all the time when she was younger because our mother was gone and her twin was as wild as Neve. Isolde was more reserved. The bookworm. The good girl.

"You aren't." She sits up straighter and steels her spine as she stares at me, like imparting a secret. The secret being . . . there is no secret.

"As for Saint . . . I say, if you like him, what's it hurt to try and make it work? Or at least, work for now," Isolde adds.

Work for now? I don't know if I'm built like that. For short-term flings, but I also don't want to miss my chance with Saint. A little holiday miracle to spice up the season.

He's certainly done that so far, between cookie baking and making out on my couch.

My sisters are both right. I do deserve to let loose. If I can't explore the world, maybe I can explore the man who has crashed into mine.

At least for a little while.

Gladys returns to our table. "Ready to order, girls."

Yep. I'll take an order of one hot Santa lookalike with a side of sexy time.

CHAPTER 15

December 12

[Saint]

*L*umi is avoiding me.

The other night, I'd wanted to shower quickly, to get the stink of hot buttered rum off my body and take care of my hard-on despite her offer to assist me. If Lumi had touched me, things would be over embarrassingly quick, not to mention I didn't want the night to turn into a tit-for-tat situation. I hadn't intended to make her come, but her body responded so quickly to mine. I felt her tensing, tightening, begging for me to take her over the edge, and I couldn't deny her.

I didn't want to deny myself the experience of watching her let go from simply kissing me.

Stepping out of the steamy bathroom with the hope we could cuddle on the couch and watch a holiday rom-com, something in her expression said she couldn't get away from me fast enough.

I hadn't fucked up kissing her even if I was out of practice.

But I'd done something wrong. She dashed off to her room like Jack Frost himself was chasing her.

I hated the look on her face as much as I hate the possibility that she might regret kissing me.

My game might be a little off, but everything about Lumi feels like a win. Like falling out of a sleigh but getting back up and trying again. The concept of kissing wasn't foreign, yet kissing Lumi almost felt familiar.

Like I'd been waiting to kiss her my entire life.

Unfortunately, she was gone early yesterday morning, leaving me a note to explain she went to the gingerbread competition with her sisters. Funny, she hadn't mentioned the activity before we kissed. Then, she stayed out later than I'd expected, when I didn't deserve to have any expectations.

Still, I was certain she was avoiding me. Which meant the best place to catch her was at work.

Entering the post office mid-morning, I linger as Lumi helps patrons shipping packages and stacks of cards for the holiday season. The post office is quaint with its rows upon rows of mailboxes and an antique counter for filling out forms. The mail window almost looks like an old bank teller or train station ticket office, minus the glass barrier.

I patiently wait until the lobby is clear before I step up to the counter and hand her one of two to-go cups.

"One ticket for the Hot Chocolate Express, please."

Lumi smiles, her top teeth sinking into her bottom lip, while she reaches out for the cup I offer her. "What's this?"

"It's Hot Chocolate Appreciation Day, and I wanted to show you I appreciate you." I wink.

"You mean, hot chocolate." She lifts the cup and pops off the lid, blowing over the steam rising from the hot chocolate-y goodness.

"No, I mean, I appreciate you." As much as I've tried to tell myself kissing her was only a kiss, the moment meant so much more to me. Like that first gift on Christmas morning.

I wanted to unwrap Lumi and savor the excitement, the mystery of who she is.

"I want you to know, again, how grateful I am that you've let me stay with you." Let me get to know her as a person. Sure, I had lots of friends throughout the world, but not anyone who knew me for me. The *real* me. Lumi seems like someone I could trust.

As much as I want to bring up her disappearance yesterday or ask if she regrets our kiss the other night, the way she's smiling at me stuns me a little bit. Like she's put a spell on me and all is right. She's making me a believer in the unknown.

"Is this from Love at First Sip?" she asks, ignoring my gratitude and staring at the paper mug.

"What an appropriate name," I whisper, lifting my own cup of piping hot chocolate and taking a first sip, keeping my eyes focused on Lumi over the rim.

That kiss with her was the same sensation. Warm. Satisfying. Comfort. *Love?* Something you can't physically hold in your hand. You simply believe it exists.

With her bright eyes on me, she fights another grin. "Eileen named the place because she's in love with love."

Ah, Eileen Burrows. I've learned all about the local matchmaker who lost her husband but still finds love everywhere she turns. Sometimes even meddling to make it happen. Like a mischievous elf, she might have worked her magic the night Lumi invited me to stay at her place. I'll always be grateful to Eileen.

With her eyes on me, Lumi takes her first sip, and my dick stirs. My insides heat. I want to reach across this counter and pull her to me. Taste the chocolate on her tongue and feel the warmth of her mouth.

"So why a career with the postal service?" I ask, attempting to distract myself.

Lumi shrugs and glances down at her to-go cup. "The post office seemed like the closest to traveling. All these letters coming and going." She pauses. "Then again, letter writing seems to be a dying art. Most people only mail bills."

Slowly, she leans over the counter, and I lean closer to her.

"Sometimes." She licks her lips. "I even read the postcards people send or receive."

The little world-traveler wannabe takes any scraps she can get about life outside of Hideaway Harbor.

I chuckle softly at how scandalous she makes her admission sound, but then our eyes lock again.

Would she like to travel the world with me?

The idea feels too hopeful and preposterous at the same time, and I break our staring contest to glance around the post office, noticing a red mailbox near the front door. One that is roughly half the size of a standard box and reads: Letters for Santa.

While I know what the box is all about, what puzzles me is the large mailbag beside it. As if reading my mind, Lumi explains.

"Each year, we collect the letters and then distribute them to local businesses willing to help a family make their children's dreams come true."

With my elbow on the counter, I turn back toward her and take another sip of my hot chocolate, noticing Lumi is still leaning toward me. "Why not leave it up to Santa?"

Lumi narrows her eyes, the look cute and playful.

"What?" I innocently ask, lowering my to-go. "You don't believe in Santa?"

Lumi chuckles. "When I was a kid, yes."

She pauses, and in the break, I add, "Until he didn't bring you a Barbie airplane?" A child's heart is so easily broken.

"Until the responsibility of Santa fell on me." She sighs, glancing at the mailbox. "When Danny was little, he was skeptical of the big man. And I worked hard, even when money was tight and I couldn't give Danny everything on his wish list, I worked damn hard to make this time of year magical for him. Give him faith in something unseen."

I like her explanation.

"However," she continues, "he thought it was creepy that some strange guy dressed in red velvet was entering our house, through the chimney, which was only a stack up a narrow passage poking out the roof." She shakes her head, lowering her eyes. "The practicality of that kid."

Pride fills her voice along with the sorrowful disappointment that she won't be seeing him at Christmas.

"Did you write Santa a letter?" I ask, despite her saying she doesn't believe. I glance back at the red box before pulling my attention back to her, taking a moment to admire her wine-red hair pulled into a loose knot at her nape. Soft, shorter pieces fall around her face. Her nose is red from the steam of her hot chocolate. Her lips are enticing when she slowly smiles.

"Not this year." Her quiet tone is sarcastic.

"What would you ask for?" *Say me.* But instantly, I know the real choice she'd make. She'd want her son to come home.

"Pick anything," I quickly amend. "Something that might seem frivolous, but really fun." I dare her, narrowing my eyes as I rest both forearms on the counter, drawing us closer while I cradle my hot chocolate between my hands.

"Anything?" she whispers, her eyes on mine, the blue as bright as today's sky. "A trip around the world."

Ah, the Barbie plane and the desire to travel.

I'd like to draw a wish in the air and send it off, but she'd certainly question me after I did the same thing when little Samantha asked for an American Girl Doll during the harbor tree-lighting ceremony.

"Anyway." Lumi sighs. "Since National Write Santa a Letter Day, the box has filled at least once, and we've had to move the requests to the bag beside the box in order for other kids to experience slipping their letter into the mail."

"You've had an overflow," I confirm, glancing over my shoulder without moving from my position of leaning on the counter toward Lumi.

"Record requests this year. Not that so many families are hurting financially, but the number of kids filling the box has been unusual. Even kids as old as high schoolers have snuck in here."

She pauses another second before stating, "It's like their faith in Santa has been restored or something."

"Or something," I mutter, lifting my hot chocolate and taking another sip, averting my eyes from Lumi despite sensing her looking at me. Her gaze burns against my forehead.

"Well, I should probably get—"

"It's strange how National Write Santa a Letter Day was December fourth, and that's the day you arrived in town," she interjects, cutting off my weak attempt to excuse myself.

"You keeping tabs on when I arrived?" I arch a brow. "Obsessed much?" I tease, trying to distract any thoughts linking me and my accidental arrival in Hideaway Harbor to the national date.

Her gaze flips from my beard to the mailbox and then back to my face. Her forehead furrows, thoughts nearly visible in those blue eyes, dancing across them. She isn't imagining sugar plums.

"Like I was saying . . ." I snap my fingers and Lumi shakes her head, like she's been caught daydreaming. "I should probably get going."

"Working on your car?" she asks, although her voice is tight. Neve informed me another box arrived this morning.

"I need to get my baby girl put back together." My tone is meant to tease, cooing over my green machine, but the quick dulling of Lumi's eyes has the sweet comment thickening my throat. Like I've reached the end of my mug, and the only thing that remains is the hot chocolate sludge at the bottom.

"Bet you can't wait to get out of this town." Her tone is equally meant to taunt me, but her question is more of a statement, one full of hurt, confirmed by her eyes dropping to the counter.

She has no idea the pressure I'm under. The rush I'm in to exit Hideaway Harbor. And yet, I don't want to leave. Not without her.

With a heavy sigh, because something like Lumi coming with me can never happen, I turn toward the red mailbox again.

"I have places to go," I whisper, unable to look at her. Promises to keep.

The post office goes quiet. Not that I'd been paying attention to the Christmas music piped into the lobby or the movement of someone in the background, behind the wall separating the front counter from the back workspace. But a discomforting silence, like the calendar is flipping faster, and the end of my time in Hideaway Harbor is drawing closer.

"Maybe you could give me that overflow bag. I can probably put a dent in the letters." Not probably. I know that I can. I run a toy company after all.

"The entire bag?" Lumi questions.

"Sure." I shrug, turning back toward her one more time. "Toy company, remember?" I point to my chest, then wink. "I might have an in with the big man in red."

Lumi's questioning gaze continues while looking at my face. What does she see? The beard. The hair. The red jacket. Does it appear too coincidental? Or impossible?

I'm not portly or jolly. I certainly do not have the apple-colored cheeks of an elderly man or a twinkle in my eyes. Those images evolved from the original political cartoonist drawings in a magazine to the jovial design used to promote a soda.

Times have changed; so has Santa Claus.

"Any*way*," I sing, mimicking Lumi, while setting down my hot chocolate cup. I step toward the mailbag and tug the strings to seal it closed, then sling the sack over my shoulder and stand.

When I face Lumi again, her eyes widen once more. She's the one with a gleam in her gaze.

I cross back to the counter and pick up my nearly empty hot chocolate and salute her with the cup as I take a giant step back. "I'll let you get back to work."

Her mouth falls open, but no words tumble out.

"I'll see you tonight," I add before exiting the post office and nearly running into a teenage boy who should probably be in school on a Monday morning. The local schools have not closed yet for winter break.

"Sorry, bub," he says, finally looking up and giving me a hard once-over. His mouth gapes a second.

Eventually, he holds up what he'd been looking at while he was walking without paying attention.

A letter.

"From my little sister." His cheeks were already rosy from the chill in the air, but they turn a deep crimson color.

Sure, bub, I want to counter, but instead I offer a smile. With my hand holding my nearly empty cup of cocoa and my other hand holding the long strings of the mail sack, I shift my hip toward the teen.

"Can you slip it into my coat pocket?"

With hesitation, he opens the pocket of my jacket and tucks the letter inside.

"Thanks, man," he whispers, adding, "She's been really good this year."

Maybe the letter *is* from his sister after all. It will be the first one I read once I return to Lumi's house.

I nod at the boy who stalks off in the direction he came, before risking a second glance toward the post office, where I have a clear view of Lumi watching me through the window, with more questions in her eyes.

Or maybe, she has all the answers she needs.

CHAPTER 16

[Lumi]

$\mathcal{W}$hen I enter my house after what felt like the longest day, I inhale and instantly smell the mouth-watering scent of garlic and tomato in the air. Although Mondays are typically for martinis and a rushed dinner of soup at The Chowder House Rules, Saint sent me a text, requesting I come straight home after work, and I was intrigued. Actually, I couldn't wait to get home to him. Which was all kinds of confusing.

"What is that delicious smell?" I praise, entering my kitchen after hanging up my long jacket and stepping out of my boots. I rub my hands together, then pause when I see Saint's broad back at my kitchen stove.

Jeans hang loosely from his hips beneath an apron tied across his lower back. He's wearing only a white tee, and when he turns to face me, I read the front of the apron.

Cooks like it best in the kitchen.

"Where did that come from?" I chuckle.

"Hidden Italy," Saint explains, glancing down at the apron.

"Is that where the delicious smell came from?" I step closer to a pot simmering on the stove, glancing inside to see thick tomato sauce, heavenly scented with additional ingredients, which explains the aroma in my house.

"Well, the smell is coming from your kitchen." He arches a brow at his cheeky response. "And I made the sauce with ingredients from Hidden Italy, so if you must give the delicatessen credit, then, yes, picture the Cafiero brothers in this kitchen."

He pauses. "On second thought, don't. Those *boys* cannot do what a man can."

He's kidding, both about the Cafiero brothers being in my kitchen and their boyishness, although they are considerably younger than me.

"And what can said *man* do?" I tease, leaning against my counter.

"Make you dinner." He leans toward me like he intends to kiss me. Quick, casual, carefree, without thinking, but he stops just short of inches from my face and abruptly straightens himself.

"Anyway," he mutters, turning back to the sauce on the stove and giving it a stir. "*Santos* spaghetti for dinner. There's wine on the butcher block." The tilt of his head implies the slim table that serves as my kitchen island.

For a moment, I just take everything in. A sexy man in my kitchen making me dinner, caring for me after a long day. The small kitchen always feels smaller with him in it but not cramped. This feels intimate, domestic even, and my pulse flutters. I cup the side of my neck, overcome with emotion, while savoring this experience.

While I wished he'd kissed me moments ago, I should be the one kissing him. Appreciating him, like he said about me earlier, because I'm overwhelmed with gratitude for him right now. Being cared for is unfamiliar, and a little unsettling, but a rather pleasant feeling on top of everything else.

Eventually, stepping toward the bottle on the island, I find it already uncorked. "Would you like a glass?"

Saint only peers at me over his shoulder. "I'd love one. I've just been waiting for you."

There's no other meaning in the words than an expression of patience, and yet goosebumps form on my skin.

Has he been eager to see me?

I've been waiting to see him all day, after the sweet hot chocolate delivery and the puzzling moment where he looked like a modern-day Santa. I have questions, but for now, I pour him some wine before filling a glass for myself. As I finish, Saint turns toward the table and picks up his glass.

I hold up mine. "To cooks who like it better in the kitchen."

He chuckles, the sound deep and rich. "To postmistresses who like it better without snow or rain or heat or gloom of night."

I snort at his reproduction of a rather ancient statement about postal work made by a Greek historian, Herodotus. *Neither snow, nor rain, nor heat, nor gloom of night stays these courageous couriers from the swift completion of their appointed rounds.*

Saint takes a sip of the dark red wine. "Delicious," he hums after his drink, keeping his eyes on me, making me wish I'd been the wine he'd sampled.

Even earlier, I was jealous of a fucking hot chocolate and the way the liquid got to cross his lips, experience his tongue, and fill his mouth.

On that thought, I take my own hearty drink of wine and close my eyes.

"Long day?" Saint asks.

"Long . . . everything." I exhale. While I meant the years and days, my gaze drops to the lower region of his apron instead.

Saint runs his hand down his chest, right over those words about where cooks like it best, and I wonder where toy makers prefer their sex.

A workshop? An office bent over a desk? How would one particular toy manufacturer feel about *my* kitchen? Or better yet, my bed?

Thoughts like this have raced through my head since the result of the other night's kiss and the double orgasm I gave myself with Saint's appreciation *gift*.

"I'm sorry," he says, compassion in those coal-colored eyes, softening them from deep black to light ash.

"Nothing is your fault." Not my upset over Danny not coming home for Christmas. Nor the financial state of Rusty's Wrecks, which will struggle once again to make the payment for this month's re-mortgage. While Saint mentioned paying for his stay, I'm not taking his money. Especially after we've both crossed a line in the snow and kissed.

"I'm still sorry," he states as if he can read my overall sadness. The lingering depression of never having fulfilled a dream. Travel. See the world. I hate that I admitted to him earlier that I still have such a dream.

Budapest will still be there.

Wales can wait.

Argentina is always open.

But how much longer will my dreams be on hold before I'm too old to really appreciate the places I want to visit?

I shake my head, dismissing his apology while appreciating his understanding.

"Life happens," I state, as if the throwaway comment is any comfort.

"Make every moment magical," he adds, lifting his glass and taking another sip of wine.

I scoff. "Meaning?"

"Life shouldn't happen to you. Living shouldn't feel like it's on pause. Live every day. Make everyday moments magical. Find the little things to appreciate."

"Like a belief in Santa Claus," I tease, circling back to this morning's discussion.

"A belief in magic or mystery or love." His eyes, ashen only moments ago, darken again, with a fleck of silver popping into them. A starburst of magic itself. "Or Santa, if that works for you."

I half-smile, then take another sip of my wine before I speak again.

"I'm not dismissing Santa as only for kids. And I'm not saying I no longer believe in the beauty of Christmas. The hope. The joy. I'm just . . . tired."

Tired of feeling alone despite my sisters and son.

"I get that." He offers me an equally compassionate smile, like he really does understand. "The pressure. My dad and the company. The responsibility of being the oldest and the next in line. Upholding tradition."

"What tradition?"

Saint flinches like he hadn't meant to say as much. He shakes his head, as if waving away the admission.

"You don't mention your parents much. Is your dad part of the family business?"

Saint chokes, lifts his wine glass, and speaks into it. "You could say that." Then he finished the remainder of his wine and reaches for the bottle to refill it.

"You're really under pressure to get out of here, aren't you?"

His gaze flicks to me, and he pauses pouring more wine. "Can we not talk about it tonight?" His tone isn't harsh. In fact, his words are gentle, like he really doesn't want to discuss something heavy. "I just want to make you dinner. Maybe tempt you into a holiday rom-com on the couch."

I laugh. "You really want to watch some silly Christmas romance?"

"I want to know what all the fuss is about."

"Certainly, you've seen a few in your time."

"Are you implying I'm old?" he laughs, finishing the pour on his wine and topping off my glass.

"I'm implying you've had dates. Or girlfriends who have conned you into watching something ridiculous and strangely romantic."

He chuffs. "No to the dates. No to the girlfriends."

"What?" I choke. Is he a one-night stand kind of man? Was our kiss a one-night-only feature?

He sets down the wine bottle and leans on the butcher block table, arching toward me on the opposite side.

"No dates. No girlfriend. No wife, former or present. No special someone in my life." He arches a brow. "Yeah, I haven't forgotten you asked me three times in The Perfect Package."

"Really?" I don't know why I sound so surprised, other than he's him. He's gorgeous and funny, flirty and kind, sexy and sweet.

I glance over his shoulder where pasta boils and sauce simmers, and garlic bread is prepped for the oven.

"This feels like a date," I blurt, bursting what's surely a dinner between friends; no, roommates; no, a woman and her long-term houseguest who—

"It'd be a first." His eyes observe my face before I notice his cheeks pinken.

"A first date," I repeat, like I need clarification, making the moment even more awkward.

"Let's call it that," he counters, still watching me.

"A first date," I whisper, my gaze pinned to his eyes. "A Christmas miracle?" I weakly tease to settle the crackling tension sparking around us. The energy of the unknown, other than a man I hardly know who is making me dinner in my kitchen and suggesting we watch a movie together afterward.

Make everyday moments magical.

"No miracle necessary," Saint says, pressing off the butcher table. "Just you."

With that, he turns for the sauce, and I'm left stunned a moment, staring at that broad back, wanting to rub my hands over the expanse, and then drag my nails into it while he's cradled between my hips.

And that . . . would be a Christmas miracle.

CHAPTER 17

[Lumi]

Dinner is better than any first date I've had in decades. The food was exceptional. The company divine. And I might be the teeniest, tiniest bit buzzed from laughter and wine.

During our meal, Saint told me stories about his childhood, growing up in a remote area, living near his father's factory, and learning to appreciate toys as more than just children's playthings. Each story was a nugget of information. A long winter season with only bursts of spring or summer. His love of snow, especially a memory of making snow angels with his grandfather. I learned his grandparents had lived with him as a child. How living amid a toy company did not mean he had endless toys. How Nick got caught stealing one he really wanted once, and Saint took the blame.

"From an early age, Kaye was always making her dolls *romantic interests*." He smiles. "She had a future in sex toys even back then."

I'd laughed, recalling the number of times I'd made Barbie

117

kiss Ken, although she'd wanted to run away with Neve's G.I. Joe guys.

When we finally clean up after dinner and slouch into my couch, I don't miss how close we sit to one another. Shoulders nearly touching. Heads tipped back and angled toward one another. Fingers twitching and inching by each of our sides.

When I watch holiday romances with my sisters, we sometimes play drinking games, like take a drink every time someone says Christmas or mentions Santa Claus. With Saint beside me, I feel like I can hardly concentrate on who says what, and before I know it, the final kiss is happening, always within the last five minutes. A rousing rendition of "All I Want for Christmas" highlights the end of the movie.

"Well, what did you think?" I turn my head on the couch cushions and meet solid black eyes, glittering in the reflection of the television, the only light in the room. At some point, I should have turned on a light, but didn't move from Saint's side, the energy between us still buzzing.

"I get the gist. In a small town, if I have a flannel shirt and a dog, I can get the girl."

I laugh at his assessment.

He shifts just the slightest bit and gently presses his fingertip against the right corner of my lip. He strokes up along my nose to the middle of my forehead and back down the other side of my nose to the opposite corner of my mouth. From there, he trails beneath my nose to a point on my right cheek, up and over the bridge of my nose to my left cheek, and then back down, beneath my nose to the corner of my lip where he started his strange drawing.

As his finger moves from cheek to forehead, his voice is rugged and low as he says, "All."

On my forehead, he whispers, "I."

While his finger drags along the opposite side of my nose, he says, "Want," in a way that's a little more commanding, demanding even, and a shiver ripples up my spine, tickling the back of my neck.

As the pattern continues, he adds in "For" and "Christmas."

While I'm trying to decipher the pattern drawn over my face, my cheeks heat. My forehead, too, as if a sudden fever has taken over. My lips separate the slightest bit while I hold my breath, waiting on his desire.

He punctuates his drawing but tapping my nose. "Is You."

I'd laugh at the silliness, the mockery of the song, but the depth of his voice, like the crackling of a fire, and the blaze in his eyes, dries my mouth.

Then just like he did with Samantha, the child at the lighting of the harbor tree, he pinches all five fingers together, brings them below his lips, and blows while spreading his fingers apart, like a starburst.

My eyes blink. My head flinches back the slightest bit at the suddenness, but the tenderness in his eyes keeps me focused.

The corner of his mouth curls upward in that lazy way it has, but the smile never reaches his eyes. The seriousness of his holiday request is written in his expression.

He wants me, but maybe he doesn't believe he can have me.

Reaching for his bristly cheek, I cup the side of his face. "Let me see if I can get this right."

I try to mimic the pattern he drew on my face, retracing his steps from lip corner to top of nose to lip corner, like a triangle. Then across his mouth to his cheek, over his nose, to the other cheek. Finally, down to the original tip of his lip. As his mouth slightly hooks, perhaps even laughing at my deep concentration, I meet his eyes. I press my finger to the top of his nose, swipe down it, and rest my fingertip against his lips.

"I want you too," I admit, like I'm whispering into Santa's ear with my secret Christmas wish.

As I focus on Saint's face a second, the pattern becomes clear, almost like I can see it in my mind's eyes.

A star.

He drew a star using the features of my face and then blew on the wish.

I don't know who moves first, but suddenly we are lips on lips. My hand is cupping the back of his head, and his fingers are in my hair, holding me tight to him.

Saint slips his opposite hand along my hip, guiding me to climb over him and straddle his lap. With my knees on either side of his hips and my center resting against the obvious wedge in his jeans, I grind against him, momentarily breaking the kiss.

"Is this where I sit on Santa's lap and ask him for my wish?" I rub my cheek along his, shivering at the tickle of his rough beard on my softer skin, while I whisper near his ear.

In an instant, I'm flipped to my back on the couch with Saint between my thighs, hovering over me.

"Let's cut the Santa talk for now." There's a warning in his eyes. Not a threat but a soft plea.

Watching as my fingers stroke over his eyebrow and around his ear, I say, "I'm finding I'm a huge patron of Saint instead."

He chuckles at my silliness and then rolls his hips forward, pressing his hard bulge against my hot core. My thick leggings allow me to feel the length of him, but I want him closer.

"How about if I worship you for the evening?" With his mouth at my ear, he works his way to my neck while his hands move to the bottom of my bulky sweater, tugging it up and over my head. My hair crackles with static, matching the energy sizzling between us.

Saint takes a moment to visually admire my body. I'm wearing a form-fitting tank top without a bra, and he runs his hand up my side and over one breast, squeezing the heavy swell before pinching my nipple, forcing it to an even sharper point than it already is.

"I dream about your body," he admits, watching as he circles his fingertip over the nipple straining beneath the tank top.

Slipping both hands over the white T-shirt he wears, I admit, "Same."

"You dream about your body, too?" he chuckles.

While I could give a cheeky retort, I admit more. "Yes. My body joined with yours."

"Fuck, Lumi." Our mouths are smashed together again, like a match struck and bursting into the first flame. Hands roam wild, stripping away leggings and jeans. Underwear and boxer briefs. He tugs his T-shirt off, and I remove my tank top.

His gaze ricochets over my exposed skin. "I don't even know where to look first." His tone is light, playful, excited. Like a kid on Christmas after unwrapping the package he knew contained the gift he wanted most.

With him on his knees between my thighs, and my legs over his, I reach for his wrist, tugging his hand in the direction where I want him most.

He softly scoffs. "Don't worry, snowheart. I promise to find it on the first pass." The comment reminds me of what I'd said to him after fumbling beneath the front fender of his fancy car.

"That's what *he*—" I'm cut off the instant his forefinger finds my clit. That sensitive nub that triggers everything, like the purr from my lips and the slight lift of my hips.

His strokes are sharp and circular, and wind me tighter and tighter before he slips his finger lower, easily gliding into me.

"*Ah*," I sing, tipping back my head, instantly filled in a manner I haven't been in years. When he draws back and adds a second finger, stuffing me full once more, I hum.

"Already so ready," he chuckles, like he knew I'd be this wet.

I've had a week of dreaming about this moment, and yet nothing compares to the reality of it.

"But how ready are you for this?" He removes his fingers and nudges the tip of his hardness against my entrance, moving his fingers to play at my clit.

My eyes roll back at the tease of his swollen tip and the pressure of his fingers where I'm most sensitive.

"Tell me, Lumi. Have you been a good girl this year? Or bad?"

"I thought you wanted to cut the—" A short flick snaps against where I'm already tender, cutting off my next words. Strangely, I liked that crack.

"Just answer the question, snowheart."

"Snowheart?" I scoff, but he flicks me again, and I arch my back, wanting this strange sensation again and again.

"Good," I whisper. "I'm always a good girl."

He hums in appreciation, returning to the torturous circles on my clit, while that teasing tip remains pressed against me. Restrained but patient.

I wrap my leg over his hip, nudging just beneath his backside with the heel of my foot.

"Come closer," I whisper, practically begging him to enter me.

"Want to be a bad girl? With me." His voice strains, matching the pressure he's placed on himself to keep the tip at my eager entrance without breaching it.

"Only with you," I admit, groaning beneath the growing pleasure, the spinning, winding, twisting sensation.

"Got one question. You okay with this?" He isn't wearing a condom.

"I'm safe." On the pill and in my mid-forties, along with not having had sex in so long I can't count, I'm clean.

"Another first," he whispers, as he glides into me, keeping up his attention on my pleasure point while faltering only a moment as he fully seats himself inside me.

"Holy . . . Lumi . . . This . . ."

I smile to myself at his rambling words. Maybe he feels as scattered as I do. As puzzled. As pleased.

And when he draws back and then glides forward once more, the speed a little faster than the first time and hitting me in a new way, my body spirals, releasing the taut tension and unraveling, like a loose thread suddenly wild, spinning in reverse, and flailing in the wind.

My leg slips from his hip, dropping down until my foot hits the floor. I hunch forward, drawing him deeper within me, as I continue to let go. A ribbon tugged free from a package. A gift unwrapped after being confined in pretty paper. A woman released of tension and fears and allowing this man to set me free.

With a deep exhale, I come and I come, savoring the orgasm by running my hands up his back and holding him tighter against me.

"Saint," I whisper into his shoulder before I drop back to the couch.

With his hand on my hip, he's braced on his other elbow and moves in a new way. His hips rocking faster. His abs tighten. His heart races beneath my palm, like he's chasing time, trying to outrun something.

For the moment, I consider it's only him seeking the same level of release as me. That euphoric, proverbial jump off a roof, like taking flight. An inhale of breath. The liberty of being suspended. The sudden rush of freefall. And just before you hit the earth, a swift catch, and you're climbing again.

Saint moves in such a way, like he's followed my thoughts. The leap, the linger, the drop, the climb. A rollercoaster of sensation before he stills, finally having lost control, while only one part of him rustles, deep within me.

Saint cries out like a man who hasn't let go in a long time as well. His head tips back. The vein along his neck protrudes, and he buries himself within me, like he never wants to leave.

And I add an amendment to my Christmas wish.

I want him . . . to stay.

CHAPTER 18

December 13

[Saint]

*I*n the early hours of an officially new day, I follow Lumi upstairs and directly into her shower, where we wash away the lingering sweat from our couch exercise and begin a second round.

Lumi's hallway bathroom has a claw-foot tub with a loose curtain for water protection, so shower wall sex is out of the question. Instead, I bend her forward, place her hands on the edge of the raised tub, and slide into her again.

Rubbing my hand up her spine, I grip a fist full of that red-wine hair and gently tug, causing her to hum. A sound that has quickly become a holiday favorite, and one I'll remember all through the year, forever marking this season in my memory. We fit so easily together, and in the steamy heat of the confined space, I realize I never want to leave her.

Not that I hadn't had the revelation at other times during my stay, but the desire to stay stitches into my heart the way I weave into her body, filling her, connecting us, binding us together. Every moment is another memory that will be woven into me.

Lumi is something homemade with love.

Love.

It's strange to be loved by many and yet feel so alone. Strange to be considered something magical yet not feel magic in your life.

Lumi.

As I glide in and out of her, her name becomes synonymous with the glitter of wishes.

"Saint," she cries out, drawing me deeper into the moment. The mystery of this woman who feels so familiar. As if, despite decades of travel, what I've been searching for my entire life is right here. In a bathroom. In a claw-foot tub. In Lumi.

"That's it, snowheart," I grunt, feeling my back pinch and my balls tighten. I can't hold out much longer. I'm surprised I even got it up a second time after the release I had earlier, but Lumi does this to me. She puts a spell on me.

Magic.

As her hips thrust backward, I surge forward, and she snaps, crying out loud and proud as her orgasm slips free. The tension breaks within me and I come undone as well, knitting us deeper together, as I jet off within her.

My legs shake as I lean forward, wrapping my arms around her waist and setting my forehead on her back. Whether she's supporting me or I'm holding her upright is to be determined.

"I could sleep for a week," she jokes about the energy drained from each of us.

"I wish I could," I kiss her shoulder blade. How I wish I could sleep beside Lumi for weeks on end, but I have less than a week, as it's technically the thirteenth and I promised I'd be home no later than the twentieth.

Make everyday moments magical, I told her earlier.

There aren't enough minutes with Lumi.

IN THE MORNING, I jolt awake to the rousing sound of "Here Comes Santa Claus" blaring from my phone. Pressing upward, like I'm about to start a round of push-ups, it takes me a minute to register the floral sheets and the fact that my phone is on the nightstand beside the bed.

Lumi's bed.

After our shower together, we curled into one another in her room.

As the first line of the holiday song repeats and repeats, I hesitate, desperate to ignore the call. With cell service spotty in the area, Lumi's wi-fi secures the connection better.

"Is that your ring tone for someone?" The light laugher comes from the end of the bed, and I flip to my back, staring at a vision.

Lumi in that too-large-for-her flannel robe, loosely tied at her waist, gaping open to expose a sliver of her bare body underneath. She's squeezing her long hair in a towel, as she is freshly showered. Her eyes glimmer in the bright sunlight streaming into her bedroom.

She needs to head to work. I should get to the repair shop.

My phone rings again.

Lumi pauses rubbing her hair. Her gaze flicks to the phone on the nightstand. "Should you answer that?"

Her eyes linger in the direction of the phone. The shimmering blue dulls a bit, dusting the bright color with questions.

Especially as the ring tone ends but immediately starts up again.

With my eyes still on Lumi, I reach for the phone, smacking my hand on the device in hopes to hit Dismiss. I can talk later.

But as I've misjudged which button is which, I must have hit Accept.

"Saint, baby?" The sweet coo of my mother's voice projects from the phone. I shift for a better grip of the device and fall back to the bed, hoping to meet Lumi's eyes again. Only she's dropped her gaze to the floor, her brows pinched tight.

"Ma," I groan, closing my eyes and scrubbing at my head.

"Astan Saint Santos," she begins.

Every kid dreads the middle name treatment, and yet it's made worse with three names that mean nearly the same thing.

"Ma," I lower my voice, sighing heavily and opening my eyes to find Lumi has left her bedroom and closed the door to the hallway bathroom.

"Saint, honey. Where are you?"

"I sent a message. I'm in Hideaway Harbor, Maine."

"Yes, but for how much longer?"

"A week," I choke out. I'll need at least a week to finish working on my car. Ideally, I should leave the Martin in the capable hands of Neve Snowe and hire a car to take me to Bangor, where I can catch a puddle jumper to Nova Scotia. Once there, I have a plane waiting to carry me to North.

Just as I say the word, Lumi opens the door to the bathroom. She doesn't look at me, but her lips purse, mouth twisting. She's dressed in loose jeans and a fitted Henley with her hair knotted in that twist at her nape. The local postal office doesn't require a uniform, so Lumi dresses casually for her position at the counter.

"Ma, let me call you back." I sit, prepared to disconnect when another voice crosses the line.

"Astan." The deeper, masculine tone reeks of his authority, and even Lumi pauses, hearing my father's voice escape the phone.

With her eyes finally locked on mine, I swing to my knees and crawl on them to the foot of the bed. Wearing only my boxer briefs, the room is cold without the heat of her body beside me and the three layers of blankets over us. As I near the foot of the bed with my awkward knee-crawl, I reach for Lumi with my free arm, wrapping around her waist, and dragging her back to the bed with me. We fall against the piles of blankets while I hold the phone in one hand and trap Lumi with the other.

"Da." My exhale is deep as I prep for a lashing about responsibility. How unacceptable it was that my road trip took me to the last minute. How impractical to get caught in a snowstorm when I understood weather patterns. How frivolous it is to own a sports car.

"Son, we're waiting." His tone suggests I should know what he means.

"Now, honey, you know he always comes through in the end." Ma has returned to the line, announcing I'm on speakerphone with the two of them.

"Yes, but I'm tired of him waiting until the end. You've cut it too close this year."

"There are two weeks," I remind him.

"Eleven days," he states, like he doesn't understand the concept of rounding up. "I expect you to be here in less than that, by half."

I could argue you can't divide eleven in half, especially when it comes to days, but flippant responses like that often garner a warning that I'll indefinitely be on the naughty list.

"A week," I state, as I told my mother. "I'm still waiting for the specialty tire and—"

The deep grunt from my father cuts my explanation short. He doesn't want excuses. He wants my presence.

Silently, I curse Nick for so easily getting out of the family business as the second son. I could step away as well, if I really wanted to, but I'd be disappointing so many people.

Our staff. Our employees. The countless number of families depending on us. The children.

With my eyes still focused on Lumi, and her body pinned to mine, she lowers her head into my shoulder, and I breathe in the green apple scent of her.

Could I walk away from it all?

Is living for every moment about them or me?

I shake the selfish thought and press a kiss to Lumi's wet hair before responding to my dad.

"I'll be there, Da. I always am." With that, I click off the phone, never expecting a sign of affection or hint of appreciation from him for all I do. I expect nothing, and yet it still irks me all the same.

Tossing the phone to the mattress, I wrap my other arm around Lumi, squeezing her tighter.

"So that was your dad?" she says after a few minutes, where I'd been dreaming of us crawling back beneath all these blankets and sleeping for a week after all.

"Yeah," I whisper.

"And your mom." She chuckles quietly, as an exhale leaves her.

I pull back to better see her face, but when she doesn't look up at me, I hook the edge of my fist beneath her chin and lift her head.

"Hey," I question, brows pinching together, evidence I've missed something.

"I just thought . . . and I'm sorry I thought . . . but . . ."

"You thought what?" I ask, eyes wide and curious.

"I just heard her call you *Saint, baby*, and it sounded so sweet like a lover—"

"Oh my God." I gag, exaggerating the choking sound before clarifying. "Or a mother to her son," I emphasize. "Don't you call Danny sweet things?"

"Yeah, but—"

"Have you ever been mistaken as his lover?"

Lumi chuckles, the sound awkward. "Well, sometimes people hesitate like I'm his *older* girlfriend."

The idea of Lumi being mistaken for her son's girlfriend isn't laughable. She's beautiful and could easily pass as a woman with a cougar fetish. Young guys are probably attracted to her. Still, I laugh, light and easy, that she's so hot she's mistaken for the sugar mama of a twenty-something.

"I'm going to start calling you sugar mama."

"Don't you dare." She grips my chest hair and playfully pulls.

"Ow," I lie, slapping at her hand, until it's flat against my chest. Her palm to my heartbeat. "So, let me get this straight. You didn't believe me when I called the woman who called me baby Ma?"

Lumi chews at her lower lip. Her gaze drops to where I've imprisoned her hand against my chest.

"Why?" I ask, softening my tone.

Lumi shrugs. "I just thought maybe . . ."

"I told you last night. No one, Lumi. There is no one else but you." *And I wish I could keep you. I wish I could have all the magical moments with you. Weeks of moments. Only with you.*

Silence falls between us as my thoughts climb over themselves.

"For a week," she whispers, breaking apart those thoughts and disassembling me.

"For a week," I confirm quietly. "I have to go home." I urge her to understand with the plea in my voice.

"To the toy factory?" She lifts her gaze to my face.

"Yes."

"Where you make toys?"

"That's right," I state.

"What is it your dad does again?"

A pause follows her question because I can't answer her directly. It's not like I don't trust her. Or I'm bound in some blood oath and can't speak the truth. It's more that I've never told anyone *exactly* what he does. Or what I do.

"He manufactures toys."

"Does he deliver them as well?"

My heart races, setting off from a steady beat to a giant leap, like harnessed reindeer eager to be set loose.

"What do you mean?"

Ignoring my question, she asks another. "On December twenty-fourth?"

I swallow thickly, certain no one has ever asked me so directly. Ever paid enough attention to me to form questions and make connections. To see me as me.

"Lumi," I whisper, like her name is that magic I'd felt last night. That shimmer of hope. That belief in something unknown and special. Faith in something unseen. Love.

With her eyes still questioning mine, she cups my jaw and strokes her thumb along my cheek. The rustling of her skin over my coarse beard is the only sound between us.

"I've got to get to work," she eventually says, her voice quiet. Her eyes are suddenly sad as I've taken too long to explain myself.

"Don't say goodbye," I plead, squeezing her tighter to me once more. *Not yet. Not ever.* We still have a week, I want to argue. More moments for magic.

"No goodbye," she says, just below a whisper, before she kisses my cheek and tugs her body free from my grasp.

I should have held tighter, but in the end, I'll need to let her go.

CHAPTER 19

[Lumi]

As I'm locking up the post office that evening, I find Saint leaning against a lamp post behind me.

"Hey," I respond, startled by his sudden appearance.

"You must have been deep in thought not to see me standing here for the past ten minutes."

I chuckle when I realize from where he stood, I could have easily seen him out the post office windows, but I didn't. I had been deep in thought, puzzled by our morning, recalling the details of last night.

The way he worked my body. The way we moved together.

I've been a walking time bomb of sexual urgency all day. As in, I'm desperate to repeat the experience again and again.

For a week.

I hate how that little clause creeps into my thoughts every time I think about Saint over me, behind me, filling me.

"Yeah, something like that," I mutter to cover the awkward seconds before answering him.

He steps closer to me and tugs at my jacket until I collapse against his chest, eager for his arms to wrap around me, which they quickly do. I snuggle into him despite the layers of outerwear. Today is surprisingly mild for a mid-winter day in Maine. A brisk, perfect thirty-two degrees.

"Smells like snow," I state, when I pull back, realizing I would curl up with him right here on the sidewalk if it wasn't something the local gossip, Lady Lovewatch, would write about in her column.

"What?" Saint chuckles, wrapping his arm around me and reaching for the large tote I carry to work. He easily slings it over his shoulder.

"Snow. I can smell it in the air. Like Bodhi Wilde, Wren's dad, says it's going to rain when his elbow hurts. I smell snow."

Saint smiles, wide and bright, before tugging me closer beneath his arm. "Lumi Snowe, you are a wonder."

"Is that some kind of compliment? Like calling me snowheart?" My voice sours on the endearment.

"You don't like snowheart?" Saint turns his head to look at me as he leads us up Main Street.

"It makes me sound like an ice queen."

Saint chuffs. "It's because your last name is Snowe and you own my heart."

My feet falter, causing both Saint and me to halt on the sidewalk.

"What?" I glance up at him, holding my gaze on his eyes.

"It's better than sugar mama," he jokes, trying to dispel the moment or backpedal from a slip up.

I own his heart. Impossible.

Trying desperately to let the comment go, I shift, as if I'm leading us up Main Street when I have no idea where Saint intended us to go until we come to the corner of Main and Lobstah Lane.

The Winter Market fills the street from Main Street to Hideaway Avenue, in front of the town hall and library. The street is blocked off and packed with tourists and locals alike. Wooden huts house merchants and their wares, from holiday specialty items to foodstuffs. The nutty, subtly sweet aroma of roasted chestnuts fills the air and my mouth waters for a mug of Glühwein, a German tradition of mulled wine made from red wine and mulled spices.

"The Winter Market?" I question as Saint takes the lead once more, directing us into the fray of people.

"I haven't been yet," he explains as we slow due to the number of locals and visitors, but also as Saint begins to admire the different businesses represented, including one that has wooden carvings of Santas, snowmen, and toys. He picks up a biplane. A propeller plane with a double set of wings stacked on top of each other and seats for two.

"My great-grandfather was still alive when I was a child." Saint's voice drifts, like he's slipped into a memory. "He was a wood carver. A toy maker back when toys were made of wood."

He smiles softly, fond of the memory. "He made me something like this when I was a child." He's silent for a second. "I wanted to be a pilot when I was a kid."

Quiet heartbreak fills his voice, and I can relate, having not accomplished all the things I thought I'd do.

"A little smaller than a Barbie plane," he says, lightening his tone before admiring the plane one final time and setting it down.

"This looks more your speed," I tease, picking up a replica racecar. "It only needs a post attached to the side of it."

"Ha-ha," he scoffs, tugging me back underneath his arm and moving us on.

"I'm sorry you never got to be a pilot," I say as we walk, wanting him to know I sympathize in every way with lost dreams.

"Oh, I'm a pilot."

I stop short, causing his arm to slip from my shoulder.

"I have a private plane in Nova Scotia."

A private plane. An Aston Martin. Just who the hell is this guy? "Is that where you were headed when you crashed here?"

Saint looks away and I realize we've crossed into a topic he doesn't want to discuss. Slipping my arm around his waist, I let the subject go.

We pass sweater makers and knitwear, ornaments and bells, more toys and wooden trinkets before pausing in front of another booth.

"Danny had one of these as a kid," I say, tugging at a string hanging between the wooden legs of a Santa. Pulling the string makes the legs jump to the side and the arms flap. "He'd pull this string for hours."

Jump, Santa, jump. The thought of making Santa dance in such a manner has me instantly dropping my hand. I glance at Saint, who has been watching me.

"Your face glows when you mention your son, but your eyes . . ." He swipes his thumb over my eyebrow like he's erasing the sadness.

I hadn't been thinking so much about my son as the strange interaction between Saint and me this morning. Could he be a descendant of Santa Claus? The idea seems preposterous. Santa doesn't exist, right? Not *really.*

Still, I take in the hair and beard and pleasing smile. The solidness of his shoulders and flatness of his abs certainly dispel the thought. And then there are the naughty ways his body worked with mine. Santa be damned. This man is not the son of some legendary being.

He's a man. He owns a toy company. He owns a fucking plane. He's under pressure. Christmas is their biggest season. It makes sense. It's logical.

So what if he lives in the ambiguous town of North? Who cares if red is a very complimentary color on him? Santa can be sexy. Look at the modern memes and viral images of him.

Then I shake the thought. Santa is not sexy; Saint is sexy.

Saint. Saint. Saint.

"Lumi?" His voice pulls me from the rambling thoughts that had collided throughout the day, questioning him and his background when it shouldn't matter. Santa is make-believe, and we are playing a game of pretend anyway.

For another week.

"Yeah?" I respond, confirming that I hadn't heard him.

"How about some Glühwein?"

Slowly, I smile, dismissing my questions. "Toss in a bratwurst and you have yourself an easy date."

His brows instantly arch, dark eyes sparkling beneath the string of lights illuminating the street fair.

"Too bad. I was hoping for things to get a little hard." He leans closer to me and rubs that bristly jaw against my cheek, making me shiver at the nearness and the contrast between rough hair and sensitive skin.

I'd strip him right here on Lobstah Lane, if I thought I could get away with it. Instead, he leads me to the hut selling mulled wine and then a spot selling authentic German brats, and our easy date is filled with heated mugs of red wine and mustard on a sausage.

CHAPTER 20

December 15

[Lumi]

"Fuck," Saint grunts beneath me as I ride him hard, the sensation deep as I straddle his lap, knees at his hips, gliding up and down his thick cock.

For three nights, we've been like this. Insatiable for one another.

This round, we've made it to my bedroom, but earlier he pinned me to the front hall wall and fingered me with my face pressed into his red jacket hanging on a hook. His hook. The one next to mine, where the placement looks right.

The night of spiced wine and mustardy brats we hardly made it past the hallway to the kitchen, where Saint set me on the butcher block island and made me his dessert. I returned the favor, teasing that he was better than the average sausage. The comment earned me a moment bent over the butcher block table with Saint at my back, filling me, like he fills me now.

"So deep," he groans.

I've lost the ability to speak as I trot up and down on him. When he adds his hand to the mix, thumb flat and teasing that trigger point he has learned well, I take off on a sprint, galloping along his thick shaft, racing with the friction.

My responding moan comes from the depths of my throat. "You feel so good," I admit.

"So good," he grunts again, matching my rapid sprint over him, tapping my clit against his thumb before he moves his hand and presses at my hips, holding me tighter, so that pressure point kisses his pelvic bone.

"Holy peppermint," I cry out at the shift. My body moves as if it isn't my own. Every thought erased. Every emotion confused. My body simply takes the reins and leads me on a wild ride before I break, breathless and spent. I come with my head tipped back and my hair tickling Saint's thighs.

He is better than any sugary treat.

With the last dregs of his energy, Saint surges upward. His hips bucking and I fling my head back in his direction, eyes wide as he takes over. He pummels into me, as if he can go deeper, force me to ride him harder.

"Saint," I cry out, letting him lead my body, take it for another trip.

"I love when you surround me. Come on me." His breath catches. "Mark me."

Like the stallion he's suddenly become, he has no idea how he's branding me, not the other way around. Sex has never been like this before. So raw. So desperate. So fulfilling.

He anticipates my needs before I express them. Sometimes I can't even formulate what I want, but Saint is there, satisfying me.

His fingers. His lips. His wicked tongue. He's definitely on Santa's naughty list, and I'd like to be on the list with him as a footnote.

Indent. Number one. Naughty like this only with Lumi.

"Lumi," he cries out, breaking my name in half, like it's two separate words.

Lou-me. Snow-heart. Mark me.

He goes off inside me like an avalanche, without warning and then a sudden collapse of piled up snow. He fills me up, cracking something within me.

I want him to stay mine so badly it aches. Like wanting that special toy as a child and putting all your faith in the big man in red that it will happen.

Sensing Saint's grand finish is complete, I fold over his chest, tucking my face into his warm neck and inhale. Peppermint and chocolate will never be the same.

Eventually, I slide off him and slip from the bed, finding it easier to sneak into the bathroom for a quick clean-up. When I return, Saint has hardly moved, but he pulls back the covers with one swift tug, and I climb beneath the flannel sheets and layers of blankets.

Saint reaches over the side of the bed, using his T-shirt for clean up, and then crawls beneath the layers as well, both of us remaining naked for now.

We face one another on our sides, and Saint uses his finger to trace around the edge of my cheek. The tenderness of his touch causes me to smile.

"Tell me again about the places you want to visit," he asks.

We've played this game often over the past few days while eating dinner. Where I tell him about a place I'm certain he's been, as he's quite the world traveler. Still, he listens as I explain what I want to see and what I don't even know I want to see that's special to a location.

Italy, I'd told him the night he made us Santos spaghetti for dinner. The Colosseum. The Vatican. And experience a hidden treasure restaurant.

Germany, I'd said as we ate our bratwurst and sipped mulled wine. The Bavarian castles and the Romantic Road. And eat an authentic pretzel.

The Netherlands, I mentioned, referring to fishing villages outside of our Hideaway Harbor.

Tonight, I had to think hard about a location, keeping to my theme of relating our daily experience to a grander one.

"Montana."

"Montana," he chokes. "What's special about Montana?" He isn't being facetious, just curious, as he has been each night when asking me about my desired destinations.

"Mountains and valleys. Rivers and streams."

"You have that here," he reminds me.

"I know, but you asked. And I want to see those things . . . rivers and mountains . . . outside of Hideaway Harbor." Bigger mountains. Grander valleys. Larger rivers and streams.

Saint hums, tucking his hands beneath the pillow that has become his. Like his side of the bed. His nightstand.

"And what would you do in Montana?" he questions.

"I'd ride a horse. Maybe camp underneath the stars." Make a wish on one or a million of them.

"Don't forget the food." He smiles, lazy and comfortable, like he knows my pattern. Like he sees me.

"Hmm. What's Montana famous for?"

"Fish," he blurts. "Or big game meat, like bison."

I gasp. "I would never eat a buffalo." The idea of eating the endangered species, even if some are purposely grown on farms, makes me shudder. Then again, fish is not overly enticing either, as we have plenty right here in the harbor.

"What about a reindeer? Would you eat one of those?"

I blink several times. "And upset Santa? *Never*," I groan.

Saint chuckles. "You can eat caribou, though. It's actually better for you than cow meat. Less fat."

I stare at him before laughing. "Are we really discussing the merits of meat while naked beside one another?"

"That's what couples do."

I blink. The casual way he's been tossing out compliments and comments about us is unnerving, because I'm nervous about the end. Of us.

"I wouldn't know," I admit, having always been a single mother and never really forming a deep commitment to someone else with Danny present.

"I wouldn't either. I'm just guessing." He pauses a second. "But it's nice, isn't it?"

Not once in the time I've known Saint has he come across as vulnerable. Yet his hesitation gives me pause. Is he just as unsettled about us as I am? Does he not want to leave, just like I don't want him to go?

"Yeah. It's nice," I confirm.

He reaches out for my face again, brushing my hair around my ear. "We need to get you a Christmas tree."

"I don't need a tree." I decorated my house after Thanksgiving like I always do. Getting a live tree is a tradition. Each year, I'd wait for Danny to return from college, and then we'd go get one. Spend the day decorating it together. We'd crank up the Christmas tunes and marvel at each ornament as we unwrapped them, because we hadn't seen them in a full year. There was one to commemorate every year of Danny's life. His interests from toddler to teenager and then adulthood.

When Danny said he wasn't coming home, I passed on the tradition, making the instant decision not to get a tree. I'll go to Neve's this year, and we'll celebrate with her tree.

"Blasphemy," Saint counters. "Tomorrow night. Christmas tree date night."

I laugh at his emphatic decision.

"What about you?" I ask. "What places have you never been that you'd like to visit?"

"Oh gosh." He rolls to his back and stares up at the ceiling.

Already knowing he's been to so many places, I imagine his answer will take a minute.

"In the Himalayas, there are monasteries built into the mountains, and I'd love to see them. And the Tianzi Mountains in China. Or the Badab-e Surt in Iran."

"Why does everything you're mentioning sound dangerous? Heights. Political unrest."

Saint shrugs and rolls back in my direction. "The world is a beautiful place."

I smile at the innocence of such a belief. The world is beautiful. I've just not seen much of it.

"Well, I'd need food," I tease about the locations he'd visit. The adventures he'd certainly have. I'm just not certain I'm *that* adventurous.

"So, you want culture more than climate?" he questions.

"I'd want food, yes." On cue, my stomach growls like I hadn't eaten hours ago.

"Excuse me," Saint says before pulling the blankets over his head and diving beneath them, heading for my belly.

"What are you doing?" I laugh.

"Your stomach and I need to have a chat."

Only when he gets to my midsection, he peppers it with kisses, and I lift the sheet over my head as well to watch him. With my other hand, I brush over his head.

"When I had my accident here, I was coming back from a cross-country road trip," he admits, sucking at the loose skin near my belly button. "Would you be interested in a road trip?"

"Of course," I state. "The U.S. and Canada have so many beautiful places to visit as well."

"Places with food," he adds, moving his kisses closer and closer to my breasts.

"Yeah, food." I sigh, then gasp when he nips the underside of one.

"Would you take a road trip with me?" he asks, his eyes as

hesitant as his tone, as he peers at me over the swell he nipped. "If I promised to feed you."

"Abso—" My answer is cut short as he opens his mouth and sucks on my nipple, hollowing his cheeks to pull me into his mouth, then releasing me with a soft kiss before circling his tongue around the peaked nub.

My stomach rumbles again.

"What was that? I didn't hear you. This belly has so much to say," he teases as he moves to my other breast, while his hand flattens over my stomach, as if willing it to stop grumbling.

I laugh again, threading my fingers through his hair.

"I'd go anywhere you asked," I admit.

His head pops up, the release of my breast from his mouth sharp.

"Anywhere?" he questions, lowering his hand between my legs, where my thighs slide apart to welcome him as if I didn't just ride him like I was chasing the wind.

"Any—" My word is cut off again as he easily slips two fingers into me.

"Would you be willing to take an adventure with me?" he asks, withdrawing his fingers but quickly returning them deep inside me.

"You're the adventure," I admit as my eyes roll back at the delicious way he draws forward and back, dragging out the pleasure.

While my head says this is all pillow talk, my heart has packed bags for wishful thinking. Do I really have anything binding me to Hideaway Harbor? Could I go wherever he wants to take me? What would an actual adventure with him be like?

"Now, that's what I like to hear," he teases as my stomach gurgles despite his attention lower on my body.

"You need something to eat, snowheart?" His tone is salacious, like he has something he can feed me.

"Don't you dare stop," I warn about what he's doing to me. "You can have your turn next," I joke.

"I'm going to take my turn right now." He disappears farther beneath the sheets and dives between my thighs, making me climb a different type of mountain. Taking me on another new adventure.

One where I forget about any place in the world other than him.

CHAPTER 21

December 16

[Saint]

As much as I wanted to just wander into the woods and chop down a fir tree like I do at home, Lumi warns that most land around Hideaway Harbor is private or protected, and we cannot simply walk into a wooded area and take down a tree.

Instead, we go to Pine & Dandy Christmas Tree Farm, where I cut down a seven-foot Fraiser fir Lumi swears is too big for her living room. I don't believe her until we cut the netting snugly holding the branches, and they spring apart. The tree is huge inside the smaller room and takes up an entire corner of her living space near the front window, even after we trim the top and saw off a portion of the bottom.

It looks ridiculous, and beautiful, and smells heavenly.

"Just what this room needed," I state, proud of our purchase, while standing back and giving the monstrosity another glance.

"You think my living room needed an extra-large, live tree?" Lumi teases.

"This room needed more holiday cheer." Just looking at the naked tree is bittersweet. A reminder of obligations yet deepening emotions about how wonderful this time of year can be.

"You don't like my house?" she counters next, and I turn to face her.

"I love this house." I hold her gaze because I mean it. This cozy two-story home is so full of love and touches that scream all-Lumi, and although I live in a house three times larger, I wouldn't give up this house unless I had to.

Which I have to do.

But that thought is for another day, so I turn back to the tree and clap my hands once. "Okay, what's next?"

At home, we have staff who decorate all the trees around the factory, and Ma has helpers who set up many of the trees within the house. Because I'm so busy with work, I no longer participate in decorating the family tree. Which makes tonight's activity all the more exciting and meaningful.

This moment will be for Lumi and me.

"Lights. Ornaments. Garland." Lumi sighs like it's all too much, but I'm all in.

"On it." I turn toward the boxes she had me bring down from her attic earlier in the day. I don't know that I've ever seen a more organized attic than hers, with everything labeled and similar items stored near one another.

"Music and beverages, snowheart." I point at her, doling out her mission.

Despite rolling her eyes, her smile is warm and sweet. As much as the endearment might sound awkward, it works. Like I told her the other night, admitting a little too much perhaps, she owns my heart. Lumi Snowe plus heart. And now I sound like a love sap, as sticky as the needles from this tree.

When music fills the living room from Lumi's phone, I turn toward the tree, eager to begin with the lights.

Twenty minutes later, I'm frustrated. "Who the hell rolled up these lights?" The delicate cords are a tangled mess, wound like a ball of yarn, only not nearly as neat or as easy to unravel.

"I think Danny did it." Lumi sighs beside me, managing her own issues as she works on a twist of fake cranberries and plastic popcorn garland. At the mention of her son, I power on because I want this Christmas to be special for Lumi with or without Danny.

I can only imagine how difficult it must be when parenting transfers from the trials and tribulations of child-rearing to the release of one's child as an adult. I'm certain Lumi's raised a good man. He's grown up and left home, as one does when raised well, encouraged to dream, and given the opportunity to fly. Still, I can feel her quiet sadness, amid her understanding. Her son won't be home for the holiday.

I don't like to think of her alone, especially as I cannot stay with her.

The resolve in her voice further breaks my heart. She isn't upset to spend the holiday with her sisters as she always does. She'll just miss those who won't be present. Like Danny. Her sister Icelyn. Maybe even me.

For the next fifteen minutes, we work without speaking, allowing the cheerful holiday music to fill the space, but on the sixth rendition of "Santa Claus is Comin' to Town", Lumi stands and picks a new selection of songs.

The playlist includes famous artists singing holiday originals about home and family, winter and love.

When we finally have the lights strung and the garland secure, we start on Lumi's ornaments and she shares little anecdotes about each one of them. The golden-plated Santa image with Danny's name engraved on it for his first Christmas. His Bob the Builder phase, which abruptly ended and moved on to Batman. His obsession with every sport imaginable. His love of cars.

Lumi also had ornaments that remind her of her mom, who

died in a car accident, and her father who eventually succumbed to a broken heart nearly two decades after his wife's death.

She smiles with fond memories, though, not every smile reaches her eyes.

For half a second, I worry this might have been a bad idea. The memories. The reminders of those missing from her home, but not her heart.

"You okay?" I eventually ask as she stands back and admires the hanging ornaments she worked to arrange and rearrange, so they look just right to her.

"Yeah," she whispers, turning from the tree to glance at me. "Thank you for this." She tilts her head toward the evergreen with ornaments only on the front three-quarters because it's so large.

No one will notice the back, I'd told her, because it was tucked into the corner.

"Anything for you, snowheart," I state, wishing I could make that statement one hundred percent true. I'd love to give her anything she asks of me, but there are a few things I cannot offer.

When she swipes at her cheek, I notice a single tear has escaped her eye.

"Hey." I set down the final ornament I hold in my hand and step closer to her. "Hey, hey, what is this?"

I swipe at a second tear while she presses at the corner of her opposite eye.

"I don't know." She chuckles, the sound awkward and uncertain. "It's such a beautiful tree. And getting one was such a thoughtful idea. And you're such a *good* man."

My cheeks heat with the compliment and the sincerity in her voice. I press a kiss to her forehead, lingering a moment, while she takes a few seconds herself.

Eventually, I lean back. "One final thing to do." I point toward the cord beneath the tree. There's a giant button to press with your foot to switch on the lights. "Want to do the honors?"

Lumi shakes her head and steps back, pressing the corner of her other eye, but the tears are gone for now. I practically skip to turn off the lamp in the room and quickly return to the power button for the tree lights.

With ridiculous pride, I tap the button with my sock-covered toe, and the tree illuminates.

While I've seen hundreds of trees lit in my lifetime, there is something extra special about this large tree in a small living room, decorated with worn-out garland and sentimental ornaments.

"It's a good tree, Saint," Lumi says, her voice soft as she stares at the lights. The selection is mini bulbs in multiple colors, and in the darkness, they reflect back on her face, giving her a rainbow glow across her nose and cheeks.

"It's beautiful."

"You're beautiful," I whisper, unable to take my eyes off her, and the mosaic display over her skin.

And as a new song begins, I step closer to her, slip my arm around her back and tug her toward me.

"Dance with me."

"Here?" she laughs, the sounds like miniature bells, lighter than minutes ago. She sounds equally surprised by my request.

"Here," I confirm, taking her hand in mine and pulling it upward. Under the masculine crooning of Michael Bublé, singing "It's Beginning to Look Like Christmas," we sway to lyrics that are not traditionally meant for dancing until the next tune begins.

"Ah, the Pentatonix," I groan, recognizing the beat of "White Winter Hymnal".

"Got something against them?" she teases as I reach for the hem of her sweater.

"Nope. Just want you against me." I tug the sweater up and over her head, revealing a fitted long-sleeve shirt.

"You're very corny tonight." She smiles and continues the pause on our dance to remove my flannel shirt.

"And you . . ." I reach for the hem of the second shirt on her. "Are overdressed for this dance party."

"Now we're having a party?" She is pure flirt.

With her long-sleeve shirt removed and dropped to the floor, I tug off my Henley by reaching behind my neck and pulling it up and over my head. It meets the pile of clothes beginning to build near our feet.

I'm in no hurry to undress her. I just want her skin against mine, but she beats me to it by running her palms over my belly and then across my pecs. Her gaze follows the trail she treads, taking her time to feel my abdominal muscles contract.

"Ticklish?" she slowly grins while retracing her pattern over my flesh.

"No." I hadn't ever considered myself ticklish but something about her tender touch sends a shiver down my spine.

"Cold," she whispers at the evident shiver.

"Nope." I rub my hands over her shoulders and along her back, pulling her closer to me to unfasten her bra, then drop it to the floor as well.

Bringing Lumi against me, I wrap my arms around her, feeling her naked breasts pressed to my sensitive chest. Our hips gently sway as we move in a slow circle that doesn't match the snaps and claps of the song. Which doesn't matter in the least.

As the rhythm comes to an end, I press at Lumi's leggings, shoving them down her thighs before squatting to help her step out of them. Her cabin socks are in the way, and I tug them off as well.

Standing to my full height, I shuck off my jeans and step out of my socks too.

"A naked dance party." Lumi giggles.

"No party," I confirm, pulling her body back against mine,

breasts back against my chest. Securing her in my arms, I press a kiss to her temple. "Just us, Lumi. You and me."

The music shifts to something more somber, almost mournful. "Winter Song" by Sara Bareilles and Ingrid Michaelson fills Lumi's living room, and she looks up at me.

"I love this song. There's something so sad but beautiful about it."

I don't know if I've ever listened to the lyrics, so while we dance, I concentrate on the soulful song about winter wishes and keeping memories inside my heart.

Pulling back, I kiss Lumi, slow and sweet, taking my time to memorize the curl of her lips. The slight pout to the lower one, the perfect bow of the upper one. I savor the taste of wine and peppermint on her tongue as she sucked on a candy cane between sips of the holiday blend we bought at the winter market the other night. I drink in the quiet sound of her. A soft purr as we bring our lips together.

As with all things with Lumi, I cannot stop time, though, and the kiss begins to heat. Tongues meet, hesitantly at first, as if trying once more to savor the flavor of the other. Our tongues connecting only edges the pleasure. As they swirl together, I draw her closer. My knee slips between her legs, and her arms tighten around my neck.

I'm hyperaware of the coarse hairs on my thighs meeting the silky smoothness of the inside of her leg. The heat of my palm spreads over her bare lower back. The curve of her jaw against my other hand, cupped on the edge of her face.

Lumi lifts her leg, entangled between mine, gently nudging at my balls. The evidence of what she does to me is long and hard and poking at the waistband of my boxer briefs, eager to be set free, but I'm in no hurry.

I just want to drink her in, freeze the moment, and store the memory . . . *inside my heart.*

When the song finally ends, Sia begins singing "Snowman,"

and I tug Lumi down to the floor, littered with our clothing and the discarded tissue paper previously wrapped around her ornaments.

Beneath the Christmas tree, the only illumination in the room, I marvel once more at the kaleidoscope of color over Lumi's skin. The blue on her breast. The green near her belly. The red on her face.

She's so beautiful and I slip my hands between her thighs, watching her eyes roll back and her back arch at that first touch. The one that confirms I turn her on. I make her wet. I cause her to hum and eventually beg for more. Of me.

When I sense she can't take anymore, I slip between her legs, spread open and welcoming my cock at her entrance. Slowly, I slide into her, filling her, treasuring her.

"Lumi," I whisper. Depending on the language, there are anywhere from forty to seventy words for snow.

There is only one word for love.

Lumi.

"Saint," she counters, running her hand along the side of my head, as I take my time to glide in and out of her. Teasing that I'll leave her body. Assuring with a gentle rush forward that I want this to last as long as it can.

I want us for as long as we have.

Her hips roll in response to how mine rock, and we write a new holiday song. One sung about an oversized tree, childish ornaments, and two bodies beneath evergreen branches, making love and memories.

I cup the back of Lumi's thigh, pressing her bent knee toward her shoulder, opening her wider for me. Her head turns to the side as her mouth gapes.

"Come, snowheart." Fall apart around me like the flutters inside a snow globe. The downy flakes that float from the sky. The swirl as it drifts across open fields.

Lumi lets out a long moan of relief as she clenches around me, pulling from me a release only she can provide.

An explosion of color painted on skin. The twinkling of bright blue lights against a pine tree. A blast of holiday music, full of cheer and excitement and enthusiasm.

Faith. Hope. Love.

As I come down from my own ride through the sky, I collapse over Lumi's body, blanketing her while she hugs me to her chest like a beloved pillow.

And we hold tight to this moment. One lived to the fullest, drawn out to the end, until there is nothing that remains but just Lumi and me.

Pure magic.

CHAPTER 22

[Lumi]

More tears prickle my eyes as Saint covers me. The weight of his body is heavy yet welcome after the profound moment we just experienced beneath my Christmas tree.

The tree is a little lopsided, but I didn't have the heart to tell him.

With my palms pressed to his back, I keep him in place for as long as I can before I feel the familiar shift of his body. The desire not to crush me with his weight. I'm happy to bear the burden.

However, Saint rolls off me, falling to his back while I curl to my side to face him. He drapes his wrist against his forehead.

"That was . . ." He blows out a breath. "Magical."

I chuckle at the term which falls nothing short of the truth. What happened was transcendent. Like angels singing on high. And elves really on a shelf. And believing in Santa Claus.

With that in mind, I trace his profile. Thick brows on a solid forehead. Strong nose. Perfectly puffed lips encircled by a delicious mix of silvery facial hair.

Could he be . . .

The thought seems ridiculous. I'm merely projecting a sexy Santa fantasy onto him. And yet, so many little clues suggest . . . maybe.

When his head sharply turns in my direction, I let out a little squeak at the sudden movement and disruption of my thoughts.

Slowly, he smiles, the curl of his mouth taking its time to reach a full grin. Then he laughs, jovial and light.

"God, Lumi. You are the best." He rolls toward me, kissing me hard and fast, and nothing like the patience of our movements mere seconds ago. "Or should I say, such a good girl."

His tone drops, and a shiver runs up my spine while my hip digs into the rug.

"And you're a little bad." *For my heart.*

However, my voice is playful, and I punctuate the flirt with a stroke of my finger down his nose.

"Oh." I abruptly sit up and glance at the newly decorated Christmas tree. "I almost forgot I have something for you."

His brows hitches as I press up with one arm. His gaze drags from my naked breasts to my face. "And you want to give it to me now?"

The curve of his mouth suggests he's thinking something sexual, but I have an actual gift. With the explosion of Christmas in the room, because of the tree, it feels appropriate to give him this present now.

Hastily, I stand, pointing at him. "Don't move." I reach for his flannel shirt and shrug into it as I walk toward the staircase and race up them.

When I return to the living room, Saint has pulled on his boxer briefs, and I pout. "You moved."

He looks up at me with innocent, yet dark, eyes. "I was getting cold without you."

Folding down to crisscross my legs and sit beside him, I hold out the decorated box. It isn't wrapped but the design on the box is festive.

"What's this?" he smiles, while not perfectly curling his lips.

"A present. Of sorts." I clarify. I don't want to complicate things. I don't have expectations of us exchanging gifts, especially as he won't be here on Christmas day. Still, I offer him this.

"First gift," I say, nodding toward it.

"First gift?"

"You know . . . Santa has a tradition. Who will receive the first gift?"

Saint stares at me, face blank, like he has no idea what I'm talking about.

"It's from *The Polar Express*." I tilt my head, like he should know the movie when the man doesn't have any children. Or maybe he's looking at me like he's surprised *I* know of such a thing as a first gift.

"Anyway," I dismissively wave my hand, explaining the details. "In the story, Santa picks someone to receive the first gift. Danny loved the idea, and it became a tradition. Who would receive the first gift? Of course, it got a little out of hand as he'd try to pass off some handmade gift days before Christmas. Then weeks before. In order to say he *gave away* the first gift."

The generosity of my son's heart knows no bounds.

And still, Saint stares at me.

"So, you're giving the first gift to me this year?" he asks, like he needs clarification.

"Yep." I nod toward the box, suddenly feeling like I've made more out of this moment when I'd been determined not to complicate things. "Open it."

Saint acts like a child eager to open a present. Wildly shaking the box as he wrestles the lid to remove it. He shoves aside the tissue paper like it offends him and stares down at the knitted mass inside the box.

Cautiously, he pulls one item up and out of the package, watching as it unfurls and gives away what it is.

"Socks." His tone expresses his confusion.

"Woolen socks," I state. "This weekend is the annual Woolen Sock race." I shrug. "It's a fun run around the Locke Reserve property. You can wear up to three pairs of socks, but the outer ones need to be handmade by yourself or someone in Hideaway Harbor."

Saint continues to stare at the sock in his hand, made from varying shades of green yarn forming stripes around the ankle with a giant snowflake on the outer side of each.

"And you made these for me?" He sounds shocked. "In my favorite color."

I shrug again. "I mean, I'm not an expert at knitting, but I've attended the local knitting night a time or two, and on the rare occasion I have downtime at the post off—"

I'm tackled to my back, while Saint fists the sock in his hand. Staring up at him over me, I blink a few times at the sudden shift in my position.

"You made these for me," he repeats, his voice less credulous. More childlike with pleasure.

"They're only socks," I state, puzzled by both his expression and the shock in his voice. "The run is a tradition, and I thought it'd be fun to participate."

"So, you made these for me," he confirms one more time.

"I mean . . . you probably have tons of socks. Tons of woolen ones, living in North." Wherever that vague city might be.

"But I don't own a pair of socks, made for me, by Lumi." He stares at me, willing me to understand something I don't get at first. Then it hits me like a sleigh colliding with a roof.

Handmade. By Lumi. With love. Because any handmade gift takes time and love to make.

Saint's mouth crashes with mine, kissing me deep and thoroughly before pulling back, reverently setting the sock in the box with the other one.

"Lumi Snowe, I'd be honored to attend the Woolen Sock race with you. And wear the socks you made for me." He presses kisses along my sternum and between my breasts, shoving aside the two halves of his flannel shirt that I wrapped around myself like a robe. He continues kissing my belly until the expanse of his shoulders spread my legs.

And then we start another kind of race in which I'm definitely a winner.

CHAPTER 23

December 17

[Lumi]

"Mayor Locke invited me to participate in the ice carving contest." Saint shrugs, after telling me about the invitation while we stand beside one another, sipping coffee in the kitchen. I'm wearing his flannel shirt again, buttoned to my neck along with my cabin socks. After making love on the living room floor, we finally retired to my bedroom, where we snuggled into one another.

Saint is wearing jeans and the socks I made him, stating he needs to break them in for the race. Secretly, I think he just wants to wear the hand-knit stockings.

"I bet he did," I mutter, knowing a Santa lookalike would be a nice draw for the event. The contest isn't so much a competition as an exhibit. Professionals will be called in to work their mastery with ice, but serious amateurs are given the opportunity to try their hand—or chipper or saw—at carving as well.

159

"He and I got to chatting about the event, and I mentioned that I might have carved an ice block or two before."

Somehow, I don't doubt it.

"My grandfather taught me, just like he taught me how to carve wood."

"For toys?" I question, interest piqued.

Saint sheepishly smiles, bouncing one brow in answer.

"So, what are you going to carve?"

With the warm cup cradled in both of my hands, I turn my head, eager for Saint's answer.

He shifts his body to face me. "You'll just have to come cheer me on to find out." With a quick kiss to my neck, he heads for the shower.

A few hours later, we enter the Locke Reserve, where the town hosts the ice carving event on the property donated to the city of Hideaway Harbor.

Our town was founded by Alma Keye and George Locke, who were young, forbidden lovers fleeing their fighting families so they could be together. Crossing the mountains and stumbling upon this area tucked between steep forests and an ocean bay, they came upon a bubbling spring they first believed was a hallucination. Delirious and dehydrated, the fresh water saved their lives. The water is considered magical.

Or so the story goes, as every Hideaway Harbor child learns it from a very early age.

The spring remains on the plot of land donated to Hideaway Harbor. The Locke Trust was established to take care of the land, which now includes the original home as a museum and the Keye Community Building, built by their descendants some one hundred and fifty years later. The one-hundred and fifty acre property, which has gardens and walking areas amid trees and open green spaces, hosts many of the quirky events that make Hideaway Harbor, well, Hideaway Harbor, and that celebrate the Nordic roots of the town's first residents.

The ice carving contest is one of those timeless traditions.

"You're really embracing this competition." I laugh as Saint carries a leather tool bag full of ice chippers and chisels, plus a small chainsaw with a thick chain blade and a slim, serrated one.

"I love this sport."

The comment surprises me. "Something tells me you've carved more than a block or two of ice before."

A smirk and a wink are the only answers I get.

"Where did you get all this?" I incline my head toward the sudden collection of tools.

Saint shrugs. "HammerTime Hardware." His tone suggests, *obviously*.

With a quick kiss, front and center to anyone watching us, Saint says. "Wish me luck."

"Luck," I call out as he walks backward a few steps and then spins to locate his assigned block of ice.

Speaking of HammerTime Hardware, Saint is positioned next to Landon Abbott, one of the sons of John Abbott, owner of the local hardware store. Landon has made a name for himself with his adventure business, Off The Beaten Path. Dressed like a lumberjack in a thin jacket, quilted flannel, and base layer, plus a cap on his head, Landon doesn't look dressed warm enough for the cold weather.

I am watching Saint and Landon shake hands, introducing themselves to each other, when someone bumps my elbow with theirs. Quickly turning, I find Isolde beside me bundled head to toe in a dark snowmobile suit. A knit cap covers her signature braid. Her hands are tucked in her pockets.

"Hey." I smile. "What are you doing out here?"

She tips her chin in the direction of Landon. "Mr. Abbott asked me to take pictures." Mr. Abbott refers to Landon's father.

When Isolde was a teenager, she worked for HammerTime Hardware. Rusty's Wrecks didn't have a spot for all of Dad's girls. Throughout her college summers, and now during her teacher time off, Isolde still works at the hardware store for extra money.

My younger sister has never been impressed with the rumors about Landon and his habit of summer flings and weekend one-night stands with single female visitors in town. So, I'm surprised to find her here for him. Then again, I know she'd do anything for Mr. Abbott. He's like a second father to her.

As we huddle together, we listen as instructions are announced for the non-competition competition, and then carving begins.

There is something a little primeval and thrilling about watching Saint chip away at a giant ice block. His movements don't give a single hint as to what he will create, but the stranger part of the exercise is when Saint tugs off his jacket.

Landon gives a momentary glance at Isolde, then Saint, after noticing my sister watching him. Then Landon hastily shrugs out of his quilted flannel.

I assume the bulky material is getting in the way of their hasty, skilled movements. But at another point, Landon glances at Saint, looks at Isolde again, and strips off the quilted flannel over his fitted base layer. Saint catches this motion and tugs off a windbreaker he has on, exposing the waffle weave of long underwear.

"What the hell are they doing?" I mumble to my sister, whose eyes are wide, taking in this ridiculous show of masculinity . . . and lumbersnack striptease.

Like watching videos of men striking wood with an ax, several of the women near us are giggling and ogling as Landon and Saint chip away at ice. Sharp thrust. Rapid whittling. The smooth coast of a hand over the cold ice.

It's strangely titillating.

Eventually, Landon pulls up his shirt, exposing a belly of flat abs, stacked like ice bricks on top of each other.

Isolde sucks in a breath and I turn toward her, seeing her

cheeks are rosy and bright, and I'm thinking it might *not* be a result of the cold temperature.

"You got a crush on Landon Abbott," I tease, jabbing her with my elbow.

"No. *Ew.* Gross." She scrunches her nose, sounding like the eighth graders she teaches.

"Huh." I turn back to the display of two buff men, now with power saws in their hands, sculpting and shaping ice. Their own muscles are on display, bulging beneath tight clothing, like *they* are sculpted creations.

"No, *huh*," Isolde snaps.

I don't believe her.

What I also cannot believe is the shape of a giant snowflake taking form from Saint's carvings. But it isn't only a snowflake. The center is circular and flat, yet Saint continues marking up the cold surface. Once it looks like he's almost finished, the center becomes clear. Saint has hand-carved a heart into the snowflake. Upon further inspection, I notice the snowflake doesn't contain any hard edges, like a giant crystal of ice, but softer curves, suggesting hidden hearts have made up the entire sculpture.

"Holy Santa Claus," I whisper, and Saint's head instantly turns in my direction.

He gives me a quick wink, then it's back to the final touches.

"Are you serious?" Isolde states beside me, the sound sharp and harsh, and for a moment, I think she's upset that Saint made a snowflake of hearts for me. But when I look at her and follow her gaze, I see that Landon has carved a giant four-legged creature.

"It's a damn chipmunk," she says, like she's offended.

"What am I missing here?" Is it supposed to be Alvin from *Alvin and The Chipmunks*? A rather old reference.

"When I was in high school, Landon and his friends put a live chipmunk in my locker. The poor thing was scared to death, but it scared the hell out of me as well when I opened the locker and it jumped at me."

"Why would he do that?" I wonder, staring from the giant ice chipmunk to my sister and back to where Landon is finishing a holiday bow on the top of the creature's head. With narrowed eyes, the creature doesn't appear so much like a chipmunk as a mink, which are common in the area, and look almost like a house cat but with shorter ears and legs, and an almost sweet face. The longer I look, the better I see it.

The sculpture *is* a mink. Minks are considered tricksters. They also represent fertility and transformation, and I have no idea why I know that random information about them.

Landon points from the ice sculpture to Isolde, then poses beside it for the honorary photo.

"I hate him," she mutters.

"I think that's a . . ." But Isolde is already stepping closer to Landon, aiming her phone camera in his direction. As Landon watches her approach, he takes off his final base layer, exposing those chiseled abs and a smattering of dark hair on his chest. He wraps his arm around his creation, cups its chin, like he's forcing the ice structure to look at the camera. Then he licks it just as Isolde takes the photo.

Like . . . he licked it, it's his.

He smiles wickedly at my sister, and that wicked isn't referring to the cold weather but a strange steam happening between the two of them.

"Ogling the competition?" Saint asks, suddenly beside me, startling me out of this sizzling, dominant display.

"Just admiring all the sculptures," I say. "Nice strip tease act," I tease, noticing the thin sheen of sweat covering his brows.

"Had to make certain the competition didn't catch your eye."

"My eyes never wander," I state, staring into the coal-colored shade of his. "But Mrs. Ackerman and Cherice Tomforde got a nice eyeful."

He chuckles.

"You're going to catch a cold," I warn about the excessive sweating in such cold temperatures.

"Promise to warm me up?" He slips his arm around me.

"Always," I whisper, turning back for the snowflake of hearts one more time.

I'll always be right here.

WE'VE HARDLY ENTERED my home before the front door slams shut, and Saint is on me, pressing me against that wall of coats again. His mouth eager to carve an imprint onto my lips.

"You should shower," I mumble against his mouth, reminding him of my earlier warning. The man was nearly naked in freezing temperatures while working up a sweat carving an ice sculpture.

"Shower with me." His lips hardly leave mine while he walks backward toward the staircase.

With a gentle push, I shove him off me. "Just go."

He pouts before turning for the staircase, thundering up the old, creaky treads.

For half a minute, I'm in full-on girl mode, not interested in washing my hair or drying it again, but then I find myself racing up the stairs after him. Clothes are flying over his head as he enters the bathroom.

While he turns on the faucet, I make quick work of removing my pants. He spins to face me and tugs off my upper layers while I fumble with the buttons on his jeans.

Every second feels like a desperate need to fight time. To notch out another second together. Another minute of closeness. Another hour connected to one another.

He holds out his hand to help me into the raised tub, then he follows me. He lets out a sharp hiss as the warm water hits his cold skin. But then he's cupping my face, kissing me again like he did downstairs.

Like we both know time is running out. We don't mention it. We can't prevent it. But we don't want these moments to end.

I tuck my hair into a ponytail high on my head, then reach for the soap to wash Saint's body. One chiseled in its own right. Sculpted pecs. Rippled abs. Solid shoulders. His body is a work of art. One permanently etched into my memory.

As I wrap my hand around his stiffening cock, Saint cups my face again and sets his lips against mine again. Mumbling, he says, "This isn't why we are in here."

"Let me take care of you all the same," I whisper back, needing more time to touch him wherever he'll allow me.

With this long shaft in my palm, I glide up and down, speeding along the length, rubbing my thumb over the slit, seeping with excitement.

"Never going to be anyone but you, Lumi," he says. "I only have eyes for you," he adds, reminding me of the sudden side-competition between Landon and Saint during the ice sculpting.

"My eyes will never stray," I say, a version of what I'd said earlier. I'd always be loyal only to him. Always be right here, wanting him in return.

Suddenly, Saint pulls back, turns off the water, shoves open the curtain, and steps out of the tub. Holding out his hand, he guides me out of the tub as well, but he skips towels, leading me straight to my bed, holding up the covers so I can climb in. He follows me, and we snuggle beneath the flannel and layers of blankets while resuming to kiss one another.

I easily find him still hard while his hand runs along my side before slipping between my thighs.

"Let me take care of you, too," he whispers, his tone as hungry as mine. We want to please and be pleased. To care and be taken care of. To love and be loved.

My eyes prickle with tears, but quickly I blink them away as my hand jerks faster along his thickness and his fingers do their magic against that sensitive nub. The spot he's been a quick study to find and perfect touching.

While I'm still crying out from my initial orgasm, Saint climbs over me. His hands slip beneath the pillow under my head, gripping at the edge of the mattress, like he needs the leverage to launch into a frenzy. Our bodies suddenly move like we are racing time, attempting to beat it, as we glide together. Dashing and daring, we are a tangle of limbs, and I cling to him as he leads us up and over, like a sleigh rushing over hills and dips, and sweeping curves. The bed practically bounces beneath me as my hips buck upward to meet his.

"Lumi," he calls out like my name means everything words cannot express.

"Saint." I grunt, unable to talk, unable to think about anything other than this man surrounding me, blanketing me, filling me up.

"Get there, snowheart. Fly with me," he begs, and I slip my hand between us, working myself where we slide together, and I'm slick and sloppy.

Within seconds, I'm coming again, crying out a sound I don't recognize while he continues to pump into me, soaking up the heat of my cry and the tension of the connection before he stills himself.

His forehead gently lands on mine as he groans, loud and feral, letting everything wash out of him and into me.

When he collapses over me, his arms wrap around me, tugging my body tighter to him despite him being above me.

"Lumi," he whispers once more, like again, my name says it all.

And with my eyes squeezed shut, I embrace him as tightly as I can in return, as if holding onto him helps me hold back time and keep it from moving forward.

CHAPTER 24

At night, Saint and I attend the annual Christmas carol event in the town square renowned for the largest group of people singing carols while wearing Santa hats.

The fountain in the middle of the square is covered by a large platform in the winter months, and the leader of the caroling will stand on the raised section.

"This is ridiculous," Saint mutters under his breath as I hand him the commercially-made plush cap with a rim of fluffy white trim and a ball on the top of the triangular shape.

"*Santa . . .,*" he grouses, "does not wear a hat like this."

"Oh yeah," I tease. "And what does Santa wear?"

"A red knit cap, like any other person when it's cold and you want to keep your head warm."

I stare at him for a second, prepared to ask him how he's an expert on the man in red. Then chuckle instead, deciding it's silly to question, just like it was silly for him to offer an explanation.

I don't know why I'm in a funk this evening, my mood having drastically shifted from this morning's easygoing event and this afternoon's delight to this evening. Perhaps it's the darkness. Or the omniscient glow of the tree. Danny's absence is hitting harder. Saint's leaving feels suddenly inevitable.

Maybe it's a result of exhaustion. Being fucked into oblivion can have that effect, but Saint and I took a quick winter nap after our earlier escapade, continuing to cling to one another even in our sleep.

Deep down, I know the shift has more to do with how we eventually had to part. Climbing out of bed to dress and eat, and carry on with the holiday activities, each one acting like a checklist, propelling the season pass faster.

With my arm tucked in his, I lead us toward Neve and Isolde, both bundled up against the harsh cold, and donning their own version of a fuzzy, red and white Santa cap.

When the caroling begins, we run through the typical gamut of songs from traditional and somber to classic and lighthearted. At one point, people are distracted by a couple kissing off near a corner of the activity.

I give Saint a hesitant look. How much longer will we kiss? How soon before we share our last one?

When we come to "In the Bleak Midwinter", I focus on the lyrics while looking at Saint.

In the Christian faith, people believe the coming of a savior arrives in winter as a small child born in a barn. And kings and commoners alike recognize he was someone special, but they didn't know what to gift him for his birthday.

While all of this was more religious than I am, I still stare at Saint, wondering, like the singers of the song, what do you give someone special in your life? When he owns an Aston Martin. When he has a private plane. What could I give him that would express my feelings for him?

He was clearly thrilled by simple woolen socks, but I want to give him something more meaningful.

As the song comes to an end, I realize the only thing I can give to Saint is my heart, like the lyrics suggest.

My heart is the most valuable thing I have to offer, and I'll willingly hand it over to him as my Christmas present. My permanent gift.

If only he could stay. Or I could go with him.

When a tear escapes my eye, his brows severely pinch, and he stops singing to watch as the single drop travels down the edge of my nose. Using his teeth, he pulls his gloves from his hands and catches the drop before it hits my mouth. He brings the tip of his fingers to his lips and sips it free.

"Lumi?" Isolde says my name.

I twist my body but not my attention. "Yeah?"

"If you don't sing, you break the record," she teasingly warns. Like I'll break the link of chain letters sent in hopes of a prize as the chain spreads and letters travel.

If I don't sing, I'll break the spell Saint has on me. Or maybe if I don't sing, time will stand still a little longer.

Instead, Saint pulls me under his arm and sings the next song softly to my ear, where I don't hear the words, only the beat of my heart, caroling for him to stay.

CHAPTER 25

December 18

[Lumi]

On Sunday, the Woolen Sock run takes place on the Locke Reserve property, just like the ice carving contest had. From this vantage point, we have a nice view of the town, which sits a little lower than the reserve, plus the cold-looking harbor. As the snow starts to build, the water looks sluggish but angry. The sky is gloomy and gray.

Tents are set up, offering food and drinks for those waiting for the run to begin. There are two portions of the race, one being longer for those tackling the run as a serious competition. For the rest of us, the 3K will be in the tradition of our Nordic founders. A more casual jog or walk.

Then again, Alma and George might be laughing from their graves at all of us fools running through snow in our socks.

Our little contingent of my sisters and Saint gather near the starting point in our stocking-covered feet. Our boots are safely stored in cubbies provided for the event. Saint proudly displays his woolen socks, often lifting his foot to show willing race members the cool design, as he calls it.

His excitement over a pair of socks is absurd while gratifying at the same time. I'm tickled that he loves them so much and flattered that I've brought him joy. This is the very essence of gift giving, and I've nailed it without knowing how much he would adore a pair of homemade socks.

Neve scowls at him when he tries to lift his foot in front of her face, like a brother might do to annoy a younger sister.

Isolde chuckles beside me. "I think it's kind of sweet how excited he is about a pair of socks."

"Not just any socks," Saint interjects, catching her comment. "Socks made by Lumi. She marked them with snowflakes, her namesake."

"We're all named for snow," Neve grumbles as each of our names represents snow in some manner from a variety of cultures.

"Well, Snow Snowe," he addresses Neve. "Prepare to have your tush *tushed* in this race, snowflake."

Saint expands his arms, stretching them wide like he'll need the upper body strength for a silly leg race around this reserve. His chest puffs forward, displaying how firm he is beneath a base layer and thin outerwear made for protection against rain and wind. Both items are forest green and coordinate with his socks.

When I glance at Neve, she's a bit shellshocked. When she finally looks at me, my brows pinch in question.

"Daddy called me snowflake." She glances off toward the trees, squinting at them for a second. Whatever runs through her head, she quickly shakes it off and turns on Saint.

"You're going down, Santa-man." She points at her eyes with her index and middle finger, then aims them at Saint.

"Challenge accepted, snow snow."

While I could be offended that my sister has just earned a nickname from Saint, I'm tickled inside by how easily she's taken to him and he to her. My sisters are important to me, and a barometer of a man's worth.

"I like him," Isolde says, slipping her arm into mine and leaning against me a second. She's had limited interaction with Saint due to her busy schedule, but now that school is out for three weeks, she has time to be lazy.

I glance at Saint with Isolde's declaration, and he winks at me, as if he heard what she said.

I stick my tongue out at him, and he laughs.

"You know what they say about a tongue, the cold, and a steel pipe?" he quips.

"Double dog dare ya," Neve counters.

Saint doesn't take his eyes off me. "I'll show you where to put that tongue later."

"Ew," Neve groans.

Isolde giggles, tucking her forehead against my shoulder, but I just stare at him, cheeks flaming by his blatant admission that we are intimate.

Not that my sisters don't have an inkling.

"Alright, Woolen Sock race fans," the mayor calls out, and all talk of tongues, the cold, and steel pipes is forgotten.

When the run begins, Neve takes off like she's on a mission. Isolde walks, falling in line with a teacher friend. Saint and I move somewhere in the middle. Not the sprint of Neve nor the slow pace of Isolde.

As we weave through the Locke Reserve, following the designated trail for the race, Saint tilts his head.

"Is that running water I hear?" Surprisingly, he's not even the least bit winded from the jog in our stocking feet.

Oh no, the spring.

"What about the spring?" Saint asks, because apparently, I spoke out loud about the place shrouded with legends about true love and making babies.

"Uh . . . it's a spring?" Surely, he's seen it. He's gone for an occasional run, and the Locke Reserve is a local destination.

Saint chuckles. "Sounds like a little more than just a spring."

I explain the history of the water saving Alma and George, then add the modern take.

"People like to go there to make out."

Saint stumbles.

"And it's said that lovers go there for a blessing on their union. And even couples struggling to conceive have sex near it to help them get pregnant."

The last one might be a little far-fetched, but recently Daryll and Carol Hemingway swear that's what happened to them.

Suddenly, Saint takes my hand and tugs us off the race pathway toward the sound of rushing water. We stumble through piles of snow until we come upon a stone bridge over the slim stream where the flow of water prevents the spring from freezing.

The bridge has a wrought iron railing on both sides to prevent people from falling into the water despite the nearly non-existent depth. The spindles of the railing also contain stacks upon stacks of locks, like the Paris Pont des Arts bridge. Love locks on this bridge are a nod to our original settlers and all the lovers who have followed, wanting to have their union blessed or their families to grow.

On the bridge, Saint pulls me into his arms and stares down into the water.

"Strange that people have such blind faith in something, right?" He glances back at me, my face close to his, causing our warm breath to mingle in the cold air. "Like Christmas miracles and Santa Claus."

"Saint," I groan, tucking my head into his chest a second before popping it upright again. "I never said I don't believe in Santa."

He arches a brow, suggesting he knows I don't. "But the spring is magical?"

"I'm saying the spring represents something. Hope . . . maybe." Hope for love to endure forever. Hope for babies to happen. Or just hope for a horny night to become a sure thing.

"And I'm saying Santa represents something as well. Faith. Magic. Like a spring that blesses love unions and helps couples conceive children." He rubs his cold nose against mine.

"If you think I'm getting pregnant by standing here with you, that sleigh has flown, along with eight feisty reindeer."

Saint tips back his head and laughs, deep and loud. When he finally looks back at me, he says, "If only we were younger, I'd make all the babies with you."

What a nice dream.

"For now," Saint pauses, glancing at the water spitting out from beneath the bridge. "I want this spring's blessing."

"For what?" I ask before realizing what he's asking.

Perhaps a blessing for us as a couple. Hope for a future together.

"Saint," I whisper, as my eyes start to prickle with tears. I clutch the front of his windbreaker as he squeezes me tighter to him.

"Love is magic, too, Lumi. You can't really see it. Can't fully describe it. But you feel it." He moves my hand from clutching his jacket to cover his heart, which thumps through three layers of winterwear. "The great thing about love, like all things unknown, is you don't *need* to see it. You just trust that it's there."

"I feel it," I admit, as if preaching *I believe*. Because I do believe in love, the unexplainable emotion I have when I'm near this man. Despite how short I've known him and how brief our time together will be, I love Saint Santos.

And he loves me. Without words, I know he does. From a sensory kit to a crooked Christmas tree, spaghetti dinners, and dancing naked in my living room, Saint feels the same way I do.

We don't need to say it.

We feel it. We believe in the magic. Believe in love.

"Promise me we'll come back here one day and hang a lock together," he asks, his voice quiet while he tips his forehead to mine.

He once told me he couldn't make me any promises. The night we first kissed. So I don't want to lie to him or myself.

"It's a nice thought," I whisper to his chest and close my eyes.

He pulls back and tips up my chin. He kisses me, long and deep, warming my insides. But what really heats me up is all this kiss means.

Faith, hope, and love.

Magic.

And I fall even deeper for Saint.

No double dog dare necessary.

CHAPTER 26

December 19

[Saint]

I love the quaintness of Hideaway Harbor. How everyone knows everyone else. How they care for one another. And I especially love their traditions, like the traveling calendar that counts down the days until Christmas. However, as I draw closer and closer to my end date with Lumi, I've come to almost resent that wandering countdown.

And I feel gutted when I approach the post office, carrying a coffee for Lumi before I head to Rusty's Wrecks, and see Miriam from the Almanac, the town's newspaper, setting up the wooden easel in front of the post office. Miriam is an older woman, short and jolly, with curly gray hair, and she's the one responsible for the rotating countdown, taking it from business to business each day. She could easily pass as a traditional-looking Mrs. Claus to some.

"Saint," she calls out to me. "Would you like to do the honors?"

The honor being ripping off a date on the calendar to

177

continue the countdown toward Christmas. The giant calendar is almost poster board size with perforation at the top of each page, allowing for a dramatic *rip*—as Lumi imitated a few weeks ago—of one more date from the month.

"Sure." As I step closer to the calendar, I'm almost knocked over by a surprising and unexpected heavy weight just below my knees. Before I stumble off the sidewalk, I catch my footing while trying to balance two to-go coffee cups. I glance down to find a giant Saint Bernard who has wedged himself between me and the easel. He plops down right in front of the wooden triangle, practically on my feet, and rocking the easel for a second before Miriam steadies it.

"Skippy," she groans, while her voice is full of tender affection for the town dog that I've seen here and there over the past few weeks but never up close. Like he is in this moment, barring me from reaching the calendar and tugging off another day.

"Uhm," I hesitate, reconsidering Miriam's invitation. "Maybe Lumi should do the honor." She's the postmistress, and the calendar is set up outside the post office. Maybe that's what Skippy is trying to tell me. I'm not from here and shouldn't have the privilege to touch the calendar.

"Good idea." Miriam cheerfully enters the post office while I wait on the sidewalk, glaring down at the dog who gives me a look with those large, sad eyes.

"Why are you in my way again?" I grumble, dismissing the niggling idea that this dog might be purposely meddling with my life.

When Lumi steps outside, she smiles widely at my presence.

"For me?" She tips a brow at the Love at First Sip cup in my hand while rubbing her hands up and down her arms. She's only wearing a turtleneck sweater and jeans.

"Of course." I hand over a paper cup. "And where is your coat?" I wrap my arm around her shoulders and tuck her into my side, glancing down at the large dog between my feet and the wooden easel.

"Oh, I'm only going to be out here for a minute," Lumi says, wrapping her hands around the to-go cup in her hands and hunching her shoulders against the cold.

"Okay, Skippy, move along," Miriam gently chides, but the dog doesn't budge. He continues to look at me, like he's trying to tell me something.

Get lost, he says. Or maybe he wants me to stay put.

I can't, I glare back at him, like I know dog mental telepathy.

Eventually, Miriam instructs Lumi to just stretch over Skippy and rip off another date.

December 19 stares at me.

Six more days until the big day—Christmas.

Which means only five more days until an even bigger day for me—Christmas Eve.

With a heavy heart, I turn away from the calendar and press a kiss to the side of Lumi's head.

Time has gone too fast.

Skippy meets my gaze, as if he sympathizes with me. I could curse my current position being all his fault, yet I don't blame the dog one bit.

My heart is the culprit, falling for the beautiful woman beside me.

In fact, I might actually owe the giant beast my gratitude for pausing my travels. With another glance at the calendar, I wonder if the dog can also stop time.

With his eyes still on me, I swear he arches a brow. Like he tried to prevent that calendar date from being ripped, but us humans just don't get it.

When I glance at Lumi, she offers me a soft smile. One that doesn't reach her eyes. Like she's read my mind about time as well.

"I need to get to Rusty's," I state, my voice ringing almost too loudly.

The specialty tire for my car finally arrived. It was the last piece to restore on my green girl, but with all the activities over the weekend, I didn't go into the repair shop like I should have. Like I could hold off time a little longer.

Instead, I snuggled my woman and made out with her on the couch between festivities.

Yesterday, we even took a long nap with Lumi tucked into my chest. We cuddled on her couch, eating popcorn and drinking warm treats, until the chill of the race wore off and the warmth of her fireplace filled the room.

"Yeah, I'll see you later," Lumi says, bursting the memory bubble. I have so many moments already collected, like a sack full of letters. Each stamped with a heart.

"Later." The word nearly chokes me as I step closer to Lumi and press a quick kiss to her cheek. "Get inside, snowheart. Before you freeze."

If only I could freeze time.

Jack Frost, where are you when I need you, man?

AT NIGHT, Lumi and I have sex like there won't be a tomorrow.

With her on her hands and knees in the middle of her bed, I slam into her, wrapping her hair around my fist and the other around her waist, until I pull her upright. Her back to my chest. I sit back on my calves, positioning Lumi over my lap. Her legs spread wide. Her hands on her thighs.

"You wanted to tell Santa what you'd like for Christmas," I growl near her ear. "Tell me all your naughty thoughts, dirty girl."

Lumi's breath hitches but she rides me faster, harder, pulling me deeper into her as her backside brushes my abs and her channel swallows my cock.

"Speak," I demand, needing to hear her words. I've already touched her, licked, and now I'm taking from her whatever she'll give me.

"You," she cries out. "I only want you."

"Beneath your Christmas tree," I grunt, a smile crossing my lips as we've already been there.

"Anywhere. With you." She stammers as she rocks faster with the aid of my hands on her hips, lifting and lowering her as she reverse-cowgirls me.

"That's my girl." I scrape my teeth across her shoulder. "My good girl."

I reach around her, dipping my hand between her spread thighs, easily finding the sacred spot that drives her wild. Not that she isn't already out of control over me, and I'm loving every second of it.

With my fingers against that trigger point, I can feel every ripple and ridge as I enter her over and over again.

"Fuck," I grunt as skin slaps against skin, and I fill her. "You feel like heaven, baby."

She's perfect in every way. From her smile to her tears. Her kindness to kisses. Her body and soul and heart.

I want it all. That's my Christmas wish, only . . . I don't get wishes.

Instead, I take what I can get, unwrapping this precious woman on my lap. Stealing her orgasms, like pulling the bow off a package. Then clutching her to me as she clenches around me like the hesitant tape holding gift wrap. But at the first cry from her lips and the stillness of her movements, the pretty wrapping comes free, exposing a much-desired gift.

Lumi is my gift.

She is everything I never knew I wanted.

"So good," I hum to her neck as she comes undone around me.

Then I'm pressing her off me and flipping her to her back, pushing her knees to her shoulders and opening her in a new way. I watch as I dip into her warm center, the place swollen and pretty pink and still dripping for me.

"Again," I command, wanting another round, another gift. More time. More of this.

Clinging to her shins, keeping her legs up and open, I easily hammer into her, admiring the way we fit. Watching how I disappear inside her, connecting us, linking us, wrapping us together.

"Ask me for anything," I demand. Tell me to never leave you. An impossible request, and yet I'd try to make it happen. I'd put everything into us, if she asked.

"Make me come," she hums, sticking only to the present moment. The edge I've built for both of us.

"Yes," I grunt. "Yes."

As she's already sensitive, she easily unravels again, and I slam into her, allowing her body to pull from mine, drawing me deep into her depths as I unwind as well.

A ball of yarn spooling out until I'm nothing more than loose thread in a heap.

I collapse over Lumi, then fall to the side, keeping her attached to me. With her leg under one hip, I pull her other leg over my opposite hip and cradle her ass in my hands. On our sides, we remain pinned together with Lumi's arms around my neck, clinging to me like she never wants to let go.

And I don't want to release her either.

But I must.

CHAPTER 27

December 20

[Saint]

In the morning, hail hammers the area, and I panic that
I won't make it out of Hideaway Harbor.

I've run out of time.

With my car repaired, thoroughly inspected by Neve, I have
the green light from her to exit Rusty's Wrecks.

Handing over a hardy check that's double what's owed for use
of the auto repair shop, I'm hoping it will help them keep the
garage doors open and the lights on for another six months or
until they can make a unified decision on what to do with Rusty's
Wrecks. Keep it or sell.

"You're really going to leave her?" Neve questions, admon-
ishing me like she's the one scorned.

"I have to go," I repeat like I've said to myself through a sleep-
less night and a barrage of texts from Da and Ma, and even Nick,
who wondered what was up with me. I'd always been a rebel, but
not a rebel from my duty.

As my brother finally found love with the single mom living next door to him two years ago, I'd hoped he'd understand. But I couldn't talk to him yet. I knew what he'd say.

It's your life, man.

With the hail over, I have a narrow window of time to slip from Hideaway Harbor before poor weather strikes again.

Neve gives me a scathing look that could skin a moose, but I drive away from Rusty's, reminding myself I have obligations. Responsibilities. People who depend on me.

I rush to Lumi's for a goodbye I don't want to make. I could have said everything this morning when she slipped from bed and prepared for work, but I couldn't speak then. One final time, I simply watched her dress, tie up her hair, and smile at me, still tucked in her bed. That last kiss wasn't enough, especially after last night's sex fest, but enough was never going to happen with Lumi. I'd always want more.

The second I enter the post office, she glances up at me. She's on the customer side of the counter, straightening envelopes in a display. Her smile is bright until she reads my face. Sees the truth in my eyes.

+ + +

LUMI

"You're really going, aren't you?"

As I stand frozen in place and cold to the bone, with a handful of bubble-wrap envelopes, I don't know why I say it. Why I question it. I've known since the moment he arrived in Hideaway Harbor, he'd be leaving. He'd been adamant in silent ways, over and over again, that he'd be going.

The excitement for every new car part that arrived. The attention to detail to restore his green machine, as he called his precious vehicle.

I'd known, and yet I hadn't wanted to accept the truth.

He'd really leave me.

Just like Danny's father came and went.

Flatlanders never stayed.

And I always did.

"Lumi." He steps closer to me, but I shake my head and shove the packing envelopes back into the display. Let them be crooked. The world isn't straight anyway.

When I turn back for Saint, I hold up a hand. "Don't."

"Don't say goodbye?" His silver brows are tight. Coal-colored eyes stricken.

"Not goodbye," I whisper. *Never say goodbye.* I swallow the silent plea. The desire to beg when I'm not like this. I don't ask. I don't demand.

Despite my protest, Saint closes the distance between us and tugs me to him, crashing his mouth against mine. Claiming me. Taking from me. The kiss is aggressive and urgent. Hard even.

Like he wants to imprint it on me.

Stamp it on my heart and send me off without a return address.

As quickly as he kisses me, he pulls back, releasing me, and I nearly fall over from the rush of it all. The finality of it.

"Safe travels," I choke around the lump of coal in my throat and the sack of emptiness in my belly.

Saint doesn't respond. His booted feet scrape the tiles as he exits the post office in a rush.

I watch him drive off, leaving the space in front of the post office vacant, like he was never here.

CHAPTER 28

December 21

[Saint]

The moment I left, I wanted to turn around. Steer my green machine back into that small harbor town and anchor there. Instead, I carried on to Bangor where I left the Aston Martin in the private garage, safe and secure for a hoped-for future road trip and powered through the persistent pain in my chest until I arrived home.

North.

The house was glowing in the winter setting surrounding it. Piles of snow were heaped on either side of the front door and the drive. Evergreens dripping with the white stuff, like heavy frosting on holiday cookies.

I exit the Jeep I typically leave at the local airport for use in the extreme weather, and enter the house. The heat is blasting. The house is decorated from floor to ceiling with garland and lights. Ornaments and knick-knacks.

"Saint? Saint, is that you?" Ma rounds into the hallway, her full face a warm greeting like the subdued brightness of the house. She's short but round, and I love everything about my mother.

"My baby," she coos like I'm five, not fifty, as she pulls me in for a hug I willingly return.

"We've been so worried about you," she says, pressing me back and taking me in like I'm not an entire head taller than her.

"Ma. I'm fine," I lie.

The sharpness in my tone directed at her isn't necessary, and instantly her brows crease.

"Astan, what's wrong?" Sometimes I think a mother's read on her child, even an adult one, is almost eerie.

"Nothing, Ma," I lie again, gently pulling free of her grasp and stepping out of her hug because the inquisition is suddenly too much. Like I'm fragile and I'll break if she keeps poking at me.

"Where's Da?"

She waves her hand and *pffts*. "You know him. Always working."

If the comment was intended to remind me that I've taken months off, it misses its mark. I don't regret one moment of my road trip, especially getting lost in a small East Coast town for the past three weeks.

By dinner that night, under the inquisitive eye of my father, I snap.

"While you were dilly-dallying—"

"I was in a car accident, Da," I remind him, jabbing my fork at the caribou steak prepared by Ma, like a welcome home cele-bration.

"And we were so sorry to hear that," Ma interjects, giving Da a pointed look.

"In that unnecessary vehicle," Da adds another poke at me. His voice is deep, gentle toward all, but me. And I stare at the man, worried that one day I will look like him. Portly and proud. Ruddy-cheeked and snow-white haired.

"A car I've earned."

"You're too old for toys," Da continues like he didn't catch the underbelly of my statement.

Earned. Because I work hard for this company. For this family. I can afford nice things and deserve to spoil myself once in a while.

Like I want to spoil Lumi.

The thought has me dropping my fork, the metal clattering against fine holiday-themed china.

Ma sits up straighter.

"You took an extra three weeks, Astan," Da continues. "Skating in here with less than three days to go."

Shoving my hands into my short hair and leaning back in my seat, I glare at my father. "I met a girl, okay. A woman, actually. A beautiful, amazing, kind woman who gave me a place to stay after the accident. And I . . . I fell in love with her. Her and this crazy little town with traditions that rival our own about the holidays. Ice carving and carol singing and woolen sock races."

"You ran around in your socks," Ma asks, shock on her rosy cheeks.

"That's all you're taking away from what I've said?" I question, shocked myself, as I meet my mother's soft blue eyes.

"Don't talk to your mother in that tone."

"I'm not—" I cut myself off like I'm fifteen and being scolded as I often was then. "I fell in love." I beseech my mother to hear me. She's the ears of logic and the voice of reason with Da.

"And I want to bring her *here*." I'm tired of keeping secrets and being so fucking alone.

Fifty years and my parents still aren't listening to me. They don't hear me. Don't understand me. Why can't they be happy for me? See that I deserve what they have. Devotion to one another. Commitment as partners. Love.

What good is the idea of Christmas and magic without love?

If *I* can't celebrate having a love in my life.

Da gasps. "What?"

"What?" Ma says a little softer, her tone more compassionate.

Nick has never brought Holliday here. Instead, Ma met her in Chicago, where Ma keeps a second home for the less hectic months. Da uses the same excuse he always uses to never visit Nick and his wife. He's too busy.

But I don't want to be too busy to live. Too busy to love.

"You'd love her, Ma. She's witty and kind. And she knows how to knit." Not that *that* is a major selling point of Lumi's abilities, but it reminds me she made me woolen socks. And homemade gifts are always made with love, right? Because she loves me, even though I broke her heart. I could practically hear it shattering in her chest before I left her standing in the post office.

The cracking of it matched my own.

"Once this holiday is over, I need an extended vacation," I tell Da.

"You just took a vacation and added three additional weeks to it."

"Da, are you even listening to me? I met a woman. Lumi. Her name means snow."

"I know what Lumi means," Da counters.

"Then you know that Lumi also means love. To me," I poke at my chest and press away from the table. "I bring her home. Or . . . or this is my last Christmas."

The collective gasps from my parents are echoed by the staff, listening from this corner or that.

But I don't care. On hasty feet, I storm the hall and then skip up every other stair to my apartment on the third floor of the house. I slam the door like a child and pace back and forth in my living room, desperate to call Lumi. Desperate to text her.

I want to tell her everything. Need to tell her everything.

Not yet.

But soon.

"Nick." I breathe my brother's name into the phone.

"Ma called me." The statement is explanation enough. Ma has the same soft spot for Nick as he does for her. If she feels she cannot reason with me, she calls Nick.

"What's going on?" he asks, his voice kind and concerned. I don't fault my brother for skipping out on the family business. Even with the name Nick, he'll never need to fill the boots unless something happens to Da or me. Jack Frost forbid.

Still, some days I'm jealous of the freedom he has. Running into burning buildings isn't an easy job, but a small part of me envies the heat compared to the constant, frigid cold of where I live.

The coldness of my empty bed, as well.

"I was late," I admit, reminding him that I had an accident.

"Da told you that car was worthless in snow, didn't he?" Nick chuckles.

"He doesn't understand," I admit. Then, softer, I add, "I met someone, Nick." I sigh, like a love-sick elf.

"Really?" I can almost see his dark brows hitch. "What's she like?"

"Beautiful and kind. Snarky but sweet. Sexy as fuck." Just the thought of Lumi makes me hard, but it also makes my heart hammer, the beat irregular without her near me.

"Sounds special."

That someone special in your life, she'd hinted.

"Yeah. Very special."

A heavy pause fills the phone.

"Gonna step back?" Nick asks.

"I told Da this would be my last Christmas if I can't bring Lumi here."

"Her name is Lumi? Like snow?"

"That's all you're getting from this," I tease, reminiscent of my response to my mother's reaction earlier to socks in the snow.

"She sounds perfect for you." He pauses for a second. "But you know you can't quit."

"I know." I exhale heavily. This is my destiny.

Too many people are relying on me. And Da is just too old to continue the tradition.

"Look, I'm not one to give advice, but have you considered just telling her the truth and bringing her to North to prove who you are?"

He already knows Lumi would most likely have doubts. About our location. About our purpose.

"Have you told Holliday?" I ask.

"I don't keep anything from her. It's called trust. And love." The affection for his wife resonates in his voice.

I trust Lumi. I *love* her. Yet I haven't told her. How could I say I love you, but goodbye?

"Just be you, Saint," Nick encourages. "If she loves you, she'll accept you."

"It isn't her." I sigh again in frustration. "It's Da."

Nick exhales. "*Ah*. The perpetual lump of coal in our stockings."

It's funny to hear our father referred to as such a thing, and I laugh, knowing only my siblings would truly understand the joke.

"I'd say ignore him, but I know you can't."

I'm too entrenched in the family business.

"But it's still your life, Saint. If you want her, you can make it work. No matter what."

No matter what.

"What if she can't accept this life?" I chew my lower lip, finally falling into a leather club chair in my living room and tipping back my head.

"Then she isn't the woman for you. But everything else you

described says she is. So why wouldn't she believe you? Believe *in* you?"

I don't know. Am I putting doubts where they might not be warranted?

"Be the love in your life," Nick reminds me. Don't just exist with hopes for it.

Make every moment magical.

I can't do that without Lumi.

Which means I know what I need to do.

Make a wish, then make it come true.

CHAPTER 29

December 23

[Lumi]

The first night of Saint's absence, I blindly climbed into bed, wishing I could sleep for a month. I'd been exhausted from the night of sex, then empty when I thought about it. Carved hollow by his absence.

In the morning, I woke numb. Showered. Dressed. Drank coffee. My day began like every other day of my life.

Wash. Rinse. Repeat.

The second night after my true love left me, I did a double-take as I walked past my living room.

After the Woolen Sock run, Saint hung our soggy socks along the mantel by small hooks permanently attached to the wooden plank above the fireplace.

Hanging the stockings by the chimney with care, I'd joked.

He'd only smiled, never confirming nor denying what he was doing. Who he was. Who he might be.

My thoughts scrambled that night. He couldn't be Santa

Claus. It was all a legend. A story written for children, based on small truths that grew into an epic tale.

One single man who delivers presents to every child in the world in a single night. Impossible.

Still, I stared at those stockings, now dangling from the mantel. Two sets. One pair for him. One pair from me. Just like his red coat on a hook in my hallway, the woolen stockings looked right hanging there.

Somehow, I made it through the third day of his absence, putting on my long, puffy jacket while ignoring the vacant hook that once held Saint's red one. I'd learned to dismiss the empty hook because Danny once hung his things there as well.

At work, I stamped letters, registered packages, and organized the mail scheduled to leave our little town and travel the world.

All the same, I took in the mail. Love from everywhere across the globe. Packages marked 'handle with care' as they headed out to that special someone.

And like every other day, I read the postcards sent from Hideaway Harbor or those coming into our town, and dreamed of escape.

Some day. Maybe.

Each night, when my workday ended, I wasn't hungry. Heading home to an empty house felt daunting. Yet I didn't think I could ever look at The Chowder House Rules or enter The Shore Thing again.

One day, the sorrow would pass. The melancholy would subside. I lived here. Eventually, I'd give in to the pull of local restaurants and bars, turning back into who I was before him.

Saint.

But the heartbreak, I was certain, would linger forever.

Finally, on the fourth day after my true love left me, which is also thankfully a Friday, the most exciting thing to happen is a downed tree that blocks the main road leading into and out of

Hideaway Harbor. The news doesn't matter to me as no one is coming into town to see me. And I never leave.

That evening, I fold onto my couch which hasn't dulled from the scent of peppermint and chocolate embedded into it.

"Thank the elves for Friday," I mutter, pre-gaming the pre-planned evening with my sisters, by breaking into the holiday wine before their arrival.

The next week is a vacation from the post office, as I put in for PTO—personal time off—as soon as the new year began, so I'd be assured of the days off when Danny came home for the holidays.

I never questioned that he wouldn't be here.

"Hello, hello," Isolde cries out, entering my house, while Neve greets me with, "Ho, ho, ho."

The phrase nearly brings me to tears, but I hike myself off the couch and hug my sisters.

Neve gives me a concerned glance, but I shake my head. After hanging up her coat, Isolde comes in for a hug, despite my stiff response at first. Neve must have warned Isolde that Saint is gone.

Neither sister mentions his absence.

In town, a dance is happening, which I'd always known I wasn't going to attend, much like bachelor auctions and speed dating opportunities. I hadn't been looking for love or incredible sex. It crashed into my life and then left just as suddenly.

Instead, tonight, the annual Snowe sisters make-fun-of-holiday-movies marathon is in order, which includes popcorn and mint chocolates as our dinner and copious amounts of wine to wash down the bad decision meal.

In years past, my sisters end up spending the night, and the three of us would climb into my bed together like we did as children. Which sounds great until one of us farts during the night or someone snores. Not to mention, three adult bodies don't fit well in my queen-sized bed.

The space works best for two.

With popcorn made and a bowl of mint chocolates, we huddle on the couch together, sharing the extra-large knitted blanket, and begin one holiday movie after another, finding a few new ones that are surprisingly entertaining, if a bit heavy on the romance.

Between shows, a teaser for *It's a Wonderful Life* comes on, and Neve pauses the commercial.

"I love that movie," she says.

"It's the story of my life," I mutter.

"What do you mean?" Isolde asks.

"I've never left this town." I tip my head back on the couch cushion, feeling the weight of it along with the heavy fog rolling in from too much wine and no solid food.

"Why not?" Isolde innocently asks, and I pop my head upright to stare at her. I don't want to remind her that our mother died when she was still in high school. And I got pregnant. The twins needed someone in their final years at home, and Dad had turned selfish. Neve never intended to go to college, so she slipped into the auto shop and did what she could to win Dad's favor and keep the business afloat.

Between raising Danny, keeping an eye on my family, and working at the post office to have a steady paycheck and benefits, there wasn't time to roam the world.

"You know, an entire town isn't going to walk in and hand over tons of money to save your bank," Isolde innocently says.

"I don't own a bank," I mutter, thinking if I did, I'd pay off Rusty's debts then take a long overdue vacation.

"What she means is, you can't rely on others to bail you out," Neve adds.

"Preach," I counter, lifting my wine and bringing it to my mouth for a sip, but Neve's hand covers the rim, and I end up kissing the back of her hand.

"What the hell?"

"He wasn't going to save you," Neve says, taking a proverbial hammer to my chest.

"I never said he was," I counter, glaring at my sister.

"No one is going to whisk you out of this town," she continues. "You need to get yourself out of here."

"Thank you for reminding me of the pin in my dreams." I scowl at Neve.

"You don't need to pin your dreams," Isolde says on the other side of me. "Danny is taking care of himself. Neve has the shop. I have teaching. You only need to take care of you."

She makes it sound so simple, and yet she isn't entirely wrong.

Danny's absence proves he doesn't need me. He'll always need me in some manner, but not for all the basics of life. He is a functioning adult, employed and responsible for himself, and I am so proud of him for living his life to the fullest.

Neve and Isolde, and even Icelyn, have taken the reins of their lives, running a sleigh along whichever road they wanted to travel.

I was the only one stuck.

"Plus," Isolde tips her wine glass toward the television. "That movie"—implying *It's a Wonderful Life*—"ends with a happily ever after. George Bailey learns that every day of his life has been an adventure. Marriage. Kids. A rundown house. A failing business. He contributed to his community, and they worshipped him in return."

Isolde shifts on the couch, jabbing her bent knees into my arm.

"Tell me three good things about your life."

I sigh. "What is this, Lumi intervention night?"

"Humor me," Isolde asks, combing her fingers through her long dark hair.

"Danny, obviously."

"Obviously." She taps my wine glass with hers, then drinks.

"Oh, is this a drinking game?" I take a sip of my own wine.

"You guys." I glance from Isolde to Neve and back.

"Obviously," Neve counters, and we all sip again.

"And . . ." I pause on the third gratitude, considering that Dad living longer than Mom was certainly a blessing, but also a small curse. Draining the business. The financial constraints after his passing.

"Saint," I whisper. For the blip of a couple weeks, he was a great adventure. Like the one he'd once asked me if I'd go on with him.

Instantly, I recall his vulnerable tone. The fear that I'd reject his invitation. Maybe he was afraid I'd reject all of him if he told me more about his life.

The secrecy of his home. The absence of the toy company's name. The pressure of whatever his position was within the family business.

"Saint," Isolde whispers, and I catch her watching me. "No matter how long you had him, you still had him for a little while."

Her sigh is wistful, dreamy, as if she pines for someone herself but has never obtained his attention.

Neve snorts, breaking into our little bubble of unrequited love.

"Fuck that. No man defines me." She drinks heartily from her glass and stands for another bottle, although she wobbles when her feet hit the floor.

"And Saint didn't define Lumi," Isolde defends. "He simply gave her a few good weeks to see that she could have a wonderful life, even in Hideaway Harbor."

I stare at my younger sister. "When did you get so wise?"

"Or romantic," Neve hollers from my kitchen.

"When I'd been the other half left behind." She offers a sad smile, as she implies our sister, her twin, Icelyn, who ran off for a bigger city.

Icelyn hasn't been home for years. I don't want Danny to turn out the same way.

When Neve returns with a newly opened wine bottle, Isolde reaches over me for the remote and bypasses the teaser about the classic black and white holiday tale.

"Round two," she states.

"I think we're on round four," Neve counters.

"We've already made it through four movies?" Then I realize I've made it through four nights without Saint.

Only three hundred and sixty-one more days to go, give or take a few days until next Christmas.

I've already decided to skip it this year.

CHAPTER 30

December 24

[Lumi]

The pounding in my head matches the rattling on my front door.

"Alright, alright already," I mutter, as I fling my feet off my bed and stand on shaky legs. I slept in last night's clothing, which includes long underwear pants, cabin socks, and a tank top, covered by a flannel shirt Saint had left behind.

Pulling it up to my nose, I inhale, hoping for the peppermint and chocolate scent to right my brain and soothe the hammering in my head.

Instead, I realize I really should wash the thing. I've been sleeping in it for four nights in a row.

With a quick glance at my bed, I find Isolde curled up on her side. Her back to my side of the mattress. She looks exactly like she did as a college co-ed. Still beautiful. Still book smart. Still shy.

As I wander down the stairs, I worry Neve left but find her

sprawled out on my couch like she had a rough night. One arm flung over her head. The other is dangling down toward the floor.

How she can sleep through the *rap, rap, rap* on the door is beyond me.

When I finally twist the deadbolt and flip the lower lock, I open the door on a rush and stare at the man in front of me.

Long camel-colored wool coat. Polished leather shoes. Thick gloves on his hands and a giant bag in each one of them stuffed with Christmas presents.

"Merry Christmas, Mom."

"Danny," I whisper with trembling lips before I launch myself at my grown son, hugging him tight and choking on the expensive cologne along his neck.

I hold back the cough and just breathe him in.

When I pull away, I stare at the vision in front of me. He's so grown up. A handsome man who looks a little like his father but more like a Snowe with jet black hair and deep blue eyes.

"What are you doing here?" I whisper, the shock still in my throat.

"You didn't think I'd really miss Christmas, did you, Mom?"

I did. He told me he wasn't coming. He was too busy.

"How did you get here?" I glance around him, looking for a rented car in the road. Then I remember the downed tree yesterday, blocking the entrance into and exit out of Hideaway Harbor.

Must have been removed.

"I could have picked you up." The airport is in Bangor.

"I wanted to surprise you."

"I'm surprised," I admit, clutching at the flannel shirt around me as the cold of the outdoors slowly seeps in.

"So . . . are you going to let me in?"

"Of course," I anxiously giggle as tears well in my eyes. "Oh, honey. Yes." I step back, announcing, "This is always your home."

He sets down his large bags in the entry hallway as I shut the door behind me.

"That's why I'm here."

Home. Where he'll always find me. Where he'll always come back to me.

Neve rouses from the noise, groaning as she slowly sits up.

"Snowe sister movie night?" Danny arches a brow at me as he takes in the living room. The empty bottles of wine. The giant, empty bowl for popcorn.

"A family tradition," I remind him.

"Another reason to be here. I'm sorry I'm late."

"You're never late as long as you're here." I reach for him again, pulling him into another embrace despite him being taller and broader than I remember.

Then Neve cries out his name, jumping up and over my couch to tackle my son.

Isolde follows, ambling down the stairs. When she reaches the bottom, Danny picks her up and spins her around, causing her to grip her head in pain.

"Who wants breakfast?" I ask.

Four arms go up because Neve raises both of hers.

With several of my favorite people all in one place, I realize it really has been a wonderful life.

CHAPTER 31

December 25

[Lumi]

December twenty-fourth was another day spent with holiday movies running in the background of our conversations about Danny's job and the potential for a promotion, plus life in the big city. He mentions how he's seen his Aunt Icelyn, and I'm so grateful to learn my younger sister has checked in with my son once a month, even if she hasn't reached out as often to me.

The day is full of appetizers as meals, and then the splurge of a lobster dinner. More wine is consumed. More stories told. And laughter that my heart severely needs to press down the sadness over Saint's absence.

His name isn't mentioned, and I'm thankful my sisters don't expose my aching heart or recent affair.

Some things aren't necessary to share with your child, even if he is an adult.

I had a winter fling. It's over. The end.

Still, my chest hurts at the thought, because nothing felt casual about the time Saint and I spent together.

On Christmas morning, I quietly sit on the couch, staring at the crooked, oversized Christmas tree, glancing from one sentimental ornament to another. The decorating of the tree this year was different without Danny, but no less special. Saint made it that way.

I smile into a mug of hot chocolate with a splash of peppermint as I bring it to my lips.

"Merry Christmas, Saint," I whisper to the quiet room.

Neve and Isolde stayed over another night, and the three of us attempted to share a bed again. Instead of drunk sisters, we curled into one another. The only thing missing was Danny, but he was a bit old to snuggle in bed with his mom and aunts.

The thought only momentarily makes me sad. My son has grown into a wonderful man.

When I hear heavy footfalls on the staircase, I close my eyes briefly, envisioning all the years a younger Danny raced down the steps, eager for Christmas morning, where he'd be spoiled by his aunts, his grandfather, and Santa.

Things look a little different as an adult, and as I thought he wouldn't be home, I mailed all his presents to him a week ago.

"Merry Christmas, Mom," he says from behind me, squeezing my shoulders before leaning down to kiss my head.

"Merry Christmas, honey."

"Are you drinking already?" he chuckles, and I shift on the couch to look up at him behind me.

"Made hot chocolate with a splash of peppermint extract, but if you want schnapps, it's above the refrigerator."

Slowly, Danny smiles. "Hot chocolate with a splash of peppermint sounds good."

As I lower my chin to the edge of the couch and watch Danny head toward the kitchen, my heart pinches.

Yes. Peppermint and chocolate is a nice combination.

When Danny returns to the living room, he plops down beside me and stares at the tree.

"How did you get such a big tree in here?"

"I had a little help from . . . a friend." I sip my hot chocolate to disguise a smile.

"A friend, huh?" Without glancing at my son, certain my cheeks are pink and will give me away, I sense his questioning glance on the side of my head.

Thankfully, Neve rushes down the steps like she's still a child and cries out, "Merry Christmas. God bless us, everyone."

Danny and I twist to see Neve dramatically standing with her arms stretched wide like she's part of *A Christmas Carol* production.

Isolde slowly ambles down behind our middle sister, and more quietly greets us with her wishes.

"Happy Christmas, family."

A round of "Merry Christmas" and "Happy Christmas" follows before we gather near the tree and share presents with one another.

Books and sweaters. A game for Isolde. A new wrench for Neve.

"Looks like one more present is tucked behind the tree." Danny stretches around the mammoth evergreen as best he can and picks up a rectangular box, which looks professionally wrapped in bright red paper with a large white bow.

Danny reads a tag dangling from the bow. "Lumi." He lifts his head and hands over the box.

I glance from one sister to the next, knowing Danny didn't arrive with such a large present in hand.

"What's this?" I ask, shifting my gaze from Neve to Isolde.

"Looks like a present for you." Neve rolls her eyes like obviously it's for me as my name is on the package. But the stoic way both she and Isolde sit, eyes wide and just as curious, makes my heart start to hammer faster. They honestly don't know what this gift contains. Which means it isn't from them.

As I slowly remove the bow, my fingers shake. I slice at the paper like I don't want to damage the perfectly wrapped package, but the second I see the pink script of a familiar name, tears spring to my eyes.

"A Barbie airplane?" Danny questions.

"A Barbie airplane," I whisper, staring at the toy on my lap. One that might never come out of the packaging, making it triple in value, and yet this item is priceless to me.

"Who is it from?" Danny asks, glancing from one of his aunts to the other.

"Santa must have brought it," Neve states, chuckling at her own joke.

"Yeah. Santa." Isolde looks directly at me, brows pinching only slightly while her blue eyes widen, innocent and childlike despite her late thirties age.

I run my hands over the smooth packaging, staring once more through the transparent plastic wrap on the giant airplane, large enough for a slender doll, that promotes travel.

See the world, it whispers.

"That's strange. Who gave you a toy?" Danny glances at my sisters, who both look at me askance.

Who *would* give me a toy? And why? But I know the answer. The one man whom I'd recently told I'd always wanted this item.

"Looks like you have something in your stocking, too." Danny points toward one of the larger wool socks hanging from the mantel. Counting the four of them yesterday, Danny assumed they were new and represented Neve, Isolde, myself, and him. He was a little surprised I hadn't hung one for my elusive sister, because he hadn't known the set of four was actually two pairs. Saint's and mine.

I narrow my eyes at the bulky outline of something inside one of Saint's snowflake-decorated socks. The pair of treasured socks he'd also left behind.

Slowly, I rise, timidly smiling at my sisters, wondering what they've done, as I cross the living room floor, now littered with tissue paper and decorative bags. Removing the sock from the small hook, I turn toward the room and stick my hand down the length of the stocking. My fingers meet something small and wooden. Hesitantly, I remove it.

"What's that?" Danny asks.

"A toy plane?" Isolde questions like she hadn't placed it in the sock.

"Looks like a wooden biplane," Neve clarifies, her voice as curious as the others.

My inspection recognizes how this hand-carved plane is similar to the one Saint picked up when we explored the holiday market. I recall him telling me how his great-grandfather made wooden toys back when toys were simple. The design of this item looks old. A little worn in places, like a well-loved object that has often been played with by a child.

Like a hand-carved toy for a beloved great-grandchild who dreamed of being a pilot one day.

My throat instantly clogs.

"Something else is in the stocking," Isolde adds.

Glancing back at the sock, I tuck the plane under my arm and pull an envelope from the stocking. Then I switch the stocking under my arm and juggle the plane in one hand while holding the red envelope in the other.

The front simply reads my name. On the back flap of the envelope is an embossed stamp that reads North Pole Toys.

Inside the envelope are three items.

The first is a check for more money than I've ever held in my hands.

The second is a voucher for a plane ticket.

The final strip of heavy card stock is a note.

. . .

For the best hostess.
  Take an adventure.
  Eat all the food.
  XO

ONLY THE X looks like a snowflake, and the O looks like a heart.

"What is it?" Danny asks as my vision blurs.

Neve unfolds from the floor and comes to stand beside me.

"Holy shit," she whispers, looking at the check. "That's a lot of—"

"The number of days he was here." A daily fee from my long-term houseguest, multiplied by a thousand. The check is signed rather illegibly, but it looks legitimate despite the North Pole Toys imprinted in the space for a person's name and address.

I hadn't noticed Isolde stand, but her hand lands on my lower back, rubbing up and down. "That's very generous of him."

"Who?" Danny questions from his seat on the couch.

I could be offended that Saint paid me for his stay in my house but this is a gift. I feel it in my soul. He wants me to explore all the places I want to visit.

"Where would you go?" Neve softly asks, and I glance up to meet eyes that match mine. Ones that are a little sad as the truth hits her. It's time for me to live my life. Take that adventure.

I only wish I could share it with someone special.

Still holding her gaze, I ask, "Did you do this?"

Did she slip this toy into the sock? Did he set it up with her?

Neve instantly lifts her hands. "I had nothing to do with this."

I turn toward Isolde. Saint took a liking to her, but he didn't spend half as much time with her as he did Neve. "Did he ask you to do this?"

"Does someone want to fill me in here?" Danny prods.

Ignoring him, Isolde smiles sweetly. "I don't know anything about this." Her bright eyes expose the truth. She didn't place the plane or envelope in the sock.

Glancing at Danny, I rule him out as he stares back at me full of inquiry and irritation. No one is addressing his questions.

Placing the three papers back together and slipping them back into the envelope, I hold up the wooden plane.

"It's a toy plane," I announce like it's the greatest gift ever given.

"I can see that," he counters, brows creased, concern etched between them.

"Inside joke," I explain, though the gesture hardly qualifies as a jest. The well-loved plane looks like something often played with by a boy who wanted to be a pilot. Who grew up to fly a plane, one that he owned.

However, now isn't the time to explain all that's happened to my son. Instead, I glance at the front door, wondering if Saint was here.

Then something pulls my attention to the fireplace behind me.

He couldn't have.

Slowly, I turn toward the hearth. The one full of ashes and a small piece of charred wood from the fires that kindled throughout most of yesterday.

Certain I will imagine a footprint in the ash, I glance at another sock, noting it looks a little full for a dangling stocking.

I brush past Neve and reach for one of my wool socks, finding it filled as well, and I tug free another item like an eager child.

Between my fingers I hold the exact pull-string Santa I admired at this year's Christmas market. The one with loose limbs that expand, making Santa jump or dance. Flipping it over, the year has been handwritten on the decoration.

A permanent reminder of when he was here.

When Saint came to town.

"Hey. I had one of those as a kid," Danny says, standing directly behind me. He reaches around me to snag the gift from my hands, but I bring it to my chest.

"This one is mine," I argue, pouting at my grown son like I'm a spoiled child and won't share.

Because I won't. This item isn't a toy but a treasure, and Saint is a secret my heart will forever keep.

Inside the stocking is another paper item, and I retrieve it next.

On the front is an image of a large home, surrounded by piles of snow, but the lights from the house beam outward, giving the place a cozy glow. In the bottom corner is one word:

NORTH.

I flip the postcard over and read the back.

LETTER WRITING SHOULD BE REVIVED.
  Here is a postcard just for you.

I WISH you were here with me.
  All my love, S

IF I WEREN'T SURROUNDED by family, I'd sob. Instead, I rapidly blink back the tears in my eyes and hug the postcard to my chest.

Wishing I was with him as well.

CHAPTER 32

December 26

[Saint]

The day after Christmas I'm exhausted yet invigorated. The holiday could have been a disaster, but with Danny home and the focus of my attention, plus Neve and Isolde present, it was a great day.

Unfortunately, Danny left on the last flight out late last night, and because I didn't want to be alone, I went to Neve's cozy cottage for the night.

In the morning, we linger in her bed. Despite my tomboy sister's interests, her bed is feminine with floral sheets and a light-colored plaid comforter.

"Did you hear about the celebration for Audrey at Making Whoopie?" Neve asks, lying on her back and staring up at the ceiling.

Audrey Nouel is our resident baker and owner of Making Whoopie, famed for their large variations of the Maine delicacy. Of French descent with soft brown hair and deep, dark eyes,

Audrey is petite for someone who makes baked goods. She was once an in-demand pastry chef in New York. Two years ago, she decided to make Hideaway Harbor her home, and we once talked about her hopes for a Hallmark romance experience in our fair town, complete with a flannel-wearing, Christmas tree farmer, or something similar.

I'm still waiting for the same grand romance, and I've lived here my entire life.

"I haven't heard." Then again, I've been rather introverted the past few days.

"Jack Lourd hosted a party for Audrey. Invited the entire town to come celebrate her."

Jack is a lawyer and Hollywood agent who represents the famous rom-com queen, Amanda Willis, among others. Amanda was recently in town, participating in many of our town traditions.

Sounds like Jack might have become Audrey's hero, even if he is a flatlander.

"It was a real *It's a Wonderful Life* moment," Neve recounts.

"Good," I genuinely smile. "She deserves it." I truly am happy for Audrey, as she and I once talked about feeling stuck. Not fulfilling dreams or potential, especially in Hideaway Harbor.

But one thing I love about this town is that we all show up for one another. I'm proud that people came out to celebrate Audrey. She deserves the honor for her hard work and her whoopie pies.

Neve clears her throat, and I turn my head on the pillow, taking in her profile.

"I'm sorry you feel like George Bailey, Lumi." She turns her head toward me. "Like you've been stuck." Her brows pinch. "You know I don't understand the desire to leave. I've never had anywhere I really wanted to go. And well, I'm not you, full of wanderlust."

I offer her a soggy smile. "You don't need to be me. You're the best you there is."

Neve's eyes water. "That's the thing, though. You've always been here for me. For us. Dad. Danny. Isolde and Icelyn. And it's time for you to go be you."

She shifts to her side and focuses on my face. "I know you might be questioning that money from Saint, but I want you to take it and run. Spread those wings and finally fly."

My own eyes fill with tears.

"But also know there's been nothing wrong with blooming where you're planted."

"I know that."

"You've blossomed here in ways you can't see," she adds. "Danny's mom being number one."

The tears spill free, and I quickly swipe at them.

Make every moment magical.

I tried. I've really tried. But now, I have other moments to make.

"Home will always be here for you," she says, recounting something similar that I said to Danny.

Hideaway Harbor will always be here, but now it's time for me to leave.

"You'll always be Anna to my Elsa," she states, reminding me how much we loved *Frozen*, a tale about sisterly love above all else.

I chuckle, the tears choking my throat amid the watery laughter. "You remember that I'm the older sister," I chide, pointing to myself.

"Yeah, but I'm the real ice queen between the two of us." She sighs. "You've always been the romantic one. The brave one."

"Brave." I laugh again, the sound defiant.

"You stayed when it would have been so easy to leave," she whispers.

"There wasn't anywhere else I'd rather be," I counter.

"Liar." She chuckles.

"Okay, a few places." I roll my eyes. "But you know why I

didn't go before, right?" They needed me. Each and every one of them. And it's not that they still don't need me in some capacity, but now is the time for me.

"I love you," Neve says, her voice quiet and choked, expressing words Neve hardly says.

"I love you, too, snowflake." Using my dad's nickname for Neve causes her to wrap her arms around me and hug me tightly for a moment.

But just a minute.

"Okay, now this is just weird," she says, releasing me and rolling back to her side of the bed to stare at the ceiling again.

I laugh but I cherish the moment. There's nothing I wouldn't do for my sisters and son, and I know they'd do anything for me in return.

It's a wonderful life, indeed.

IN THE STILLNESS and quiet of a day after a holiday, I decide to take a walk through Hideaway Harbor. From my place, I walk down Locke Street to Love Lane and up to Buoy Street, reveling in the calming silence. Reaching Main Street, I pass the closed businesses as I head south toward the harbor.

I smile as I pass The Perfect Package, Hidden Italy, and Love at First Sip. Each location holds a new memory for me. Magical ones from a sensual sensory kit to a spaghetti dinner to hot chocolate appreciation.

For just a moment, I allow my thoughts to turn to Saint. Wondering how his holiday went. If he worked, like he said he would. If he made amends with his father, or if they fought. If he celebrated the day with family or friends, or felt a pinch of loneliness. If he missed me at all.

There was so much I didn't know about him, and yet so much I didn't think I needed to know.

He was generous. He fulfilled every wish from the letters to Santa overflow-bag. He was kind, playing along with little Samantha, and even taking the letter from Henry Ashley, a teenager having a tough time at home.

He was kind, helping Neve at Rusty's, and then paying for the repairs *he* made on his own car.

He was sweet and thoughtful. From St. Nicholas Day presents to Christmas tree dates, and more.

He'd made this holiday better than it would have been if I wallowed in Danny's absence, which didn't turn out to be an absence after all.

My heart is full. Full from Saint.

As I continue down Main Street, I head near the post office, although I don't have to work this week. An entire week to myself. The thought alone is refreshing, and I inhale the crisp winter air, full of the scent of snow.

I chuckle when I recall Saint's surprised expression when I mentioned I could smell snow. Like he didn't believe such a thing, just like I didn't believe in Santa—

My thoughts come to an abrupt halt as a tall, buff man exits a forest green sports car parked near the corner by the post office.

My breath catches, and I blink twice to clear my vision, as if he cannot really be standing there, but a mirage. My mind is playing a trick on me. I've heard of peri-menopausal fog, but this might be upper level.

With wide eyes, I take in the dark jeans, heavy boots, and a deep green puffer coat, plus that trim silver beard and hair.

As I'm frozen in place on the sidewalk, he approaches me, slipping his hands into his pockets. His eyes look weary with thin strips of purple beneath each of them. He looks exhausted.

I clear my throat, but it still sounds watery and thick when I say, "Can't park your car there, Mister." I exaggerate the accent to dismiss the *-r* in *park, car,* and *mister* as I point toward the tow zone sign.

He glances over his shoulder at the sign and smirks. Then he exhales and hangs his head a second.

"I got your Christmas present," I finally state. "It was too much." The amount was overly generous, and I considered ripping up the check, like Neve thought I might. I didn't need a handout, but Neve's comments talked me off the ledge, reminding me it was a gift with a purpose.

Saint's head lifts, and he takes another step closer to me.

"In all the holiday movies we watched, the guy always stays in the small town after meeting the girl." He pulls a hand free from his pockets and waves toward me. "Or the girl stays."

The comment reminds me of one tale about a big city land agent who came to town to steal some property and ended up falling in love with the landowner.

Only, I'm not that girl. I don't want to stay here. Not every second of every day, although Danny's visit and Neve's words this morning are a reminder that Hideaway Harbor is home, and my door is always unlocked.

"I can't stay," he states, hammering home what I already know. "I don't own a dog, but I do have lots of flannel."

Despite the abrupt jab to my heart about how he can't stay, I smile soggily at the reminder that every holiday movie has a dog and a man with too much flannel.

"I also have a reindeer farm. And a toy company that has me traveling all over the world."

My head tilts, uncertain what his point is with these reminders that he won't stay, although the reindeer farm is new information.

"North Pole Toys," he states, clarifying the name he never offered before. He stands straighter, holding up his head. "My name is Astan Saint Santos. And I am—"

I press my mitten-covered fingers to his lips.

He closes his eyes, cups my hand at his mouth, and kisses it, mitten and all. The heat of his breath seeps through the thick covering before he lowers my hand while continuing to hold onto it.

"It doesn't matter who you are," I eventually say, watching his dark eyes smolder. "Or what you do. Or where you live."

North.

"I want you to know all my truths," he admits. "Who I am."

Do I need to know if he's some legendary person? Maybe he is.

"I know what I need to know about your character. You're dedicated to family. You're committed to your company. You love to laugh and snuggle, and you are as sexy as candy cane martinis."

His cheeks turn from rosy-cold to red-hot.

"And you care about me. And you're here."

I pause at the end of my ramble.

"What *are* you doing here?" I ask, tilting my head. If he can't stay, why is he back?

"I'd like to propose a new ending to those Christmas romances."

My eyes start to burn, tears filling them despite my attempts to stop the flow. It's been quite the day of tears.

"First," he begins, squeezing my hand in his. "No ending. Only beginnings."

He releases my hand and cups my face with both of his. His palms are warm, and I close my eyes, savoring the heat of his hands on me again.

"Look at me, snowheart," he whispers. "*My* heart."

I blink my eyes open, as a tear leaks out.

"I love you, Lumi," he adds.

A sob escapes me at the earnestness in his voice.

"And I'd like to take you around the world."

"Saint," I choke, because he's already given me the gift. The means and the voucher.

"Then, I'd like to take you home. My home."

"North," I clarify.

"North." He glances to the side, a second. "It's complicated to get there, but it's—" I cover his mouth again.

"You've traveled the world and seen lots of places. And I've done lots of research on places I want to visit." Sometimes video tours and travel guides can reveal all the mysteries of a location. "So, let's leave this one place a total surprise. For me."

Saint slowly smiles as I remove my hand from his lips. "Is that a yes to adventures with me?"

"Make everyday moments magical, right?" I counter.

"So, that's a yes?" He looks vulnerable but hopeful, as his lips curve higher on one side.

"You promise there will be flannel?"

With that, he laughs, hearty and deep, and tugs me into his arms, and I close my eyes, inhaling his peppermint and chocolate scent.

"I love you, too," I say, pulling back to look up at him. His smile is wild and bright, and his eyes dance.

He wants to travel the world with me.

He wants to share adventures.

He wants to take me to *his* hometown eventually.

However, right now, the only place I want to be with him is my home.

Tipping up on my toes, he meets me halfway, and right here on Main Street, like the perfect wrap on a holiday rom-com, he kisses me.

When we separate, he tugs me beneath his arm, and we both glance toward the town square, where Skippy, the town Saint Bernard is watching us, before he trots off in the opposite direction.

Saint and I both laugh.

There *was* a dog in our romantic tale after all.

READY FOR MORE HOLIDAY FUN IN Hideaway Harbor? Next up...

The Holiday Clause by Lydia Michaels

Having three billionaire brothers as best friends has never been easy. But I'm faced with the impossible choice when all three ask to marry me. Did I mention they want my decision before Christmas?

A multi-billion-dollar empire.

Three possessive alpha males.

And one holiday clause that could destroy us all.

Who will win in this steamy small-town Christmas romance where friendship, fortune, and forever collide in a smoldering race to the finish line?

Read THE HOLIDAY CLAUSE now!

Christmas at Hideaway Harbor series

The Holiday Hate-Off by Angela Casella
The Holiday Fakers by Evie Alexander
The Holiday Whoopie by Sara L. Hudson
The Holiday Post by L.B. Dunbar
The Holiday Clause by Lydia Michaels
The Holiday Grump by Enni Amanda

ALL BOOKS ARE INTERCONNECTED standalones and can be read in any order.

BONUS STUFF

Thank you for reading THE HOLIDAY POST.

If you loved this book, please leave a review where romance
books are sold and discussed.

Want a little more of Saint and Lumi?
Read "A Very Naughty New Year's Eve"

If you adored Saint, you'll enjoy his younger brother Nick in
NAUGHTY-ish.
A naughty next-door neighbor holiday romance.

Turn the page for a sample.

SAMPLE: THE HOLIDAY CLAUSE

"Dashing Through the Snow"

"There I was, fumbling for my keys as cats coiled between my legs on the cabin porch, their urgent mewing echoing in the frigid air."

"Here we go…" Logan rolled his eyes.

Wren ignored him. "I bit the tip of my glove, precariously balancing my grocery bags in one arm, so I could dig through my purse." She could still hear the rock salt crunching underfoot.

"It had been a frigid day. Breath clouded as I spoke to the cats." The rescued strays were why people assumed she was Hideaway Harbor's unofficial cat lady at thirty. That was back when she was still single. A lot had changed since then.

"Your stories take forever."

"Shut up, Soren."

"Get to the point, Wren."

She rolled her eyes. "The metallic bite of wind promised more snow, and we already had a foot from the storm that rolled in before Thanksgiving that year."

"There was a northern wind, and the temperature was a biting seventeen degrees. Two blue jays sat on a branch," Logan mocked.

"Patience, guys." She narrowed her eyes on the men. "That's what I remember saying to Figgy and the other cats as they perched on frost-dusted chairs. Then, suddenly, the roar of a motor exploded through the silence! I spun, keys tumbling from my grasp as a black super-duty pickup rocketed over the snowdrifts—an avalanche of ice and slush erupting in its wake as it plowed straight toward me! I screamed, and the cats scattered like buckshot."

Greyson's deep chuckle rumbled as he lounged by the fire.

"I don't think it was all that dramatic," Logan mumbled.

"Get to the good part," Soren urged.

Wren continued, "Out of nowhere, a snowmobile buzzed from the woods behind the cabin! I plastered myself against the front door in a sorry attempt to avoid a collision as claws scraped wood and the cats scrambled up the walls in sheer terror! My groceries crashed to the ground, eggs exploding, as I threw my hands up to shield my face. The truck slammed on its brakes, spraying snow all over me and my midnight blue siding as it skidded to a halt mere inches from my step. I was terrified. The engine growling like a caged beast as the driver's door burst open and I screamed, *What the hell is going on!*"

"Whoa, whoa, whoa. Even I know that's stretching the truth. The snowmobile totally got there first."

"False." Logan laughed. "And you can't start the story there anyway." He sipped lager from a pilsner glass. "That makes us sound like maniacs."

Wren scoffed. "You are maniacs."

"She has a point." Greyson stretched his thick denim-clad legs toward the raised hearth of the massive fireplace.

"That's exactly how it started," Wren continued. "I'm telling the non-fiction version."

"Your version might be true, but that's not how it started." Soren brushed a piece of non-existent lint off his knee onto the oak floor. "You've got to give a little background to accurately portray the emotion."

Wren pursed her lips. "The emotion was fear."

"Nah, that kind of unhinged urgency can only be provoked by love." Soren flinched as a balled-up copy of *The Almanac* pegged him in the head. "What? Love can make a man do crazy things."

"You're an idiot." Greyson rolled his eyes.

Logan settled into the empty chair on the other side of the fire. "I'm with Soren. If you want to tell the story right, you have to go back to the beginning."

"Fine. You guys tell it."

The rocks in Soren's glass clinked as he sipped slowly, his eyes watching Wren like a predator watches prey. "All right. It was the weekend after Thanksgiving. Dad insisted we all come to the big house to celebrate. We'd just finished feasting on leftovers and were delving into Dad's bourbon collection as we pilfered his humidor when he dropped the bomb of the century on us."

"He always was a master of manipulation."

Wren cast an empathetic look at Logan. Of the three brothers, he'd had the least time with their father, so his grief always rang closer to anger and resentment than his older brothers'.

The loss of Magnus Hawthorne impacted all three of his sons differently—in ways they would likely unpack for years to come. Grief was funny like that. It didn't arrive all at once in a tidy package. It stretched out over time and seeped into unexpected crevices of life, showing up when you least expected it and teaching lessons that pushed a person to feel things no one would willingly choose to feel.

Heartache moved in phases, and over the last year, she'd watched all three brothers process the stages differently at different times. Denial, anger, bargaining, depression, every phase played a part until they finally reached acceptance. Some were getting there slower than others.

"He really was a prick when he wanted to be," Soren agreed, never one to sugarcoat the truth. "Dad came into that study knowing exactly what he was doing. It was never about the business. It was always about controlling us from the grave."

"I think you're being a little harsh." Wren tucked her legs under the fur blanket as she nestled into the corner of the sofa with her mug of cocoa.

"You weren't there. I'm telling it exactly as it happened." Soren swept up the wood shavings by his feet and tossed them into the fire. "There we were, actually believing Dad wanted us there for some quality time that Thanksgiving. Then he dropped the bomb."

"I still remember the sound of that massive file hitting his leather-topped desk." Logan laughed without humor. "He shoved Soren's feet right off the edge and gave us a look of pure disappointment."

Greyson grinned and quietly recalled, "He always got pissy when you stole his cigars."

"Well, I still have the one I nabbed that day. A nice Cuban. Never even got it lit."

Wren looked at Greyson, noting the introspective way he stared into the fire. As the eldest of the three and by far the most reclusive, he never followed his brothers' lead. But he observed everything, depending only on himself, his presence like a silent shadow in the background of all their family drama. Of all the boys, Magnus had the least control over Greyson.

Soren retrieved the bottle of bourbon from the thick oak mantle. "Dad thought he was so slick, dangling that carrot over our heads only to snatch it away as a last hurrah."

Logan laughed bitterly. "He always knew how to tease the line to get the fish to do exactly what he wanted."

Staring into the flames, Soren shook his head. "He loved finding his opposition's Achilles heel."

Another gruff, humorless laugh escaped Logan's throat. "Opposition's the perfect word."

"Your dad loved you," Wren reminded.

"Sure—in his way. But he still saw us as the enemy."

"No, he didn't."

"You weren't there, Wren. There were times—after Mom died —that I swear he wished we'd been in the car with her."

Her heart clenched. "That's not true, Logan. Your dad, just like mine, never expected to be a single father. He did the best he could with what he knew."

"He knew how to pit us against each other."

"Well, lucky for the three of you, he wasn't very good at it."

Few brothers could claim the loyalty Greyson, Soren, and Logan shared. Sable Hawthorne would have been proud of the men her sons had become.

Soren refilled his glass at the wet bar. "The company was the perfect bait to get one last emotional response from us. He lured us in, and once he knew he had our balls in a vice, he couldn't wait to tighten the crank."

"You gave him that power." There was something primal about Greyson, something wild and wise his brothers lacked. Maybe it was because he was older, or maybe it was his years at sea that had hardened him.

Not to say Logan and Soren weren't formidable—they were. But Greyson was different. He didn't need anyone.

Wren smiled at his stubbornness. Magnus could never manipulate Greyson the way he manipulated his brothers.

He didn't need his father's wealth to feel content. He didn't crave his father's approval like his brothers, nor did he waste time antagonizing the man over their endless differences of opinion. Greyson created his own security and kept to himself most days, so it made sense that he hadn't reacted when his father dropped the ultimatum that fateful Thanksgiving.

As if sensing her thoughts, he met her stare, flames flickering in his dark blue eyes, his mouth a flat, unreadable line hidden by the stubble of his beard. Those devilish blue eyes smoldered, and Wren dropped her gaze—familiar heat spreading through her belly the way it always did when he fixed her with that knowing look.

All of the Hawthorne men possessed a potency that was impossible to ignore. It wasn't easy sitting in a room surrounded by such raw masculinity, but she'd been around it her entire life. Despite their history, when any one of them drilled into her with that shameless Hawthorne stare, she was as defenseless as every other red-blooded woman. Even now, after everything they'd endured together, that intensity could still overwhelm her.

Mercifully, Greyson turned his attention back to the fire.

Wren faced Soren. "Finish the story. What happened next?"

"He laid down the law," Soren said with a gruff laugh. "Told us we'd been invited to Thanksgiving only to help him decide who would inherit the family business. We'd always assumed it would be divided among the three of us, so you can imagine our surprise when he suddenly changed the game."

"Not all of us wanted it," Greyson said, his stare turning pointedly toward his brother.

Soren scoffed. "How can you say that?"

"Because if you wanted it, you'd have it. Hawthorne men get what they want. And they own their mistakes."

"Fuck off." Ice rattled in Soren's glass. "It was never about who wanted it most."

"Wasn't it?"

Logan stretched out his legs on the ottoman, mimicking Greyson's radiated confidence. "As his sons, we all deserved an equal share."

Soren's eyes narrowed on his brothers. "But we're not talking about the company, are we?"

Together, they all turned to her, each wielding that penetrating Hawthorne stare. "Don't look at me! I had nothing to do with this."

"Wren," Soren smiled wickedly, "you had everything to do with it. You were the true prize."

She rolled her eyes. "No, I wasn't. It was always about the company. I was just a means to an end."

Logan laughed, the sound a little lighter now. "Dad wanted one last hurrah—one last chance to pit us against each other—and he got his wish, just not the way he expected."

"I was never part of Magnus's plans."

"But you were always part of ours."

"Take it easy." The low warning was enough to defuse any flirtation sizzling in the air.

The room fell silent. Even the crackling fire seemed to quiet as Greyson met his youngest brother's stare. "You never showed any interest in running the company back then, so stop acting like you did."

"How the hell would you know what I wanted? All you cared about was keeping to yourself in that secluded cabin of yours, chopping wood at all hours of the day and night."

"All right, Logan, keep it civil."

"Grey's right," Soren agreed. "You never said anything about wanting it until Dad said you couldn't have it. On paper, the fishery might look good, but you never cared about the actual work that went into managing the fleet or making sure the captains had everything they needed to keep the crews safe. You were too impatient to sit through quality control meetings, discuss logistics for managing the supply chain, or build relationships with our overseas buyers."

"Because I was never given the chance."

"Bullshit."

"Here we go," Greyson mumbled, rolling his eyes.

"Boys!" Wren snapped, slapping her hands against the fur blanket covering her lap. The muffled sound didn't have quite the effect she wanted, but it got their attention. "We were reminiscing, not having an argument. Stay on topic, or I'm going to bed."

"Maybe we all wanted the prize," Soren admitted, meeting her stare from the shadows. "At least on some level."

Greyson and Logan glared at Soren. Wren dropped her gaze to the contents of her mug, afraid to meet any of their stares in that moment.

"Dad did what he did best," Logan said, disrupting the tension. "He reminded us how much we disappointed him and leveraged his stingy affection to create a competition between us."

"Not all of us were starved for his affection, Logan."

"Shut up, Grey. I guess it was just about the money for you then."

"Watch it."

Wisely, Logan withdrew his challenging words and continued with the story. "What choice did we have? We either grew up, settled down, and acted like responsible adults, or he was selling off the company and giving the profits to the board and shareholders."

"He loved being a prick." Soren sipped his bourbon and stared into the fire.

"Maybe his actions weren't malicious at all. Maybe this was his way of making sure you boys would be okay in the end."

"There she goes, romanticizing things again," Soren grumbled. "Sometimes, people are just shitty, Wren."

She adjusted her blanket. "Everything in nature has duality, Soren. Even Magnus Hawthorne. If he could feel anger, he could feel peace. And if he was capable of happiness, he also knew sadness. I know for a fact your father loved you."

"You guys ever see Dad happy?" Soren joked, and his brothers chuckled.

"Couldn't even tell you what his laugh sounded like."

"Did Dad even have teeth?"

They all chuckled, but then the mood sobered as they each recalled a personal memory with Magnus that—despite his gruff and direct manner—brought a soft smile to their faces.

"He laid down the law before we'd even digested our Thanksgiving turkey," Soren recalled, his gaze unfocused as he seemed to relive the whirlwind of the past few months. "The doctors gave him weeks, and he wasted no time meeting with his attorney to permanently change the will."

"It was a pointless clause," Logan grumbled. "How did he expect any of us to actually change our lives that much before Christmas? His expectations were always unrealistic."

A strange mixture of guilt and relief flooded Wren as she kept her gaze down. That holiday clause was where she came in.

Magnus had changed his will just before the holidays to include a section stating that the lion's Hawthorne Fishery of the family business would be inherited by the son who married first. None of the men had been thinking about marriage until Magnus dropped that bomb. He'd wanted a reaction, and he'd gotten one.

Hawthorne Fishery wasn't just some rinky-dink, small-town operation. It was a billion-dollar, global-scale company with astronomical expenses and hundreds of vessels in each fleet built to travel deep international waters. There were inland processing plant stations off the coast, and the board wielded government-level influence when it came to ocean-related legislation and the country's environmental laws. There was an entire world of capitalism out at sea, and the Hawthornes were one of the oldest family-run fisheries still in existence.

The boys had a right to be disgruntled. It wasn't just Magnus's legacy—it was their birthright. The thought that the company could have been divided into shares and sold to the highest bidder or passed down to the board was simply unthinkable. Hawthorne Fishery needed to stay in the Hawthorne family.

"As always, Dad got his way."

Like a magnet, she felt Logan's dark stare pulling at her senses. Wren lifted her eyes and met cold obsidian. The year had changed him in ways she was still trying to figure out. Gone was the sweet companion she'd grown up alongside, and in his place sat a cold-hearted man desperate to hide all the gentle qualities he now believed made him weak.

He held her stare. "Didn't he, Wren?"

Logan had a gift for unnerving others with that penetrating glare, but she'd learned how to deflect it long ago. Despite the way her breath grew shallow, she held her body perfectly still. "I suppose he did. In a way."

Logan's cold stare slowly warmed when he smiled at her. With a past as long as theirs, every glance carried language outsiders couldn't decipher. Her tangled history with the Hawthornes harbored more secrets than anyone would guess, and their silence spoke volumes.

When the four of them were together, it was impossible not to feel the pull of nostalgia. Their shared past could be as overwhelming as their masculine intensity.

"Don't give me that look." She turned back to Soren. "Finish the story."

Soren sighed and sipped his bourbon, shifting to get more comfortable in his seat. "So he dropped the bomb on us, and we all knew he meant business. None of us woke up that morning with a single thought about marriage, but that all changed when we understood what was at stake."

"It's a big company," she agreed, and they all chuckled.

"Yeah, that's what this was about."

Her cheeks flushed. She couldn't fathom a reality where she wielded that much influence over men as unapproachable as the Hawthorne brothers. They might not intimidate her as much as they did outsiders, but that came with a lifetime of knowing each other.

Despite playing together in diapers when they were young, she still recognized the potent breed they were. She preferred to believe their actions were motivated by money, but when she found herself at the center of their family feud, she learned there was more to the story. Much more.

Logan chuckled. "There was no way you were beating me to her."

"I guess not when you stole my fucking keys."

"I didn't steal them. I relocated them into a snowbank."

"Prick." Soren reclined in the wooden rocker and stretched out his legs. "We all had the same thought. If we had to pick a wife in a pinch, there was only one choice."

All eyes again turned on her, and her cheeks burned. "Okay, take it down a notch." The testosterone radiating from the three of them was thinning the air and making it hard to breathe.

They smirked with Neanderthal-like male satisfaction.

"So Logan steals my keys, leaving me with whatever was left in Dad's garage. I grabbed the first set I could find—"

"To the snowmobile."

"Correct. Next thing you know, I'm blasting through the woods—without proper gear—in my socks—getting blinded by the snow." He shot his brother a pointed look. "I could have died."

"Don't be such a drama queen." Logan rolled his eyes. "The whole time I was driving, he wouldn't shut up on the two-way radio. It couldn't have been that treacherous if you had the ability to use the radio."

"Talking shit was my only defense! You were in a truck!"

Logan snickered. "And I got to her first."

"Which brings us back to where I left off." Wren set her mug aside and sat up. "I was carrying in my groceries—swarmed by cats—when you two maniacs barreled in like a landslide and almost killed me."

"Now who's being dramatic?"

"My whole life flashed before my eyes!"

"And like I said, that's not where the story starts."

She frowned at Logan. "If not there, then when?"

"You have to go back. Way back, to when we were kids."

"He's right," Greyson agreed, watching her with that quiet attention that missed nothing.

Wren frowned, oddly feeling as if they harbored secrets that—for once—didn't include her. "How far back?"

Soren shrugged. "Probably to the Christmas after Mom died."

The room grew silent as it usually did at the mention of Sable Hawthorne. As always, any reference to their mother reminded Wren of her own.

Haven Wilde and Sable Hawthorne had been lifelong best friends. Losing them at the same time was a sort of poetic tragedy that further sealed the bond she shared with Greyson, Soren, and Logan. Their mothers' connection had been stronger than marriage. The expectation that the four of them remain friends had been instilled from birth. Therefore, Wren's life had always been entangled with the untouchable Hawthorne brothers —even when she'd tried her best to detach herself.

As she stared at the lapping flames in the hearth, she tried to recall the fading memory of her mother's hair. It had been blonde, like hers, but with fiery copper undertones. The crackling wood put her in a trance as she fixated on the flames, searching for the exact shade of red she sometimes glimpsed in her mother's highlights when she stood in the sunshine.

A gentle hand closed around her shoulder, startling her. She closed her eyes, able to recognize and differentiate each brother's touch. The grief in her chest instantly eased as she pressed her cheek to his familiar fingers and sighed.

Their silence spoke volumes. After their mothers passed away, birthdays, holidays, and ordinary Mondays were never the same. Nothing was. They'd somehow managed to stick together.

The Christmas Magnus died was, by far, one of the most challenging, but, as always, the challenges they faced together only made them closer in the end. And, what was one of their hardest holidays, somehow also ended up being one of the most memorable and cherished.

"Fine," she eventually conceded. "If that's not where the story starts, then you tell it from the beginning."

The men shared a knowing grin. "For that, we're going to need a refill and another log on the fire."

CONTINUE: The Holiday Clause by Lydia Michaels

SAMPLE: NAUGHTY-ISH

Chapter 1

Where is that fucking elf on a shelf doll?

In preparation for the upcoming Christmas holiday, I'd been searching everywhere for that damn creepy imp that sits on a shelf, pretending to monitor my children's behavior in the weeks before the holiday.

Naughty or nice, Nash and Eloise are my favorite two people in the world.

But that elf really annoys me.

I couldn't keep the festive doll with the other decorations for fear the kids would discover him, thus ruining the ploy that he appears on the Feast of St. Nicholas. A tradition which includes setting out your shoes—in our case, by the front door—and if you are on Santa's nice list, candy fills your footwear. A kid on the naughty list receives a lump of coal.

My parents used this setup when I was a child, which was long before that shelf elf was even imagined. It was another gimmick propagated by adults to keep their children in line during the holiday season.

"If you're on the naughty list, there's still time to right wrongs."

I've said those very words myself, although my children are not bad kids. They aren't angels by any stretch, but with the year we've had, they're damn near perfect. My ex-husband is the one who belongs on the naughty list. Actually, he belongs on the dirt-bag's list, but that's neither here nor there tonight as I tackle my first holiday season without his presence. I want it to be a pleasant Christmas for my little ones. They deserve it.

"Shoes," I mutter aloud, standing in the wintery darkness of ten o'clock in my living room.

Before the kids went to bed, Nash put his gym shoes by the front door beside Eloise's Sherpa-lined boots. She thought St. Nick might bring her more candy if she had taller footwear. *St. Nick is on a budget this year, kiddo.* Of course, she doesn't know the tradition is all make-believe. There isn't a saint named Nick checking in on us. There isn't even a Santa Claus, but I'll wait a few years before breaking her heart on that one.

Lord knows she'll have bigger heartbreaks in her life. I'll shield her as best I can, for as long as I can. But what happens when she's older and on her own? What do I do if she ends up like me, marrying a schmuck?

Mitch hadn't been a schmuck when we married. He was everything I'd been looking for in my early thirties. What does the heart know though, right? Good sex brought us together, but it apparently wasn't good enough because he eventually went elsewhere.

Once. It only happened once.

On a scale of zero times it should have happened, his infidelity occurred one time too many.

His decision shattered me. No marriage is perfect, but that kind of slip-up means there was an issue I hadn't noticed buried underneath the daily life of a married couple with young children. I faulted myself in some ways. Not for him stepping out on me. That was all on him. However, I'd been blinded by a sense of security I had with my ex-husband. And blindsided by his actions.

Now I was forty, wiser, and wary.

And Mitch's construction boots are conspicuously absent from our collection this year.

"Shoes," I mumble again. Snapping my fingers, I recall what I was doing—looking for the elf. Eventually, he'll be placed on top of the fridge or the china cabinet because he needs to be out of reach from Nash, who is only five. At eight years old, Eloise is the one with questions. And shoes are the answer tonight, as the wily elf is in a shoebox on a shelf in my closet—a place the children would never go.

Climbing the stairs of my new-to-us home, I find the little rascal in an old box for heels I no longer own. Once retrieved, I look about the house seeking a good spot to place him. Eloise already wrote him a long list of questions, and I'll need to forage through her letters from last year (also placed in the box) to recall previous answers. She's a smart one, my little girl, and she remembers this shit better than me.

As the litany of her questions spans a sheet of paper front and back, a glass of wine is in order to navigate this process. As a right-handed person, I'll have to disguise my handwriting by using my left hand to write the answers. A full glass of red matches the holiday spirit, I decide, although I don't have a stitch of decoration up in this house yet. I haven't had time. Returning to full-time work after the divorce, plus carpools for extracurricular activities, and the daily grind of getting my children to and from school, then dinner and homework, baths and bedtime routines, I'm beat by the end of the day.

Besides, Thanksgiving was just over a week ago.

After a hardy drink, I focus on the first question.

Number one. Do you like peppermint dick?

I blink, certain I've misread and realize I have.

Do you like peppermint stick?

Sweet baby Jesus in a manger, my imagination got the best of me there, or perhaps it's more my subconscious, as I haven't been with a man in over a year. Feeling dirty and unwanted after what Mitch did, the dry spell hadn't bothered me at first, but now, twelve months later, I miss the sensual touch of another human. My own fingers have worked willingly but not provided the wonder of connecting with someone else.

Number two. How many—

THUNK!

"What the hell?" I glance over my shoulder, peering behind me through the small window in the eating area. Something has just hit my house.

Another thud and then something clatters outside, out of sight of the window.

"When up on the rooftop, there arose such a clatter," I mutter the famous line from Clement Clarke Moore's poem *'Twas the Night Before Christmas."*

Standing, I hold my breath, awaiting another thump when a different thought wafts through my head. The poem is actually titled *A Visit from St. Nick.*

Impossible.

Bemused, I breathily laugh at myself. Clearly, I need more sleep.

Willing my shoulders to relax, I prepare to sit back down when I hear the telltale sign of an aluminum ladder clanking and a light thud of metal connecting with my house again.

On second thought, is the verse *arose such a ladder?*

Shaking my head, I realize I'm losing my mind, but something is definitely banging on the side of my home. With wineglass in hand as if that will protect me, I slip into my own set of Sherpa-lined boots and step out the back door leading to the driveway I share with my neighbor. My single car garage is detached from the house, and I don't park in the slightly leaning building. The space covers bikes, summer furniture, and boxes I haven't unpacked yet. We've only been in the house for seven months.

Standing on the back stoop, I pause. *What am I doing?* I'm a single mother living alone. I shouldn't be out here investigating in the dark.

Then I hear the metal clang of a ladder against the siding once more coming from my front yard and curiosity gets the best of me. Despite the cold, I walk along the side of my home and down the drive toward the front. Cupping the wineglass against my chest, I slowly approach the corner of my house.

"Shit." A deep male voice whispers in the night.

My heartbeat ratchets up a few thumps. *Is someone trying to break in?* They're making quite a racket if that's the case. Not to mention, the only thing of value in this house are my two children *nestled all snug in their beds.*

Rounding the corner, I shout, "What the hell are you doing?"

My sharp voice rips through the quiet night air, causing the man standing on the low roof overhanging my front stoop to slip. With a curse from his lips and the slide of his feet, he scrambles to stay on the narrow strip of roofing. Only his left foot goes over the edge, kicking the gutter. He does an awkward split motion before his body slowly glides to the end of the roof, and his weight takes him off it.

"Oh my God!" I cry out, rushing toward the large body dangling from the overhang. Not more than ten feet from the ground to the start of the incline, his stretched form shows he's roughly six feet plus. He only has a few feet to drop if he lets go of my gutter, which is starting to strain under his weight. He's too far away to reach the ladder, which is propped up on the opposite corner of the overhang. With a swing of long legs in jeans that accentuate the thickness of his thighs and the firmness of his backside, he tucks forward before lunging back and dropping like a cat to the ground, clearing the stairs that descend from the porch. His back remains to me for half a second, and red buffalo check flannel strains over the expanse of thick muscles and flexed biceps in a shirt that hugs his body. Slowly, he turns to face me.

"Nick?" I choke.

With a bright red knit cap on his head, my next-door neighbor stares down at me. He has these intense, dark blue eyes and cheeks like cliffs, matching the mountainous stature of his body. His jaw holds an artful combination of black and white scruff, which is more snow than earth-colored despite his hair still being a shade of charcoal.

And I know these details about Nick, my next-door neighbor, because he's hot with a capital H.

Nick Santos was already living next door when the kids and I moved in. My first interaction with him was when I'd pulled into my driveway one evening to find him making out with a woman against his front door. He didn't break away from her mouth until I'd parked my car, gotten out, and walked toward my front entrance. Only a sliver of grass separates our single car driveways.

I hadn't wanted to look at them, but it was hard to pull away from the sight of his body pressing some woman against the building. His thick leg between her thighs. His hands on her sides. Her arms were around his neck, hands in his hair. He was going for a breast when he pulled back from her and turned his head toward me. Our eyes locked and his gleamed in the early darkness.

Then, like a frightened mouse, I'd scampered toward my house with my head down.

The next time I'd seen him was a week or so later. Shouts and curses came from the house next door. I had been leaving for work sans children, thankfully, as the display in his yard included him standing on the lawn and the woman who I assumed was the one from the week before tossing items out the front door, calling him names I'd never heard and stringing together profanity that might make a sailor blush.

Nick had stood stoic and firm with his legs spread wide, arms crossed, one hand lifted to his chin, slowly stroking thick fingers over that beautiful layering of ink and chrome hair on his jaw.

Hours later, he'd ripped out of his driveway on his motorcycle.

Questions had flitted through my mind at the time. Was she the same woman or someone different? Had he cheated on her or were they the same hot-for-each-other couple from one week ago? The scene had been a reminder of how quickly a relationship can flip. And for some reason I felt sorry for him.

Another week had passed before I'd seen him again, tinkering under the hood of a large pickup truck in his portion of the shared driveway. On that day, I'd been returning from work. Walking up my side of the drive, something prompted me to stop and address him despite us never having exchanged a word previously.

"Are you okay?"

He'd tipped his head. Surprise had been evident in his hard expression before he stood straighter and turned his face in the direction of his front yard.

"Nothing that hasn't happened before," he'd huffed and leaned forward, half-hidden underneath the hood again. "Might have been more effective if it wasn't my house, though."

Puzzled by his explanation, I didn't move from my spot. "Well, I just wanted to make certain you were all right."

He didn't respond at first, but his body stilled once more.

"I'm Holliday," I'd offered. "That's with two l's." There's irony in the name, and I'd waited for him to comment, but he didn't. "My children are Eloise and Nash."

I'd paused, thinking he would introduce himself. Or not.

"Just thought you should know." I'd previously lived in a neighborhood where everyone knew each other's names and the names of their children. It takes a village. Then again, that village knew everyone else's business.

Like how my ex-husband cheated on me while attending a reunion at his alma mater. A rambunctious Big Ten football game led to post-game shenanigans with his college sweetheart.

This new-to-me neighborhood, however, consisted of mainly older homes with elderly residents, and I was out of my element here.

With the growing silence between my neighbor and me, I'd turned on my heels and headed toward my back door.

"I'm Nick," he'd finally stated.

I'd stopped walking but hadn't spun to face him before he added, "You should get your old man to cut the grass."

Glancing at what I could see of my yard, I'd taken offense at several things.

One, I didn't have an old man.

Two, I was aware my grass was overgrown, but I didn't have a mower yet—it was just one more item on a list of growing necessities.

And three, I could take care of my own damn lawn, even if I wasn't certain that was true. I didn't need an old man to do it for me.

"I'll get right on that," I'd muttered, turning only my head over my shoulder and giving him a friendly salute when what I really wanted to do was give him the finger. "Nice to meet you." Sarcasm had dripped in my tone. So much for being neighborly.

However, within a few days, the drone of a lawnmower filled the air, and the sound came particularly close to my home. When I'd stepped out on my front stoop, Nick was mowing my grass.

"What the hell are you doing?" I'd snapped, wondering what he was playing at by encroaching on my yard. I'd said I'd take care of it. But I didn't have a viable plan. I'd considered asking Mitch if I could borrow his lawnmower, the one I'd bought him two years ago as a Father's Day present, but the thought of asking Mitch for anything made me sick.

The loud hum of the mower cut off, and Nick halted in my yard. Looking up at me, he clutched the handle of his mower.

"I wanted to apologize." Those dark eyes were sparkling sapphires under the bright summer sunshine. "Your kid told me you're . . ."

The unspoken word could be one of many.

Single? Divorced? Helpless?

"I'll speak to my children about bothering the neighbors." I crossed my arms and stared back at him.

His arms were covered in tattoos, and some even crept up his neck, sticking out from the collar of his tee, which was plastered to his chest from the exertion. A giant wet stain formed between the solid flat of his pecs beneath the cotton. Jeans covered his legs, accenting the curve of firm thigh muscles. He wore a baseball cap on his head. He was a beautiful man—slightly dangerous-looking but gorgeous nonetheless—and he was sweet to cut my grass, even if it was out of pity.

"I can pay you," I'd stated.

He'd tipped up a brow. "Consider it my apology."

"For what?" Kissing a woman on his front porch? Fighting with said woman in his yard? Or insulting me about needing a man to tend my lawn?

"I can take care of it." I'd nodded at the grass. I didn't need his apology. I was only being friendly that day when I'd asked about his well-being, foolishly thinking we were kindred spirits through our relationship failures. I had been wrong. He didn't need to prove anything to me.

Heading into the house for my last twenty-dollar bill, I'd returned to find the mower running again. Walking up to him, I held out the money. He'd stilled but didn't cut off the mower this time. He'd stared at the bill in my hand.

"Don't want it!" he'd hollered over the drone of the lawn mower.

"I'd feel better if you take it." My pride was on the line. I'd flicked my wrist once, emphasizing the outstretched twenty.

His gaze lifted, and those sharp eyes met mine. "Buy yourself something pretty with it, and we'll call us even."

Oh, he was smooth. But I wasn't having that nonsense.

I'd folded the bill in my hand and pursed my lips, knowing my next move was bold. I stepped back, allowing him to step forward. Then as he passed me, I slipped the twenty into his back pocket, getting an unintentional swipe of the firmness of one globe, stretching worn denim over his ass.

He'd stopped abruptly, twisting his upper body and staring down at my retreating hand.

"Buy yourself something pretty," I'd taunted and stomped away from him. I wasn't going to owe him, neighbor or not.

That was back in June.

In the cold of December, the night air is seeping through my thin, long-sleeved shirt and pajama shorts. What was I thinking stepping out here wearing boots and wielding a wineglass?

"Where's your jacket?" Nick snipes, stepping toward me, hands reaching forward to rub up and down my arms. I'd pulled them in close, huddling them against my chest as I hopped from foot to foot, waiting for him to explain what he'd been doing on my roof.

However, the freezing chill skittering over my skin disappears under the warmth of his calloused palms. His proximity infuses my entire body with a rush of heat, that ignites something in the depths of my cold bones. The faint scent of bayberry and snow tickles my nose, awakening all my senses. Forget my wine, I'm intoxicated by his nearness.

"I heard a noise," I stammer, struggling to remember what he asked me.

"Sorry about that." He removes his hands, and instantly, I miss the heat of his touch.

He tips his head, sheepishly peering down at the ground.

"What are you doing out here?" I nod at my roof, noting the ladder and some tools plus a cardboard box, resting on the shingles.

"I was hanging Christmas lights."

"On *my* house?"

"You're bringing down the block," he teases as he'd done the remainder of the summer when I still hadn't purchased a lawnmower.

My dad eventually bought me a mower from a garage sale in September, but as I struggled to start the thing, Nick appeared and told me he'd upkeep the lawn as he had most of the previous months. He continued to refuse my money.

"I hadn't gotten to it." The phrase was becoming the story of my life.

For the sake of my children, my intentions for the holiday season were well-meaning, but I haven't decorated yet. I haven't purchased any gifts. I haven't planned any seasonal activities. As a single mom, working full-time, I was doing the best I could living on a budget of time and finances. Which roughly translated to, I didn't have the *ho-ho-ho* energy I've had in years' past.

My Christmas spirit was waning this year, like that one pesky bulb causing an entire strand of lights to go out.

However, as Nick looks at me, his eyes twinkle like the little blue lights I've seen in other people's yards. And a teeny-tiny spark inside me wants to do better. Be better.

"What are *you* doing out here? It's freezing." His hands return to my arms, rubbing up and down once again. Immediately, the warmth melts over my skin, heating me up like a cozy winter fire.

"I thought you were the sugar plum fairy breaking in."

Nick laughs, hearty and full, rich like the wine in my glass.

"You don't need to do this," I remind him, repeating what I'd said dozens of times to him over the past few months. He feels sorry for me. That's why he does what he does. I'm that single mother neighbor who will one day let cats overrun her home when her children grow older and leave her alone, forgetting she exists.

The thought is pathetic and sobering.

"I want to," he states, as he's said often enough.

"Nash and Eloise will love it," I say, hoping my children's happiness means something to him. He's friendly with them. He even played catch with Nash a few times this fall when Mitch didn't show up for his scheduled weeknight visits. Nick also praised Eloise's chalk drawings, allowing her to overtake his driveway when ours is full of sketches.

"I want *you* to love it," he says, his eyes still on me.

I'd offer to pay him for the lights or his time, but I already know he'll reject the gesture. After my bold move last summer to slip a twenty in his pocket, I've never attempted to touch him again. I've made him cookies and casseroles, bought pots with flowers for his porch, and left him a case of beer on occasion. I didn't know how else to repay him for his kindness.

"It will look beautiful." I'm not really certain how it will look, but the roofline was made for Christmas lights. If he edges the front porch overhang and wraps lights over the dormers on the taller roof like he did his own home, the twinkling magic will bring cheer to my little house.

I like the place with its three small bedrooms on the second floor and its subtle front stoop raised up a few steps as typical Chicago homes are. Our previous home in the suburbs was double the size with manicured landscaping and a koi pond. Still, this place is mine and I smile in spite of myself.

"Thank you." My voice is quiet as my teeth chatter.

"Get inside." He winks with a tilt of his head toward the front door. "I'll try not to make too much noise."

"Try not to fall off the roof," I warn with a laugh in my throat.

"You startled me." His eyes narrow a bit, focusing on my face until his gaze drifts to the pebbled nipples poking out beneath my thin sleep shirt. He doesn't take his gaze from my chest.

I breathily answer him. "You surprised me."

His Adam's apple bobs, and he pulls his head upward, turning to give me the side of his face. "Go inside, Holliday." His deep voice roughens, and his jaw clenches.

The strangest sensation washes over me. I want to kiss up the column of his throat, outline the edge of his jaw with my lips, and climb his body like the evergreen he is.

The thought isn't entirely offhand as I've had several similar fantasies throughout the summer and into fall about him. I'm highly attracted to my neighbor, though it's ridiculous to feel this way.

"You're going to catch a cold," he adds, breaking into my vision of slipping my arms inside his red-checked flannel and pressing my cool tits to his warm chest.

His words are a reminder he isn't attracted to me.

He just feels sorry for the single mom next door.

CONTINUE reading: Naughty-ish

Naughty-ish

SEASON'S GRATITUDE

Thank you to Evie Alexander and Enni Amanda for creating and organizing Hideaway Harbor, and allowing Angela Casella, Sara L. Hudson, Lydia Micheals, and me to sail away within this fictional small town.

Shout out to: Judy M., Robin L., and Peggy G., who gave this work the Mrs. Clause stamp of approval.

MORE BY L.B. DUNBAR

<u>Sterling Falls</u>
Seven small-town siblings muddle their way through love
over 40.
Sterling Heat
Sterling Brick
Sterling Streak
Sterling Clay
Sterling Fight
Sterling Touch
Sterling Stone

<u>Chicago Anchors</u>
When your eyes are on the silver fox coach more than the ball.
Elevator Pitch
Catch the Kiss

Parentmoon
When the mother of the groom goes head-to-head with the
single father of the bride.

<u>Holiday Hotties (Christmas novellas)</u>

Holiday novellas certain to heat the season.

Scrooge-ish
Naughty-ish
Grouch-ish

<u>Road Trips & Romance</u>

Three sisters. Three destinations. All second chances at love over 40.

Hauling Ashe
Merging Wright
Rhode Trip

<u>Lakeside Cottage</u>

Four friends. Four summers. Shenanigans and love happen at the lake.

Living at 40
Loving at 40
Learning at 40
Letting Go at 40

<u>The Silver Foxes of Blue Ridge</u>

Small mountain town, silver fox brothers seeking love over 40.

Silver Brewer
Silver Player
Silver Mayor
Silver Biker

<u>Sexy Silver Foxes</u>

When sexy silver foxes meet the feisty vixens of their dreams.

After Care
Midlife Crisis
Restored Dreams
Second Chance

Wine&Dine

Collision novellas

A spin-off from *After Care* – the younger set/rock stars
Collide
Caught

The Sex Education of M.E.

The original sexy silver fox.
When a widowed professor decides she'd like to date again, and a
local fireman volunteers to give her lessons.

The Heart Collection

Small town, big hearts - stories of family and love.
Speak from the Heart
Read with your Heart
Look with your Heart
Fight from the Heart
View with your Heart

A Heart Collection Spin-off
The Heart Remembers

BOOKS IN OTHER AUTHOR WORLDS

Smartypants Romance (an imprint of Penny Reid)

Tales of the Winters sisters set in Green Valley.
Love in Due Time
Love in Deed
Love in a Pickle

The World of True North (an imprint of Sarina Bowen)

Welcome to Vermont! And the Busy Bean Café.
Cowboy

Studfinder

THE EARLY YEARS

<u>Legendary Rock Stars Series</u>
A classic tale with a modern twist of rockstar romance and suspense.

<u>Paradise Stories</u>
MMA romance. Two brothers. One fight.

<u>The Island Duet</u>
Intrigue and suspense. The island knows what you've done.

<u>Modern Descendants – writing as elda lore</u>
Magical realism. Modern myths of Greek gods.

ABOUT THE AUTHOR

www.lbdunbar.com

L.B. Dunbar loves sexy silver foxes, second chances, and small towns. If you enjoy older characters in your romance reads, including a hero with a little silver in his scruff and a heroine rediscovering her worth, then welcome to romance for those over 40. L.B. Dunbar's signature works include women and men in their prime taking another turn at love and happily ever after. She's a *USA TODAY* Bestseller as well as #1 Bestseller on Amazon in Later in Life Romance with her Sterling Falls, Lakeside Cottage, and Road Trips & Romance series. L.B. lives in Chicago with her own sexy silver fox.

To get all the scoop about the self-proclaimed queen of silver fox romance, join her on Facebook at Loving L.B. (Dunbar) or receive her monthly newsletter, Love Notes.

+ + +

CONNECT WITH L.B. DUNBAR

www.ingramcontent.com/pod-product-compliance
Lightning Source LLC
Chambersburg PA
CBHW011135190726
48289CB00012B/3048